M000112935

SPIDER KISS

HARLAN ELLISON®

An Edgeworks Abbey offering
in association with M Press

EDGEWORKS
ABBEY

PRESS
Milwaukie

SPIDER KISS
is an Edgeworks Abbey® offering in association with M Press.
Published by arrangement with the Author
and The Kilimanjaro Corporation.

SPIDER KISS
by Harlan Ellison®
Copyright © 1961, 1975, 1982 by Harlan Ellison.
Renewed, © 1989, 2003 by The Kilimanjaro Corporation.
This edition copyright © 2006 by The Kilimanjaro Corporation.
All rights reserved.

Harlan Ellison® is a registered trademark of
The Kilimanjaro Corporation.

Front Cover painting by Robert E. McGinnis
Copyright © 2006 by Robert E. McGinnis
Cover design by Lia Ribacchi and Amy Arendts
Book design by Debra Bailey and Krystal Hennes

No part of this book may be reproduced or transmitted in any form or by any means
electronic or mechanical—including photocopy, recording, Internet posting, electronic
bulletin board—or any other information storage and retrieval system, without per-
mission in writing from the Author or the Author's agent, except by a reviewer who
may quote brief passages in a critical article or review to be printed in a magazine or
newspaper, or electronically transmitted on radio, television, or in a recognized on-
line journal. For information address Author's agent: Richard Curtis Associates, Inc.,
171 East 74th Street, New York, New York 10021 USA.

All persons, places, and organizations in this book—except those clearly in the
public domain—are fictitious, and any resemblance that may seem to exist to actual
persons, places, or organizations living, dead, or defunct is purely coincidental.
This is a work of fiction.

ISBN-10: 1-59582-058-2
ISBN-13: 978-1-59582-058-7
First M Press edition: November 2006

M Press
10956 SE Main Street
Milwaukie, OR 97222

mpressbooks.com

Edgeworks Abbey
P.O. Box 55548
Sherman Oaks, CA 91413-0548

Harlan Ellison website: www.harlanellison.com

10 9 8 7 6 5 4 3 2 1

Printed in United States of America
Distributed by Publishers Group West

BOOKS BY HARLAN ELLISON

NOVELS:
Sound of a Scythe [1960]

Web of the City [1958]
Spider Kiss [1961]

SHORT NOVELS:
Doomsman [1967]
Run for the Stars [1991]

All the Lies That Are My Life [1980]
Mefisto in Onyx [1993]

GRAPHIC NOVELS:
Demon with a Glass Hand
(adaptation with Marshall Rogers) [1986]
Night and the Enemy
(adaptation with Ken Steacy) [1987]
Vic and Blood:
The Chronicles of a Boy and His Dog
(adaptation with Richard Corben) [1989]

Harlan Ellison's Dream Corridor [1996]
Vic and Blood:
The Continuing Adventures
of a Boy and His Dog
(adaptation with Richard Corben) [2003]

SHORT STORY COLLECTIONS:
The Deadly Streets [1958]
Sex Gang (as Paul Merchant) [1959]
A Touch of Infinity [1960]
Children of the Streets [1961]
Gentleman Junkie and Other Stories
of the Hung-Up Generation [1961]
Ellison Wonderland [1962]
Paingod and Other Delusions [1965]
I Have No Mouth & I Must Scream [1967]
From the Land of Fear [1967]
Love Ain't Nothing
But Sex Misspelled [1968]
The Beast That Shouted Love at the
Heart of the World [1969]
Over the Edge [1970]
De Helden Van De Highway
(Dutch publication only) [1973]
All the Sounds of Fear
(British publication only) [1973]
The Time of the Eye
(British publication only) [1974]
Approaching Oblivion [1974]
Deathbird Stories [1975]

No Doors, No Windows [1975]
Hoe Kan Ik Schreeuwen Zonder Mond
(Dutch publication only) [1977]
Strange Wine [1978]
Shatterday [1980]
Stalking the Nightmare [1982]
Angry Candy [1988]
Ensamvärk
(Swedish publication only) [1992]
Jokes Without Punchlines [1995]
Bce 3bykn Ctpaxa (All Fearful Sounds)
(unauthorized Russian publication only) [1997]
The Worlds of Harlan Ellison
(authorized Russian publication only) [1997]
Slippage [1997]
Koletis, Kes Kuulutas
Armastust Maalima Sodames
(Estonian publication only) [1999]
La Machine Aux Yeux Bleus
(French publication only) [2001]
Troublemakers [2001]
Ptak Smierci
(The Best of Harlan Ellison)
(Polish publication only) [2003]

OMNIBUS VOLUMES:
The Fantasies of Harlan Ellison [1979]

Dreams with Sharp Teeth [1991]

COLLABORATIONS:

Partners in Wonder: Collaborations with 14 Other Wild Talents [1971]

The Starlost: Phoenix Without Ashes (with Edward Bryant) [1975]

Mind Fields: 33 Stories inspired by the art of Jacek Yerka [1994/2006]

I Have No Mouth, and I Must Scream: The Interactive CD-ROM (co-designed with David Mullich and David Sears) [1995]

2000^X (host and creative consultant of National Public Radio episodic series) [2000-2001]

NON-FICTION & ESSAYS:

Memos from Purgatory [1961]

The Glass Teat: Essays of Opinion on Television [1970]

The Other Glass Teat: Further Essays of Opinion on Television [1975]

The Book of Ellison (edited by Andrew Porter) [1978]

Sleepless Nights in the Procrustean Bed Essays (edited by Marty Clark) [1984]

An Edge in My Voice [1985]

Harlan Ellison's Watching [1989]

The Harlan Ellison Hornbook [1990]

SCREENPLAYS, ETC:

The Illustrated Harlan Ellison (edited by Byron Preiss) [1978]

Harlan Ellison's Movie [1990]

I, Robot: The Illustrated Screenplay (based on Isaac Asimov's story-cycle) [1994, 2004]

The City on the Edge of Forever [1996]

"Repent, Harlequin!" Said the Ticktockman (rendered with paintings by Rick Berry) [1997]

RETROSPECTIVES:

Alone Again Tomorrow: A 10-year Survey [1971]

The Essential Ellison: A 35-year Retrospective [1987] (edited by Terry Dowling with Richard Delap and Gil Lamont)

The Essential Ellison: A 50-year Retrospective [2001/2006]

AS EDITOR:

Dangerous Visions [1967]

Dangerous Visions: 35th Anniversary Edition [2002]

Nightshade & Damnations: The Finest Stories of Gerald Kersh [1968]

Again, Dangerous Visions [1975]

Medea: Harlan's World [1985]

Jacques Futrelle's "The Thinking Machine" Stories [2003]

THE HARLAN ELLISON DISCOVERY SERIES

Stormtrack by James Sutherland [1975]

Autumn Angels by Arthur Byron Cover [1975]

The Light at the End of the Universe by Terry Carr [1976]

Islands by Marta Randall [1976]

Involution Ocean by Bruce Sterling [1978]

THE WHITE WOLF SERIES:

Edgeworks.1 [1996]

Edgeworks.2 [1996]

Edgeworks.3 [1997]

Edgeworks.4 [1997]

For the sixth time around, even fourty-five years later,
this one is still dedicated to the lady
who knew it ain't as easy as it looks.

For my ex-wife BILLIE,
with affection and respect.

AUTHOR'S NOTE

This is a work of fiction. It is intended, however, to convey a reasonably accurate impression of a segment of contemporary life as it existed during the period 1950-1960; a segment of show business based on the reality of the time. To convey a feeling of verisimilitude, I have employed the names of real persons, places, organizations, and events. Any such use, however, is intended strictly for story value, and it should be understood that any part they play in this fiction is a product of literary license employing figures whose public images are clearly in the public domain, and in no way implies any actual participation in reality. Of the fictional characters, woven from the whole cloth of the imagination, there may be those who seem to have counterparts in real life. Anyone attempting to "rip aside the masks" to discern the "real" people underneath, should be advised they're wasting their time. Stag Preston and all the others are composites, a chunk from here, a hand movement from there, a mannerism from somewhere else. He is many people and he is no one: he is a symbol, if you have to have labels. I have tried to tag a type. Types have no names. Or, to quote from Mark Twain: "Persons attempting to find a motive in this narrative will be prosecuted; persons attempting to find a moral in it will be banished; persons attempting to find a plot in it will be shot." It is a fable; who can be offended by a fable?

Harlan Ellison

ONE

First there was only the empty golden circle of the hot spot, blazing against the silk curtains. That, and in another vein, the animal murmuring of the audience, mostly teenage girls with tight sweaters and mouths open-crammed by gum. For what seemed the longest time that was the portrait: cut from primordial materials in an expectant arena. There was a tension so intense it could be felt as warmth on the neck, uncontrollable twitches in the lips and eyes, the nervous shifting of small hands *from* nowhere *to* nowhere.

The curtains gave a vagrant rustle and from three parts of the orchestra and four parts of the balcony came piercing, wind-up-a-chimney shrieks of pleasure and torment. Behind the velvet ropes, overflow crowds pressed body on body to get a neck-straining view of the stage. Just those purple and yellow draperies, the golden coin of the spotlight beam. The scene was laid with a simple, but forceful, altogether impressive sense of dramatics.

In the pit, the orchestra began warming its sounds, and the jungle murmur of the anxious crowd rose a decibel. There would be no Master of Ceremonies to start festivities, no prefatory acts—the Tumbling Turellos; Wally French & Sadie, the educated dachshund; Ivor Harrig with mime and merriment; The DeLaney Sisters—there would only be that golden spotlight, a blast of sound, and the curtains would part. This was one man's show, as it had been one man's show for two weeks. This was The Palace, and it had been invaded.

Two weeks before they had made The Palace alter all its precedents. The screaming, feral teenage girls with their eyes like winesoaked jewels, their mouths hungry, their adolescent bodies rigged and trussed erotically. They had booed and hissed the other acts from the stage before they could gain a hearing. They had stamped and clamored so outrageously, the booker and stage manager had decided—in the absence of the manager—to cut straight through to the feature attraction, the draw-card that had brought an audience rivaled only by the gates of Garland, Belafonte, and in days past, Martin & Lewis.

They had set the other acts aside, hoping this demonstration was only an opening day phenomenon. But it had been two weeks, with SRO at every performance, and the other acts had been paid off, told a profusion of sorrys, and the headliner had lengthened his stint to fill the space. He seemed, in fact, suffused with an inner electricity that allowed him to perform for hours without fatigue. The Palace had regretfully acquiesced . . . they had been conquered, and knew it.

Now, as the golden moon-face contracted, centering at the overlapping folds of the curtains, the orchestra burst into song. A peculiar song; as though barely adaptable to full brass and strings, it was a repetitive melody, underslung with a constant mechanical piano-drum beat, simple and even nagging. Immature but demanding, infectious.

The audience exploded.

Screams burst from every corner of the theatre, and in the first twenty-seven rows of the orchestra, girls leaped from seats as though spastic, lanceted with emotional fire. A senseless, building fury consumed The Palace and beat at the walls, reverberated out onto Seventh Avenue. The love affair was about to be consummated—again.

The curtains withdrew smoothly, the golden circle of light fell liquidly to the stage, hung in the black mouth of no scenery, no cyclorama, nothing, and the orchestra beat to a crescendoing final riff.

Silence . . .

The hushed intake of a thousand, three thousand, too many thousand breaths . . .

The muscle-straining expectancy as bodies pressed upward toward the empty space soon to be filled . . .

The spotlight snapped off . . .

Darkness . . .

Then back to life and he was *there*!

If the insanity that had ruled seventy-six seconds before was great, what was now loosed could only be called Armageddon. Seats clanged up against the backs of chairs, a Perdition's chorus of screams, wails, shrieks, moans, and obscenities crashed and thundered like the waves on the Cliff at Entretat. Hands reached fervently, feverishly, beseechingly upward. Girls bit their fists as their eyes started from their heads. Girls spread their hands against their breasts and clutched them with terrible hunger. Girls fell back into their seats, reduced to tears, reduced to jelly, reduced to emotional orgasms of terrifying intensity.

While he stood quietly, almost humbly, watching.

His name was intoned, extolled, cast out, drawn in, repeated, repeated repeated repeated till it became a chant of such erotic power it seemed to draw all light and sound to it. A vortex of emotionalism. With him at its center, both exploding and imploding waves of animal hunger.

He was of them, yet not of them. With them, yet above them.

He stood tall and slim, his legs apart, accentuating the narrowness of his hips, his broad shoulders, the lean desperation of his face, the auburn shock of hair, so meticulously combed with its cavalier forelock drooping onto his forehead.

A guardian of unnamed treasures.

Then he began to play. His hands moved over the frets of the guitar slung across his chest, and a guttural, sensuous syncopation fought with the noise of the crowd . . . fought . . . lost momentarily . . . lost again . . . crowd swell . . . then began to mount in insistence . . . till the crowd went under slowly slowly . . . till he was singing high and loud and with a mounting joy that caught even the self-drugged adolescents who had not come to listen, merely to worship.

His song was a pointless thing; filled with pastel inanities; don't ever leave me because I've got a sad dog heart that'll follow you where'er you go, no, don't leave me 'cause my sad dog heart cries just for you for you, ju-ust fo-o-o-or you . . .

But there was a subtext to the song. Something dark and roiling, an oil stain on a wet street, a rainbow of dark colors that moved almost as though alive, verging into colors that had no names, disturbing colors for which there were only psychiatric parallels. Green is the dead baby image . . .

The running line of what could be sensed but not heard was ominous, threatening, sensuously compelling in ways that spoke to skin and nerve-ends. It was like the moment one receives the biopsy report. It was like the feeble sound an unwatered plant makes in the instant before all reserve moisture dries from the tap root and the green turns to brown. It was like the sigh of anguish from the victim of voodoo at the instant the final pin is jammed into the ju-ju doll half a continent away. It was like the cry of a mother brought to see the tiny, crushed form lying beneath the blanket on a busy intersection. It was like the kiss of a spider.

And the great animal that was his audience, his vacuous, demanding, insensate, vicious audience, purred. Ripples of contentment washed the crowd. Almost mystically the surface of mass hysteria was smoothed, quieted, molded by his singing into a glossy plane of attention and silence. Girls who had been facially and bodily contorted by his appearance, who had thrown themselves forward in a spasm of adoration, now settled back demurely, seated and attentive.

He went on, singing, gently strumming the guitar, making idle movements of foot and hip and head—yet nothing overly suggestive, nothing that would rouse the sleeping beast out there. His movements, his voice, the chords he chose to pull from his guitar—all combined to lull the herd. His performance was as much a casting of hypnotic trances as it was a demonstration of musical ability.

Like some advanced breed of snake charmer he piped at them, and their eyes became glassy, their limbs limp; they stared and absorbed and wanted, but were silent, all waiting.

And he *could* sing. Granted his material was that semi-obscene and witless conglomerate of rhythmics known as rockabilly—half thump-thump of rock'n'roll, half twang and formalized beat of hillbilly—he *moved* his people with it. His voice was low and strong, sure on the subterranean notes that bespoke passion, winging on the sharp, high notes demanding gentleness. His was a good voice, free from affectation, based solidly in the sounds of the delta, the back hills, the wanderlusts of the people.

It came through. And they listened.

Until he was sure he had wrung everything from the song; then he finished. A soft rise to a lingering C-sharp, held till it was flensed clean, and a final chord. Then silence. A quick-phrased reporter from *Time* had once compared the hushed silence following the song to the silence when Lincoln completed his Gettysburg Address. Compared it and found it wanting, diseased, laughable, sexually stimulating, dangerous. Nonetheless, there it was. A long instant without time or tempo. Deepest silence. The silence of a limestone cave, the silence of deafness, the silence of the floor of the Maracot Deep. No one spoke, no one screamed, and if there was a girl in that audience who breathed—she did it self-consciously, inadvertently, quietly.

It lasted a score of heartbeats, while he stood in the spotlight, head down, wasted, empty, humble.

Then the holocaust broke once more.

The realization that they had actually felt honest emotion burst upon the constantly self-conscious teenagers, and they quickly covered their embarrassment with the protective cloak of crowd behavior. They screamed.

The sound rose up again, a cyclonic twisting outward, reaching even those beyond the sight of the stage (where the most demonstrative always clustered), sweeping all sanity before it. Carrying its incoherent message of attack and depravity with it like a crimson banner.

The noise lasted only until he struck the first four notes of the next song.

Then . . . the somnambulistic state once more.

He sang.

Sang for the better part of an hour and a half, ranging widely in interpretation, though restricted by arrangement and subject matter and the idiom of his music. His songs were the tormented and feeble pleadings of the confused teenager for understanding in a time when understanding is the one commodity that cannot be found pre-packed in aluminum foil. His songs were not honest, nor were they particularly meaningful, but they mirrored the frustrations of that alien community known as the teens.

There was identification, if nothing else.

The lean boy with the auburn hair, gently moving his hips in rhythm to his own music, unaided by the full string orchestra in the pit, unaided by the lush trappings of The Palace, was spellbinding the third largest audience in the theatre's history.

Here he was, a twenty-two-year-old singer with a faint Kentucky accent, dictator of emotions to a horde of worshipful post-adolescents. Humble, handsome, heroic in fact. He did nothing but sing, step about the stage with little regard for the bruised feelings of Terpsichore, and strum a Gibson guitar with steel strings.

Yet he ruled. Unquestionably, his was a magnetism not easily denied. His singing was clear and strong, and he *reached*. He held them. Tightly, passionately, expertly.

Stag Preston was doing the one thing in this world he *could* do in public.

From the wings he was being watched by a pair of dark eyes. The man slouched against the flats, a cigarette dangling from a corner of his mouth, burning but forgotten. He was easily as slim as the singer, but there was lacking the wiry command inherent in every line and muscle of Stag Preston's body. Rather, this man was quick-looking. Almost feral. His eyes were set back under thin but dark eyebrows, and he watched the entire scene. He was shorter than Preston, no more than five feet seven, and his clothes hung on him with good style, unlike the clinging form of Preston's flamboyantly fitted garb.

Sheldon Morgenstern, publicity man, ace flak-merchant of the Stem, bodyguard and handmaiden to the hottest talent in the game, inveterate chainsmoker and decrier of the human soul, stood silently watching his meal ticket.

There was a singular lack of expression on his tanned, planed face. But his eyes, though dark, were a-swim with flickers of emotion.

The ash lengthened on his cigarette, as he drew deeply, split among its gray folds and dropped, dusting his jacket front. He swiped at the debris absently. The cigarette burned on, unnoticed. *Sing, kid*, he thought. *Yeah, sing.*

Behind him, the many nameless busymen who always infest backstages stood silently, listening to Stag Preston. Though their expressions were not those of the girls out front, still they were being *reached*, they were being *held* by this boy in his modern jester's motley. It was that way with anyone who listened to Stag Preston.

He was that peculiar phenomenon, the natural talent. He was uniquely Stag Preston, with no touches of Sinatra or Presley or Darin in him. He was an electric thing on a stage, a commanding personality that instantly communicated itself.

That was one-tenth the reason he had become the most valuable musical property in the business, inside four years. Just one-tenth.

Four years.

Shelly Morgenstern lipped the butt from his mouth and ground it underheel, shaking another from the pack without conscious effort. He lit it and the brief lighter flame made the stage manager wince: smoking was prohibited in the wings, so close to the highly flammable scenery. But this was *his* PR man, and godlings could ignore mere mortal rules.

Four years.

Shelly Morgenstern stared at the tilted, arched body as it made a one-step, two-step in the slightest beat to the guitar's music. Stag Preston had it, all right. There was no question about it. He was Destiny's Tot. Up from nowhere, with a handful of doubloons. Nothing to sell save that which no one else had to sell. A voice, a manner, a look, a pair of hands that could innocently warp forth innocuous backgrounds to subtle oral pornography. That was all he had, yet when those components were joined and bathed by a spotlight, or trapped and grooved on an LP . . . he was more. Henri de Toulouse-Lautrec had once said, "One should never meet the artist; the work is always so much better than the creator." That, Shelly Morgenstern mused, was more true of Stag Preston than it had ever been of anyone.

Four years.

Shelly Morgenstern watched as Stag Preston finished his final number. There would be no curtain call. Stag would announce a "little private show" around back in the alley under his dressing room window, and the stampede would start out of the theatre. That, they had found, was the only way to cleanse the theatre of its prepared-to-stay-an-eternity-with-peanut-butter-sandwiches horde. The turn-over had been slow till they had employed the old Martin-Lewis dodge to empty the theatre. How they followed him; how they loved him; how they ached to touch his lean, hardrock body. It was sick, Shelly was certain of that, all arguments about Vallee and Sinatra and Valentino be damned. It was sick, and four years before, *he* had been steering for a poker game. Just that long ago he had been a hungry kid with too much moxie, too much hair, and no place to go.

Four years.

Shelly Morgenstern corrected himself. That wasn't so, no place to go. The kid would have made it somehow; he had been too hungry, too anxious, too much on the grab to ever settle for a fink's life in Louisville. If it hadn't been Colonel Jack Freeport and Shelly

Morgenstern, he would have done it another way. Yet it was phenomenal the way he had clawed his way up; even Jack Freeport—a tooth and nail career money-maker—had been amazed at the drive and verve with which the kid had pushed himself in so short a time. Amazed, a little frightened, but altogether impressed.

Four years.

Shelly Morgenstern stared at the advancing face of Stag Preston as it came offstage. One of the "gopher" flunkies waited with outstretched arm, presenting the ceremonial towel. The towel into which Stag Preston would wipe all that semi-holy Stag Preston sweat . . . which could easily be sold for twenty dollars to any of the screeching, drunk-with-adoration infants now jamming into the alley. The god sweated, yeah, it was true. But all the better. Don't put him completely out of reach. Put him just a handhold away, with the characteristic humbleness of all the new teenaged idols. A god, yet a man.

Stag Preston stopped directly in front of Shelly Morgenstern, his face buried in the towel. When he pulled it away the dark, penetrating eyes stared directly into the shorter man's face. It was a good face, Stag Preston's face, though in the eyes and in the cruel set of mouth, the stygian darknesses under the cheeks, there was the hint of something too mature, too desperate.

Now, as Stag shoved the towel under his shirt, wiping his moist armpit, the change would take place. *Watch the remarkable, magical transformation, folks,* Shelly thought. *Watch as Sheldon Morgenstern, whose father was a cantor and whose mother had wanted her son to become a CPA, subtly undergoes a sea-change from publicity man for the great Stag Preston to pimp for the great, horny Stag Preston. Watch closely, folks, the degradation is faster than the eye.*

"Shelly . . . "

Here it comes. "See one, Stag?"

The smile. The *Motion Picture / Look / Life / Teen Magazine*-famous smile guaranteed to contain 100% unadulterated sex appeal combined with bullshit. The smile, and, "A cutie, Shel. A little redhead down front with a ponytail. She's got a sign says Stag Preston We Love You. Can't miss her. She'll be out in the alley. G'wan and round her up for me, how's about, Shel." There was no question in it; it was an order, despite the lisping, gentle Kentucky voice.

Sure, Stag. "Sure, Stag."

Stag Preston made his way to the dressing room, and Sheldon Morgenstern made his way to the stage door. He paused to dump the old cigarette, light a fresh one, and open the huge metal door.

There they were. Growling, clamoring, straining for a sight of God on Earth. He watched them with the pitying scrutiny of a compassionate butcher, and found the little redhead. Stag had a good eye, there was no taking that away from him. She was too large in the chest for a kid her age, and the hair was a bit too brassy, but that was invariably the way Stag liked them.

He moved out into the crowd, reached her, and tapped her shoulder. "Miss?" The wide, green eyes turned up to him, registered nothing.

"Miss, Stag would like to meet you." He said it with no feeling, with, in fact, a definite absence of inflection in hopes she might be scared off. But they never were. Any of them.

Her breath went in like a train through a tunnel, fast and sharp and leaving emptiness behind it. "*Stag*? Me?"

He nodded. No encouragement, no deterrent.

She said something to a girl beside her, a fat girl with pimples (why did the best-looking ones always come with their comparison-friends, so they looked that much better?), and gave her the Stag Preston We Love You sign. Then she turned, with Roman candles in her eyes, and followed Shelly Morgenstern into the theatre.

Four years, he thought. Four years, and how did it all start? Was it that request from the Kentucky State Fair for Colonel Jack Freeport to judge the talent contest?

Had it started then, when they'd met Stag in Louisville? Or did it go further back, much further back to the days when Shelly had been trying to break away from the orthodox enslavement of his home, when he had discovered he could no longer believe in the terrible God of his father, and worshipped more easily at the heavenly throne of Success (and Money is his prophet)? Did it go back to Jack Freeport, who needed more, more, more of everything . . . to rebuild a name that had been shattered as far back as the burning of Atlanta? Had it begun with hungers, or with simple supply and demand?

He knew how it had started.

And as he walked the little redhead into the lion's mouth, he thought about it . . . about the four years.

Well tell it, then. Tell it, but make it quick.

We've still got three shows to do.

Two

Great White Father and the ferret. That was how they looked from the corner of the eye, in that side-of-sight glance hurriedly thrown by people at airports. First came the big man in the white linen suit. He paused at the head of the aluminum stairs, mopping his desert brow with a monogrammed handkerchief.

Even as his hand came away from his face, the armpits of his white-on-white shirt darkened through with perspiration. Almost maliciously, he turned his face up to the sun, and the Louisville heat greeted him inhospitably.

"Cursed state," he muttered, "always said it should have been plowed under by God." He spoke with a thick Georgia accent, a touch of nobility, a touch of arrogance.

He was big in small ways. His face was almost leonine, with a snowy nimbus of hair capping his massive head splendidly. His hands were blocky, yet had a suppleness suggestive of fine Swiss watchmaking or brain surgery. He stood momentarily, staring from bleached-out eyes—the image of Great White Father—framed against the open port of the big Eastern Convair 440; he surveyed the crowd jammed against the fence.

With a satisfied tone he called back over his shoulder, "Wharton sent no one, Shelly. I don't see any badges from the fair."

Then he deplaned from the twin-engine Silver Falcon.

Behind him, squinting, the wiry Palm Beach-suited ferret shied from the gagging humidity. It was not so much the olive coloring of his lean, hard face as the diamond-intensity of his black eyes that gave the impression of stealth . . . deviousness . . . attentiveness. He cursed softly, a Manhattan twang, and gripped the strap of the thin, cabretta-grain attaché case more tightly. It did not swing idly from his left hand. Shelly Morgenstern hurried after the older man.

Almost before they had passed the hurricane fence with its strict admonition of

GASOLINE FUMES
NO SMOKING
DANGER!

the younger man had forked a cigarette from his lapel pocket and had wedged it between his lips, firm in a corner of his thin-lipped mouth.

Even inside the terminal building of Standiford Field the heat was monstrous. The big man stopped abruptly and leaned against the wall. He mopped at the perspiration on his jowls. "Shelly," he said snappishly, "give me one of those cursed tablets."

The ferret jammed the attaché case between his feet and fumbled a small plastic vial from a jacket pocket. Unsnapping the lid he tumbled a pale blue tablet onto his palm, and extended it to the older man. "Water fountain up the line, Colonel," Shelly said, jerking his head in the direction.

Laboring under his bulk—not fat, just girth—Colonel Jack Freeport (Savannah, New York, Cannes, and London) made it briskly to the fountain, popped the tablet onto his tongue, and washed it down with irregular gulps of water, managing to avoid spilling on his jacket.

"I'll see to the bags," Freeport said, straightening. "You call George Wharton at the State Fair Headquarters, and under *no* circumstances are we to be bothered by their sending some incompetent down to drive us. I want to get cleaned up and rested from that cursed plane ride, without having to meet anyone." He waved an imperious hand in the direction of the phone booths. Then he moved off toward the baggage claiming area.

Shelly stared after the imposing figure of Jack Freeport, and the muscles along his lean jaw jumped. For an instant he felt like a toady. He had felt that way before. He disliked the feeling intensely. Then remembrances of debts, his unpaid balance on the Mercedes-Benz, what it cost to maintain Carlene . . . and the twenty thousand a year Freeport paid him . . . came back to him and he struck off for the phones.

He dropped the attaché inside the booth, against the wall, and slid onto the seat. From a list of numbers in his wallet he dialed a downtown Louisville exchange, and waited. Traffic moved past the booth in both directions.

When the dial tone broke and the husky feminine voice said, "Kentucky State Fair Headquarters," he was not quite prepared, and for an instant fumbled his silence.

"George Wharton, please," he said finally.

"Whom shall I say is calling?"

"Colonel Jack Freeport."

There was a soft, furry click and silence at the end of the line. Shelly flicked ash from the dwindling cigarette in his mouth, without removing the butt from between his lips.

Another click and a voice said, "Jack! When the hell'd you get in, boy?"

"This is Sheldon Morgenstern for Colonel Freeport, Mr. Wharton. We're at Standiford—"

Wharton blustered forward with his interruption: "I'll have a car right out there for you, fella, just hold on a min—" He turned away from the mouthpiece and shrieked at someone, "Teddy! Teddy, get your coat on and take the Buick. Freeport's at Stan—"

Shelly cut him off with a loud, "*Hold* it, Mr. Wharton."

George Wharton came back to the receiver from the Land of Speedy Activity. "No trouble, no trouble at all, Mr. Morgenstern. Have a car out there in fifteen minutes. We've got a bunch of hangers-on around here, anyhow. They don't do a damned thing all day but mooch from petty cash. Let me send someone out for you."

Shelly was adamant. "Don't bother, Mr. Wharton. Colonel Freeport is a little tired from the flight and wants to go directly to his hotel. Where have you booked us?"

"The Brown, but—"

"We'll take a cab to The Brown, then. The Colonel will give you a ring from the room when he's settled. Is there anything on for tonight?"

Wharton sounded unhappy, but answered, "Just a dinner, but that isn't until nine or nine-thirty. Say are you sure—"

Shelly felt the conversation had exhausted its meager limitations and said, "All right, then, Mr. Wharton, we'll call you as soon as we've gotten settled. Thanks a lot. Goodbye." He dropped the receiver without waiting for a reply.

Freeport was already leaving the baggage area, the suitcases going on before under the arms of a redcap. He turned as Shelly approached, and a questioning expression bent his features.

"What did he say?" he asked.

Shelly lit a fresh cigarette from the butt of the one before and answered, "He wanted to send out a car; I told him we wanted to make it on our own."

Freeport snorted. "They'd take us down to the Headquarters and before I'd even gotten a bath—some Momma would have her little Agnes tapping and bawling at me. These cursed talent contests are all the same. Where are we staying, The Brown?"

Shelly nodded. "At least we'll have good rooms. No money in this, but I suppose it's good relations. Any plans for Louisville, Colonel?"

Freeport pursed his lips, shrugged the question away. "Well, Shelly, we'll see, we'll see."

They followed the redcap to the line of waiting cabs and settled themselves for the ride into Louisville. "The Brown," Shelly advised the hackie. When the bags were loaded, they pulled away, and he settled down, closing his dark eyes. Freeport continued to squint, even in the absence of sunlight. He mopped at his face and neck constantly, with nervous, spastic motions. "Cursed state," he muttered once.

Shelly considered what Freeport had told him about this untimely, uncomfortable trip to Louisville. The taxi, weaving down the expressway, was so close Shelly felt as though he was knotted into a bag, and the cab smelled faintly of urine. It added to the ease of contemplating what Jack Freeport had said about misplaced loyalties.

Because of the lack of foresight of his parents, some fifty-three years before, of having resided in Cadiz, Kentucky, on the day of his birth, Freeport was—at least technically—a native son. Despite the fact that the family had been recouping drastic financial losses and had moved back to Savannah three months after Freeport's birth, the Kentucky State Fair committee had still seen fit to call on him to judge their abominable talent show.

After all, thought Shelly, *first comes Sol Hurok, and then comes my big twenty thousand dollar a year meal ticket, Colonel Jack Freeport.*

Savannah, New York, Cannes, and London.

Amen.

So we are in Louisville, Kentucky. Shelly dropped the thoughts like pigeon excretion. *Navel of the nation. And we are preparing to judge a Talent Show (cast of thousands . . . all nonentities). While back in New York that damned jazz show needs a shot of digitalis, in Chicago the poetry readings are drawing about as well as a Sunday picnic at Buchenwald, and in L.A. the Go-Kart races are about as popular as an acrobat in a polio ward.*

Everything was dying on the vine. *And here we sit warm and cuddly on the same vine, in Louisville. Say one for me, Agnes, we'll all be in the soup line tomorrow.*

"But well dressed," he murmured under his breath.

"What was that, Shelly?" Freeport turned from the view outside the taxi.

"Nothing, Colonel. Nothing at all," he answered, without opening his eyes. *Not a damned thing, Massah.*

Beyond the cab, the red loam of a housing project-in-progress swept past like a raw, naked wound in the arid flesh of the land.

As they pulled into the center of town, Shelly sat up in the seat, and tried to shrug some composure—lost during the flight and this heat assault since the airport—into his wilted frame. It didn't do much good. It was no use; he resigned himself to a weekend of heat, boredom, and too-sweet martinis.

Fourth and Broadway. The Brown Hotel.

The bags were carried by an old man whose black pants had two distinctive attributes: a red stripe down each leg, and several hundred thousand wrinkles. A butter stain adorned the uniform tie.

Colonel Jack Freeport marched through the lobby, signed in with a maximum of notice while Shelly limply autographed a check-in card, and made the sanctity of his suite without undue delay. Once in the air-conditioned sanity of his room—separated from Freeport's by a sitting room of unparalleled dinginess—Shelly stripped off his jacket, shirt, and tie, threw them across the bed, and bare-chested, crucified himself before the cool air ducts of the big Fedders.

"Shelly," the call came from Freeport's room, "let me have the attaché case."

The flak-man ran a hand through his dark hair and retrieved the leather case from where he had dumped it on a big Morris chair. He carried it through the sitting room and into Freeport's bedroom.

The Colonel was stripped to fancy nylon shorts, dark socks, and shoes, the garters tightly clinging to thick, hairy legs. Shelly was once more—as always—startled by the hard-muscled, trim condition of Freeport's big body.

"Fetch me those papers on the key clubs, will you, Shelly?" He said it over his shoulder as he lifted the big three-suiter onto the bed and unsnapped it.

"I think you'd better call Morrie in New York, Colonel, and find out how he did with MCA," Shelly said.

Freeport nodded without turning around. "Good idea. Get him

for me." Shelly shook his head feebly, in resignation, and picked up the receiver.

After an interminable wait: "I want to call long distance, operator, New York City, MUrray Hill 2-4368, person-to-person to Mr. Morrie Needleman."

When the call went through, a bored, "Yeah, this is Needleman, go ahead," at the other end greeted him.

"Morrie? Shelly in Louisville. The Colonel wants to speak to you." He handed the receiver to Freeport, who continued brushing his hair with one hand while he fastened the instrument to his head with the other.

"Hello, Needleman? Did MCA come through for us?"

The eternally weary voice of Morrie Needleman, entrepreneur second-grade, raced down the wire . . . slowly. "Yessir, but they asked for more for Satch so I met 'em halfway."

Freeport scowled. "You went beyond your authority, Needleman. How much more?"

"Another three yards, Colonel. That was as low as they'd show." He paused a moment, seeing his job fly South for the duration. "I tried to do better'n that, Colonel, but they had us over a barrel. We'd already announced Armstrong; papers, radio, billboards."

Colonel Jack Freeport scowled more intensely. "Well, hmm-hmm. All right, Needleman. No real harm done, I suppose. We'll make it up at the box office." He handed the phone back to Shelly.

Morgenstern took over as though he were merely a surrogate for the older man. "Morrie? Shelly again. Listen, baby, sit on the damned concert till the sonofabitch's SRO. So meanwhile, how's everything else? What d'ya hear from L.A.?"

The faint rustle of paper came from the New York end of the line, and Needleman's absorbed, "Ummm," filtered down with it. Finally, as though he had been consulting briefs, Needleman said, "I'm going to call Buddy Halpern out there and get him to pull off a stunt. Maybe soup up one of them Go-Karts and drag the L.A. cops down the main stem. Get the papers on it, and we might have the in we need."

"Wild, baby," Shelly said blithely, "keep us posted. We'll be back by Sunday night the latest."

Needleman's lazy voice lost its business edge. "Anything shakin' down there?"

With a disgruntled grunt Shelly replied, "Sure, sure. The whole damned town's a bacchanalian orgy. At least I'll be catching up on my sleep. So long." A reply, and he hung up.

As he turned, Freeport said softly, "Mark it down to let Needleman go, Shelly."

That easy. Five years with Freeport, and mark it down to let him go. It was always that easy with the Colonel. *I'll mark it, Boss Man. I know the Bible says you're a jealous people.* "Yes, sir," he said.

While Freeport pored over the proposed plans for a nationwide chain of key clubs to be leased by major sports figures under their names (but run through Freeport's holding company, with gigantic kickbacks to Freeport's syndicate), Shelly returned to his room, visions of showers dancing in his head. He tried not to think of Needleman and his wife's breast cancer.

The shower was cold and sharp and good, and when he had toweled himself pink (*like a baby shrimp*, he amused himself), he returned to his room, the towel around his waist. He surveyed himself in the full-length mirror, ignoring the slight protuberant bulge of his stomach, and struck a wholly ineffectual Muscle Beach attitude.

"I can do the Mr. America bit with *either* arm," he told his reflection, pressing first one fist to his temple, then the other, while maintaining a ferocious expression.

"Shelly, come in here, please," Freeport called.

Sighing, he hastened to do as he was bid, thinking:

But Mistah Lincoln done tole us we was free.

THREE

For the better part of four and one half hours, a superlatively trained corps of yawn-makers had dispensed boredom by means of platitude, homey homily, grandiose visions of Kentucky futures, and soggy reminiscence.

The testimonial dinner had been a walloping success.

Shelly Morgenstern contemplated killing himself.

There had to be easier ways to go. Boredom was such a slow, despicable demise. "Oh, God, oh for a barrel of absinthe and free passage to dissolution," he burbled into the too-sweet martini. "Bartender, give me another fruit punch." He indicated the martini glass.

When the bartender brought the refill, Shelly stared at his bald head for a long instant and refrained from saying: *Your head, sir, is shining in my eyes.*

That's pretty damned cornball, Morgenstern, he chided himself.

I know, he snapped the reply, *but I'm not nearly drunk enough to be quick and clever. Oh, God, this town!*

"Where's the action tonight, fella?" he asked the passing bartender. The man paused on his way to the orange squeezer and assayed the questioner.

"What are you looking for?"

Shelly shrugged. He was too tired for wenching. Maybe a good cool game of cards. He relayed his desire.

The bartender said, "Wait a minute." He moved up to the other end of the bar, took out a pad and pencil, and jotted down a quick address. He came back, handed it to Shelly, and said, "Ask for Luther. He'll know what's on tonight."

Shelly thanked him, paid for the drinks, and slid off the barstool. The note said: *Dixie Hotel, 5th and Broadway.*

Louisville at night was a combination of Coney Island at ten P.M. and deepest Brooklyn at five in the morning. A short stretch of naked neon insensibly wiggling—and then silence. The center stripe rolled up like a long tongue. The fleshpots, and the closed shops. He walked quite steadily, waiting for the right recognition symbol to be tripped in his head.

Ding!

The sign was a bilious green. DIXIE HOTEL—ROOMS.

He pushed through the revolving door, finding himself in one of those B-movie sleazy lobbies cut from the same cheap pattern. Brass lamps with hanging beaded pull chains, sofas that gave off small puffs of dust when sat upon, a long oak table from some esoteric period covered with copies of *The Farmer's Weekly*, *Look* from seven months before, and three battered copies of *Radio-TV Mirror*. The three *Radio-TV Mirrors* had subscription stickers on their covers. One of them had been left out in the rain; it was wrinkled.

"Room, buddy?" The voice drifted to Shelly from behind the high plywood counter. He turned and saw the top of a balding head.

Stepping closer, the head-top became only the top of a head that topped a shrunken, yellowed body barely in the same species with Morgenstern. "Where can I find—uh—" he consulted the slip of paper, "somebody named Luther?"

"Luther?" The room clerk sighed resignedly. "Wait a minute." He reached across with a foot and jabbed a red button on the board. "He'll be right down."

The little man continued to stare at Shelly from dark eyes with yellow rings under them. "Is my monkey bothering you?" Shelly asked.

"What?"

"The one on my back."

The clerk looked disgusted. "Comedian," he mumbled. Shelly lit a cigarette, staring at those obscure places in every room that seldom command attention: the juncture of ceiling and wall, ornate filigree along the upper walls, worn spots on the seedy rug. *I should have gone with Freeport to that business conference. Couldn't have been any worse than this.*

The elevator sighed open, and a tall, thin kid with too much hair came out. He wore a faded blue bellhop's uniform, and the most monumentally bored expression Shelly had ever encountered.

The boy walked to the check-in desk. "George-O," he said, and the balding dwarf jerked a thumb at Shelly. "He asked for ya," George-O said. The boy turned to stare at Shelly. His eyes narrowed.

Morgenstern could see the question *process-server?* in the gleam of them.

"Bartender over at The Brown told me I might find some action here; told me to ask for Luther. You Luther?"

The boy nodded. "What 'chu aftuh, Mistuh?"

The way he said it was very much like rolling out a brochure. With listings under J for junk, B for broads, Q for queers, and G for shuffle them. "I heard there might be some poker hereabouts," Shelly said.

Luther studied the man before him with casual carefulness. Then, reassuring himself by means of those nebulous signs and auras known to the hungry ones on the fringes, he nodded. "Yessuh, big man, we got a little game goin'."

Shelly made a negligent motion with his hand. "Lead the way, son."

Luther shied at the word "son" and his dark eyes narrowed. "Stakes goin' five, ten, twenny-five, big man, you figuh you can stand the action?"

Shelly dropped the butt on the rug and ground it in with his heel. "You figure on making your steering money talking me to death in this lobby?"

The bellboy turned and re-entered the elevator. Shelly followed him, watching the swaggering, self-contained way the boy walked. Loose. He had indeed been around. There was something hard, something coolly dangerous about Luther.

The elevator door closed and the machine started up. Then Luther flicked out the lights.

"Hey! What the *hell* is *this*?" Shelly backed into a corner, seeing himself being rolled by a teenager.

Luther's soft voice came out of the darkness. "Stay loose, big man. This's just so's you don't know what floor you're on. We don't want no trouble from The Man."

The elevator whined to a stop (How did he know when they'd reached the correct floor, Shelly wondered?), and Luther reached out through the opened door, and clicked another switch. The hall went dark beyond the elevator car: "C'mawn, big man," Luther said, taking Shelly by the arm.

A sharp fear clutched Shelly Morgenstern as the boy hustled him down the hall. This could be the easiest sucker trap in the world. Pow! *We never saw no New York bigmouth, Officuh; he musta got rolled someplace else. Musta been seven other guys, Officuh. We all clean around heah.* Oh, this could be so sweet a setup.

Luther reached a door and rapped on it three times, quickly, waited, then twice again, slowly.

The door opened, and Shelly knew he was all right.

The card players' smoke was thick enough to butter on bread. He fished a five out of his pocket; Luther took it.

He entered the room, Luther falling in behind, and saw the big green-topped poker table, surrounded by six men, three of whom wore expensive suits. This was no rigged roll setup in any case. The game might or might not be fixed . . . that was another matter. It would take some careful scrutiny.

"Stay loose, big man," Luther said, and elbowed past, opening a side door and disappearing beyond.

A florid-faced man with a tie too thin for his fat, too bright for his pink eyelet shirt, got up from the table and extended a hand to Shelly. "Name's Walter Swatt," he said jovially, "do me a favor and don't make any cracks about getting the Flit." He chuckled, and the men around the table smiled lamely, as though this was their five hundredth exposure to the remark.

"Sheldon . . . Lewis," Shelly answered, grinning just as widely. "In town for the Fair, thought I'd like to play a little friendly poker."

Swatt led him to the table, and the men scooted around to leave an open space, quickly filled by a chair Swatt pulled up. "This's the place, Mr. Lewis. We're all local businessmen, get together here every week for a little game. Whyn'cha sit, y'hear?" Shelly plopped into the chair.

The sound of a guitar drifted to him in the momentary silence of the pre-shuffle. He turned toward the sound; the small room where Luther had disappeared.

Swatt caught the glance, said, "Oh, that's just the kid, Luther. We let him practice in there, he's a good kid. Sings, plays a little. Ain't too good, but, well . . . what the hell . . . you know."

Shelly nodded. "Hey, deal me in this hand."

It only took him seven hands to establish that the game was neither rigged nor very deadly. Despite the stakes, which were high for a "stranger game," the other players were open-faced and easy to outmaneuver. He began winning steadily, but not outrageously. It was a friendly game.

With the solving of the puzzle of the players' methods and the gradual disinterest that comes with knowledge of superiority in the game, Shelly found himself listening more and more to the peculiar strains of music coming from the little side room.

After a while, he excused himself from the table, pocketed his winnings with the promise of returning shortly, and went to the side door. He hesitated a long moment, hearing the rhythms of back-country blues coming from the room; then he knocked sharply.

The players looked up, then returned to their hands.

Luther's voice, muffled, offered him entrance.

Shelly opened the door and saw a room as yellow and bare as a monk's cell, the only furniture being a slat-back chair and a washstand with a pitcher of water and a glass on it. "Somethin',

big man?" the boy asked, looking up from the steelstringed guitar. It was a cheap guitar, but there was whiteness around the
boy's knuckles as he clutched it tightly to himself. *He looks like
he's afraid someone will rip it away from him,* Shelly thought
suddenly.

"I heard you playing," he said.

"Sorry if ah was too loud. I'll cool it," the boy answered, surli-
ness in his tones.

"No, you weren't too loud," Shelly replied. He leaned against
the wall and lit a cigarette.

"Then what's the mattuh?"

"Nothing, just wanted to hear you play," Shelly admitted.

The boy set the guitar behind the chair and looked up from under
his awning of auburn hair. "I don't play for nothin', Mistuh."

"Well, I'm not about to pay, Elvis," Shelly retorted. The boy
started at the name, his eyes narrowing down.

"Why don't you get the hell outta heah, big man, an' let me be?
You wanted to play some pokuh, so I brought you up, whyn't you
g'wan back out theah?" His fists were white with suppressed fury.

"Maybe I'd like to hear you play?" Shelly said; he was sure he
could handle the kid, wiry and tall though he appeared, even
slouched into an "S" on the chair.

"What foah?"

"I'm from New York. I'm with Colonel Jack Freeport, you ever
hear of him?"

The boy shook his head slowly. He wasn't giving an inch. "What's
your trouble, Mistuh? You want somethin' from me?"

Like a primitive, Shelly thought, taking in the narrowed eyes, the
thin mouth, the wary expression, the hostility so near the surface.

"Nothing at all, Luther. I'm just with the Colonel, and he's judg-
ing the big talent show at the Fair; you've heard about *that*, haven't
you?" He stared at the boy openly. Interested in him, without knowing why. There was a quality about Luther that interested Shelly.
Vaguely. Disquietingly. Peculiarly.

The boy's eyes now acquired a brightness, a gleam. "I know all about it. I'm entered."

"Go ahead and play for me," Shelly said. He slouched back against the wall, waiting.

Luther stared for another moment, then reached back, took out the guitar, and slung the cord around his neck. Then he began to play, and to sing.

It was mostly rock'n'roll garbage, with occasional folk songs and Negro blues numbers included, either shuffle-rhythmed for backbeat, or delivered in a strange-to-Shelly mournful manner. He was impressed. The boy had a talent. It had been there distinctly, distantly, through the door as Shelly played cards, and now Morgenstern realized it had been nagging at him for some time.

He had *wanted* to hear this boy more closely.

Abruptly, he realized he might have stumbled on something more than amusing. At first it had been idle curiosity, then mild amusement and interest. But now . . .

"Get your coat," he told the boy, when Luther paused in his strumming.

The boy stared at him suspiciously, half-confused, half-terrified. "Whut foah?"

"You're coming over to The Brown to meet the Colonel." *You're thirty-three years old, Shelly Morgenstern,* he thought, *and you've been losing a long while now. This time, just maybe, just may-damn-be, you'll win.* "C'mon, Luther, let's get moving!"

Oh, you beautiful twanging Louisville delinquent, you!

The card players were plenty mad to see their dough slamming out of the room, out of the game. And who'd bring ice if that damned bellboy cut out?

Colonel Jack Freeport, when he slept, very much resembled a whale in shoal. Or the *Île de France* in drydock. Rousing him was very much a salvage job.

He finally burrowed out from under the covers and the oppressively stuffy closeness of the sealed, darkened bedroom, to blink at his wee-small-hours invaders.

"Just what the cursed devil do you think you're doing, Shelly?" His face grew red as a stop sign, his otherwise pleasant features contorting in annoyance and frustration, verging on an infantile expression.

"Colonel—" Shelly began, shoving Luther forward.

Freeport exploded once more. "Do you have any idea how late I was in that meeting? This is inexcusable, Shelly. I've warned you about drinking, and if this is a sample of—"

Shelly stood over the bed, his mouth tightening down into a line of ricocheted annoyance. The Colonel had a right to be angry, but he had no right to *stay* angry, particularly with what Shelly had brought. "Colonel? If you'll only listen a minute!"

"Listen to what?" the Colonel cried, frustrated fury in every syllable.

"To this goddamn kid, that's to what!" Shelly screamed back.

There was a long silence. An awkward silence, in which Luther made a hesitant step toward the door. "You stay put!" Shelly snapped, without completely turning.

Freeport sat up in the bed, running a hand through his thick, white hair. His eyes narrowed as he stared at the boy. Then he spoke calmly, as though deciding if he paid this man so much money, it might be worth his time to trust him. "All right, Shelly, explain why you want me to hear this boy."

Shelly quickly gave him a rundown on the poker game, the music he had heard, and his excitement. "I felt you should hear Luther before the talent contest tomorrow. He's entered in it, but that isn't what counts. I thought—if you liked what he sounds like—we could . . . "

He sketched a promotional plan, and at its conclusion, Freeport was sitting on the edge of the bed in a deep purple silk bathrobe, nodding carefully at each point his PR man ticked off.

"It's good, Shelly. Very good. And the contest, too?"

Morgenstern nodded, a crafty light flickering in his eyes. "The contest, too, as a starter. We can see how he does cold, with no fanfare, no puff at all. If the kid swings on his own, we've got us a hot property."

Luther stood listening. What might have passed for an innocent, confused expression rested on his face. But that was precisely what it did; it rested there, a mask. He was listening. He was hearing everything being said, and applying it.

"Well, let's hear him sing," the Colonel said, shifting on the edge of the rumpled bed. "Let me hear what you can do, son."

Shelly said, "Just take it easy, Luther, don't press. Just sing for the Col—"

"Knock it off, big man," Luther snarled. "I'm cooling it, I'm singin', and you don't hafta worry whut I'm gonna do." The hardness of the streets was in his voice, mixed with the pleasant susurration of the Kentucky accent.

He pulled a plush chair to him, planted his foot directly in the middle of it, and began tuning the guitar. He did it hurriedly, expertly, and abruptly launched into a rockabilly version of "Birmingham Train" while the Colonel stared open-mouthed. So sudden had been the explosion of sound that neither Shelly nor his employer could quite grab a breath till the second verse.

By then, Luther had made it.

He was on his way.

He had come up with a product for which there was—at the moment—no demand whatsoever. But he had two of the most silken supply-and-demand men in the country on his side, seeing him not as a tall, willowy Kentucky street-snot with a guitar, but as a seven-figure bank account in the Chase Manhattan.

Luther What'shisname was about to become famous. "Shelly," the Colonel said reverentially, when the boy had stopped playing, "you have dipped into pig slop and come up with a diamond."

Luther Whateverhisname smiled. Knowingly. Complacently. Cool.

FOUR

Big men, happy men, are often equated with stupid men, slow men ...
men who substitute camaraderie for the sleek slyness of the professional sharpie. There had been such equations made of Colonel
Jack Freeport. They had been made when he was in college, a pen-
niless undergrad with pretensions to Southern nobility. Those who
had seen in him a slightly overweight Good Time Jack had been
rudely awakened; Freeport had managed to become a power on
the campus, had talked any number of the most eligible co-eds into
his bed, had promoted several offbeat deals that had made his
financial way through higher education infinitely easier, and when
he graduated, was labeled by the yearbook NOT NECESSARILY
MOST LIKELY TO SUCCEED, BUT A SHOO-IN TO GET ANY-
THING WORTH HAVING.

Jack Freeport had started small.

His first promotion was a string of girlie shows made up of
local talent recruited from eight of the widest-open towns in the
decadent South. Ostensibly song and dance grinds, the girls were
emotionally and physically equipped to do double service as pros-
titutes, and in little over eighteen months, Freeport was able to sell
the operation to three brothers (one-quarter Seminole) and invest
his capital in the next ventures ...

Indoor, year-round ice skating rinks.

A carnival, top-heavy on grifters and nautch shows.

A dog track.

A traveling country music and revival show.

Some calculated gambling in Reno, Las Vegas, Monte Carlo, and
Hot Springs, Arkansas, utilizing the services of a gentleman with
only three fingers on his right hand, a need for twenty-seven

thousand dollars, and a face seen on posters often tacked up in metropolitan police stations.

Some gunrunning.

Another dog track.

A talent show.

Another talent show.

A third talent show, packaged by Freeport's own outfit.

A girl singer with connections.

An ill-starred publishing venture (no one was really very interested in reading), *The Alexandre Dumas Adventure Magazine*.

A Broadway musical featuring a girl singer with connections.

Some more gunrunning.

And then, the organization of

FREEPORT,
SERVICES UNLIMITED

from which foundation emerged young talents and well-known personalities in new formats that, within the space of five years, made the name of Colonel Jack Freeport a touchstone in the trade. The name no longer elicited a querulous, "Who?" in the Brill Building.

With obsessive, relentless drive, Freeport had made his way, had built his fortune, had grown older but surer of himself; to make real the dream: to revivify, in modern mold, the old days, in Atlanta, when the Freeport family had *owned* Freeport, a family name and a plantation whose fields and rooms and eyries had known blinding, glorious light. Make real the dream; to rebuild a tiny empire of regal living, on land charred by Sherman and his marauders. A great dream, a fine dream.

Too poor, too long, living with the slightly stale smell of decaying memories. This was the driving force of Colonel Jack Freeport—no more a Colonel than his great-great-grandfather (who had been a pillaging privateer) had been.

And any means to this end was a valid, honorable means. How much more potent is the drive to regain stature than mere love, motherhood, honor, security. Of this substance are made dictators, nations, dynasties, empires, rock'n'roll singers.

Colonel Jack Freeport had a good eye.

His ears were excellent, also.

He saw what Shelly had seen in Luther Whoeveryouare. Had it been necessary to rig the talent show (a small challenge to the man who had convinced America it needed a ticket to a Freeport-produced show more than it needed shoes for baby), he would have done so without hesitation.

But the need had not arisen.

The only competition had been a snot-nosed tot with Shirley Temple dimples and a head of Breck shampoo curls. Weak competition at best, whose only strength had been fatuous mommy-love. Luther had walked off with it; the pre-rigged decision by Freeport had not been necessary.

The boy had been just this side of sensational. Aside from a fleeting nervousness which had quickly dispersed as his audience warmed, his stage presence had been sharp and commanding. He had sung his heart out, received three curtain calls, and collapsed the house by singing on one knee—oddly, in no way reminiscent of Jolson—directly into the pimply face of an adolescent and the wine-bright eyes of a matron. They squealed. They squirmed. They found themselves drenched with a sweat of desire. Luther was a sneak-away success. He won the first prize, which, it miraculously turned out, was a contract with Colonel Jack Freeport, and a trip to New York. Had the tot won, the prize would have been a lovely Westinghouse refrigerator-freezer combination and a check for five hundred dollars.

That's show biz.

His full name was Luther Sellers. No relation to Peter. Mother dead, father off in the oil fields somewhere. He was—literally—a child of the streets, and it showed through with every word he uttered, with the way he carried himself, his conception of the world, and his interests. It was there all the time—but not when he sang.

He had a manager, which surprised Freeport and Shelly, and immediately made their eyes narrow, their minds begin to work. "Don't worry about Asa," Luther told them the next day. "I can handle him."

"Have you got a contract with him?" Shelly asked.

The boy shook his head. "He heard me singin' one time and said he'd help me. Got me a place to stay, an' a job at the hotel."

Freeport was in a position to be magnanimous. "Sounds like a fine man, Luther. We'll have to do something for him." He thought for a moment, pursed his lips and went on. "Of course, the corporation will have to have full ownership of your contract, but I'm sure we can make it worth this uh—"

"Asa Kemp."

"—yes, uh, Asa Kemp. We can make it well worth Mr. Kemp's time and efforts spent. I think perhaps a thousand dollars might—"

"Forget it," Luther said, giving Shelly and Freeport the first solid indication of a somewhat darker character. "I'll take care of old Asa."

Freeport smiled indulgently. He exchanged a glance with Shelly that said, *This infant knows nothing about business.* And Shelly had a Roman candle thought-burst that said very distinctly, *Freeport, we have maybe got ourselves a tiger by the short hairs.*

"Well, Luther, we'll see." The Colonel placated him, adding, "Why don't we call this Mr. Kemp, and have him come by for a drink?" Luther shook his head.

"We have to go there," he said. "He won't leave the bicycle shop during the day. He's got a thing."

Shelly and the Colonel exchanged their glances, and Freeport moved to get his pills from the table. "All right, Luther, why don't we go see Mr. Kemp right now, so we can clear things up here, and be on that ten-thirty plane to New York. How does that sound?"

Luther shrugged. Shelly thought wryly that Luther was very large on shrugs. He was also beginning to notice that Luther had very, very sharp teeth.

It was a fairly safe bet that Asa Kemp was about to get twelve or fifteen inches stripped off his ass. The hard way. Shelly felt uneasy; also greedy. *The grab is a helluva disease,* he thought, as they descended in the elevator.

He thought about it as the rented limousine pulled up before The Brown. He thought about it all the way across town to the bicycle shop. He stopped thinking about it when he saw Asa Kemp for the first time.

Only a fink could worry about cheating such an easy mark. Asa Kemp was born to be had. He wore wire-frame glasses. And a bow tie. Clip-on.

"Luther!" His face looked like a bonito bettor's at hit time. "Son, how *ah* you!" He didn't really want an answer. He grabbed the boy around the shoulders and hugged him carelessly. "Ruth was askin' after you, boy."

Then he noticed the silk-suited accompanists, and his smile broadened, became a company grin for the folks at large. "Afternoon," he beamed.

"Mr. Kemp," Shelly began, and never finished.

"Luther!" The fat little woman came through the curtains at the rear of the shop. She seemed out of place here among the frames and wheels and rubber tubes strung about the walls, yet she moved between the rough wooden benches and the racked bicycle parts with the ease of familiarity. She held Luther at arm's length and blinked at him myopically.

"Where have you *been,* Luther Sellers?" she chided him with false severity. "You've had poor Asa and me about worried to death! Do you know we didn't even know you'd entered the Talent Show at the Fair till we saw't in the paper this morning that you'd won. Lord, son, you mustn't *worry* us like that!"

Luther stared at her coldly. Even to Shelly there was a warmth here, and though he did not do it openly, he felt like smiling at the pleasant Kemps. But Luther stared at them coldly.

"This is Colonel Freeport from New York," Luther said briskly. "He wants he should talk to you." He opened the door for Freeport, and stepped back.

The Kemps turned their glances to the massive, leonine head of Colonel Jack Freeport, and a wash of fear marred the placid features of Ruth Kemp for an instant. Asa was just behind, as though the wave had found him an instant later.

Then they composed themselves, their fear of the big town strangers sublimated. "How do ya do, suh," Ruth Kemp beamed a gingerbread smile at Freeport.

"Mrs. Kemp." Freeport angled his head in that peculiarly charming and disarming manner only three kinds of people can manage: true aristocrats, well-bred cavaliers, and con artists.

"It's a pleasure to meet you." Asa Kemp extended his gnarled and oil-stained hand. Freeport took it without hesitation. Shelly noted the stepping-down to the common man's level with approval. His admiration and fear of Freeport's amazing way with all types continued to grow as their association lengthened.

"Mr. Kemp, it's more than a pleasure to meet you. Luther here has been telling us what a wonderful thing you did for him, getting him his start, and now that he's on his way, we had to come along and say thank you, thank you very much." Freeport piped his snake-charming tune while Shelly made a silent background accompaniment of nods and reassuring smiles.

Ruth Kemp's face began to alter, subtly. Shelly watched.

There was something afoot here, and while her bumpkin husband might get laid out in his grave and have the dirt dumped in his face, smiling and unaware all the while, this woman knew the slickers were here to rob her. She may not have been Polish by descent, but there was the hard, lined look of the babushka-wearing, shopping bag-toting peasant about her. Suddenly. Her voice no longer floated along in its rhythmic, pleasured style.

There was suddenly a serrated edge. "What are you heah foah, Mr. Freeport?" she asked.

"Nothing, really, Mrs. Kemp." Freeport tried to smooth out the surface of the discussion, sensing intuitively that a true light had begun to shine through his words.

Shelly interjected, "When we heard Luther sing and play, Mr. Kemp—" trying to draw Asa Kemp further into the dealings, rather than leaving them in the mouth and hands of the suddenly-too-competent Ruth, "—we felt he was destined for better things than Louis . . . "

"My husband manages Luther," Ruth Kemp inserted flatly.

"Yes, we under*stand* that," Freeport said, almost obsequiously, "and that's why we've come to—"

"Are you taking Luther to New York, is that it?" Asa asked gently.

Shelly felt a pang. He neither acknowledged nor identified it. This was big gravy now, no time for sentiment.

"Well, we—" Shelly began.

"They're taking him away, and they're here to jew us out of our share!" There was a snap in Ruth Kemp's words. At the word "jew" Shelly's head came up with anger. He stared at the woman, knowing she had not heard his name, for it had not been given. *Jew us, huh, lady . . . is* that *the word . . . well, you've never seen jewing till you've seen Morgenstern.*

Now all the compassion he had felt for these unaffected people fled, and Shelly was ready to do battle, his eyes cleared of impairing, foolish sentimentality.

"Mr. Freeport," Asa Kemp said gently, "you have to forgive my wife. Ruth gets upset sometimes." He turned to the fiercely belligerent little woman and touched her shoulder. "Ruth, please. I'm sure Mr. Freeport is here to do the best for Luther. After all we can't give him—"

"We gave him love, and we gave him our home to live in, and we found work for him, and singing jobs for him, and you'd just stand there, Asa Kemp, and let them take him away, prob'ly make a fortune with him, while we smile and say, 'It's all the best for little Luther.' Well, you've done it too many times in the past, Asa, and it's not going to happen *this* time.

"If they want to have Luther, they got to pay us for our share of his contract, or we don't have to—"

Luther's voice was as soft as a chloroformed rag: "We don't have no contract, Miz Kemp."

There was abrupt, smothering silence in the bicycle shop.

Everyone realized what the boy had done. He had left the bag open purposely, and the alley cat had crawled out to be smelled by everyone. Silence would have meant perhaps a little more dickering, and the remote possibility that Freeport and Morgenstern would cool on taking Luther with them—but it would have meant money to the Kemps. He had denied them their stranglehold, showed they were screaming into the wind, and had insured his position with Colonel Freeport.

It was the calculated move of a very smart operator.

It smelled bad, even to Shelly, so anxious to see this woman with her inadvertent prejudice stomped into the linoleum. It smelled very bad.

Ruth Kemp's face disintegrated. She sobbed once, lightly, and turned away. What she had counted on as an ally had turned out to be the enemy who had destroyed her; she vanished behind the curtains.

Asa Kemp stared with empty eyes. He was suddenly a very old man.

"Well, I feel you people are entitled to something for all the time and good will you've spent on Luther," Jack Freeport said. He reached into his inner jacket pocket for his checkbook.

Luther's hand stopped him. "You don't owe them nothin'," he said flatly. His voice was very even, much lower than his singing voice, almost unreal. "They did what they wanted to, and they wouldn't of, if they hadn't wanted to. So I'm all squared with them.

They had from me, an' I had from them. That finishes it." He turned to go.

Shelly and Freeport stood rooted for a long moment, then turned to follow. As the tinkle of the little brass bell over the door filled the bicycle shop, Asa Kemp's voice stopped Luther in the doorway.

"Ah hope you'll be happy, Luther." There was no veiled meaning in his voice. He said what he meant.

The boy turned and walked out onto the street. Shelly was the last to leave; he looked around the shop. Something had happened here. Something important. What it was, he was not quite sure; but something dreadfully important had occurred, and he knew he would think about it.

When the plane climbed above the clouds, Shelly saw that Luther was staring intently out the window, across the wing, and down into the massed cotton candy of the banks. He watched the boy for a while, then turned to snub out the cigarette in the armrest ashtray. He heard the vague murmur of words beside him, and turned back to the boy.

Luther's hand was pressed against the Plexiglas. His face was close to the port.

He was saying, over and over, very softly, but very distinctly, "Goodbye, you poor sonofabitch, goodbye."

Shelly wondered if something hadn't happened to the air conditioning.

He was, all at once, quite cold.

FIVE

Athena sprang full-blown from the forehead of Zeus, and it was later said that Stag Preston had sprung in a like manner from the forehead of Colonel Jack Freeport. It wasn't exactly like that, but close enough not to matter. Stag Preston emerged full-grown from the cast-off eighteen-year-old shell of Luther Sellers.

Once in New York, Freeport began molding the raw material he had acquired into a marketable commodity. First came the contracts, many contracts, all sized and planed and pruned and riveted at the loopholes. Freeport owned thirty percent of the boy, Shelly owned thirty percent, and—much to everyone's surprise—Luther owned forty percent. How had it happened? Well:

Luther's face at the sight of the massed grayness that was Manhattan might easily have been done by Rockwell for the front cover of the *Saturday Evening Post*. It was tanned, upturned, astounded. Shelly had thought it impossible in an age when any large city—Louisville included—was a small surrogate for New York, but Luther goggled and boggled and swept his head around in wide circles of enjoyment.

"*Jeezus*, willya look at *that*!" Luther cried as they swept over the Pulaski Skyway. The rented Cadillac convertible had seemed an unnecessary bit of vulgar ostentation to Shelly when they had found it waiting at Newark Airport. But now, as they sped across the hanging panorama of the city, Morgenstern realized it had been a calculated bit of Freeportian showmanship. Impress the kid, sway the kid, let him know there were larger gods; dealings were always simpler with someone off-balance.

The chauffeur threw the car ahead, and eventually they came down the spinning ramp into the Lincoln Tunnel. Luther's excitement was a contagious thing, and Shelly remembered the first time he had seen the city, from the window of a Greyhound bus. It was very nearly like that now, vicariously.

The bathroom-tiled tunnel echoed around them and Luther giggled with barely restrained excitement. Hey!

Out of the tunnel at 41st Street, and rising around them was the jungle. Shelly despised clichés, but to him, since that day the Greyhound had pulled into the Port Authority Building, it had been just that. A jungle. Filled with eaters and eaten. Filled with walkers and the walked-upon. Filled with those who took, and the saggy-faced ones who constantly got tooken. It was, very much, a jungle. Where the claw and the fang were Max Factored and Brooks Brothered to look like the glib line and the quick smile. He had made it in this jungle, primarily because he was one of the hungrier of the hungry ones, and he had the underlying feeling, as he caught the fever of joy and wonder from Luther, that this kid was equipped with the biggest appetite Jungle York had ever seen.

"Shelly, get Phil Moore over to the office about four; and check with Needleman—no, not Needleman—better get hold of Joe Costanza, see who he feels can do a promotion job on our boy here." The Colonel threw a hand onto Luther's shoulder.

Luther ignored the hand, ignored the Colonel, continued to drink deeply of the cup of New York.

Shelly jotted the instructions on a scrap of paper from one pocket, nodded, and smiled to himself. The full treatment. Phil Moore was known in the trade as "The Doctor." An adept at forming and styling a performer's act, he was one of the most expensive behind-the-scenes talents going. Shelly's estimation of Freeport's estimation of their property changed, just by mention of Moore's name. Freeport was certain they had something.

Still Shelly wondered. The rock'n'roll craze seemed to have reached its peak, seemed to be going downhill. Since the payola scandals, the FCC clamping tighter restrictions on the industry,

Presley's return from Germany toned-down slightly, but noticeably . . . was it a dying horse?

Or could Moore, as well as Costanza and his crack team of flak-merchants, merchandise Luther in a different manner? Did the boy have what Shelly (and apparently Freeport) had come to *think* he had? Shelly's memory of Luther at the talent contest returned. The faces of the women in the audience—he had . . . what? . . . reached them, *held* them. Yes, Luther could make it.

But first, conquer the flaws in the initial design.

A memory of Asa Kemp intruded. Flaws?

Yeah, those, too.

They pulled up in front of the Sheraton-Astor and the bellhops magically erupted from inside. Tourists with bags that overpowered them stood waiting while Freeport's entourage made its way up the steps, across the lobby, and into an elevator waiting for them alone. The floor Jack Freeport had rented six years before now no longer had a number. It might have been between the twelfth and fourteenth floors of the Sheraton-Astor . . . and it might not. It was unnumbered because it was very much foreign soil in the hotel's bosom. It was Freeportland.

"Shelly, tend to those items while I shower," Freeport ordered, heading through the amethyst- and cream-colored living room. Shelly turned to the bank of phones on the Italian marble-topped desk.

"Make yourself at home, Luther," Freeport said as he disappeared into the master bedroom. In a moment the sound of a shower filled the room. Then the bedroom door was closed. Luther took in the suite, let fly a low, meaningful (and to Shelly possessively contemplative) whistle, and threw himself onto the amethyst-tinted sofa. His feet left sliding black smudges.

"Whoooeee-*sheet*!" he exclaimed.

Shelly sniggered under his breath. *That's right, baby, be impressed. Contract time is here at last.*

"This whole joint belong to the Colonel?" Luther asked. Shelly nodded, crushing the latest cigarette into a fresh ashtray. "Every interiorly decorated inch of it, Luther." He dialed a number, waited, lit a fresh cigarette.

A querulous hello came from the other end; Shelly's face broke into a smile transmitted through the voice. Jolly. "Joe, baby! Shelly here, we is *back*, man . . ."

And that was the way it went for the next hour.

Eventually, he called Carlene.

He looked dehydrated by that time, but not from the heat. He looked like the wrinkled, sweating rubber shell of a balloon about to expire. Shirt open, hair faintly mussed, the cigarettes now pacing one after another from the corner of his mouth, he excused himself and went into one of the side sitting rooms, where he dialed the number he knew best.

The phone rang three times and he knew she had to be out. Carlene was a woman who lived on the phone, whose sole line of communication with the outside world was the Princess phone, in coral, next to the bed. Where was she? He felt the same helpless rage, the same ineffectual trapped feeling he knew every time he rang her up and found her out. At times like that he wanted to lock all her clothes away, like the whacks in the bad jokes and the mystery stories—the big-time gangster shacking with the nympho, the guy who has to keep his broad naked with only high heels or she'll ball anyone in sight—but the image was too weird and he put it away. He substituted a simple smash in the mouth.

It was at times like this that he felt he knew how junkies got hooked. He knew their feelings. He was hooked on her. On a girl whose body was a commodity, and he happened at the moment to be the biggest demand for her supply.

He hung up and ground out his cigarette, half-smoked, in the clean ashtray. He lit another and returned to the living room to continue the business calls.

Shelly set the wheels in motion.

The Colonel showered and lingered at his toilet.

Luther examined every corner and room of the suite.

And then, it was too soon time to talk contract. The evening was close, and the Colonel demanded his dinner. It always seemed that way to Shelly. Freeport would personally call room service, and order the dinner, but it never seemed to be ordering; it was always demanding.

And after the squab on Austrian toast, the potatoes au gratin, the bottle of Liebfraumilch 1957 (from Freeport's personal stock in the hotel's wine cellar), the baked Alaska, it was talktime.

"We'll need a stenographer," Freeport said, wiping his mouth, wiping his hands, dipping the end of the linen napkin in his water glass and touching the corners of his mouth.

"I'll get Jeanie Friedel," Shelly answered. He shoved away from the table, made another phone call, and returned to the table.

They stared at each other in expectant uneasiness. The animals were beginning to sniff each other; the hunting season had opened right on schedule. From where Shelly sat, the Colonel seemed to have the larger-bore weapon.

"More coffee?" Shelly asked.

Luther shook his head.

Freeport took a pill. He took a capsule. He took a pepsin tablet.

Shelly lit a cigarette. It tasted foul. He snubbed it, and almost immediately lit another.

Luther coughed self-consciously, covered it with another, a forced cough from deep in the throat.

Shelly dragged on the cigarette.

The elevator sighed open beyond the door, and the doorbell went off an instant later. They each started, and Shelly recovered first, pushing back his chair. "I'll get it. Must be Jeanie."

When he opened the door, the girl caught him with her eyes, and there was a glint of something quick, taunting, smoldering. She smiled, lowering her eyes coquettishly. "Hello, Sheldon," she said, whispering it; calculated sexuality couched in a tight challenge. One step out of reach. It was wholly incongruous: this was Shelly, or Shel or Shel-baby, but never, except by Mama Morgenstern, Sheldon.

He felt his face going tight; the bitch with the heart like a popsicle. She edged past him, her smile turned elsewhere, but somehow (Bast, you cat goddess!) still on Shelly. He watched her back as she moved across the room . . . the play of her legs, moving more than her body. She had a way of carrying herself that most tall girls had never learned. It was the movement they spoke about when they used the word statuesque.

Silkenly, gliding, coming off the balls of the feet in little, long strides that stretched the fabric of her slim skirt taut; strides that made strangely disturbing emotions run through the Colonel's right-hand man.

"Good evening, Colonel Freeport," she said, and though there was nothing in the tone, Shelly could detect a come-on as flagrant as any he'd ever encountered.

Jean Friedel was on the make.

Not for Shelly and his measly twenty grand a year, but for something bigger. Perhaps Freeport, perhaps anyone else who had wanted what she wanted. Did it really matter who?

This was the tempting shape of the hungry ones in Jungle York.

"Good evening, Jean." The Colonel smiled at her with the particular return-smile of a man who has known a woman, and further, knows what she is, who she is. Shelly found a spiteful pleasure in the knowledge that though Jean looked at Sheldon Morgenstern as small peanuts . . . still, she would never hook the Colonel. Freeport might make her, if she was offering it, but she was being conned. By an expert.

"We'll be needing your superlative stenographic abilities, my dear." Freeport leered at her. To Shelly, it was the smile of the cat, gauging tibia, fibula and femur. To Jean Friedel, it was a return image of her own come-on.

To Colonel Jack Freeport, it was getting the job done. A girl who thought she would get something for "service" would be certain to give good—service.

"Jean, I'd like you to meet Luther. You'll be taking down some things Luther has to say in a few minutes, and we want to be sure you keep it in strictest confidence.

"We have big things planned for this boy." He waved her on to Luther, who stared at the tall, dark-haired girl with an open appraisal.

It was slave-block time in the land of Luther Sellers.

The boy leaped up and shook hands with the hotel stenographer vigorously. His smile was as engaging in intensity as his scowl had been facing Asa Kemp. "I'm very pleased to meetcher, Miss—" He left it hanging the way he had seen it done in the movies.

She gave him a beggar's smile and moved the flash and fire back to Freeport. "I'm ready any time you are, Colonel."

I'll just bet you are, thought Shelly.

Freeport waved Shelly and Jean to chairs at the table, settled back with another pill and a glass of water. For a moment Luther stood staring at the trio, then he too sat down, placing himself across the table from the others. Almost as though sides were being drawn up.

"Well, Luther, it's time we dispensed with some very small business details," the Colonel said. He beamed at the boy and opened his mouth to speak again.

"Sixty percent." Luther stopped him. "I get sixty percent of my own contract."

Shelly was too amazed to notice the Colonel's expression, but he was certain it was one of blood-draining confusion. Of course, the boy would pull off no such hat trick, but the gall . . . the temerity . . .

One hour later, far less time than any of them thought it would take, Colonel Jack Freeport (Savannah, New York, Cannes, and London) had agreed to a contract the terms of which assigned Shelly Morgenstern thirty percent of Luther Seller's earnings, himself thirty percent, and the boy retained forty percent. It was not that unusual a legal form, except Freeport had never before gone that route. He owned one hundred percent (where more was not feasible) of any enterprise he dipped into, and at the end of that contract, there were several shifts in attitude.

Freeport realized he had a live item on his hands, one which was not going to be duped, and for that reason came to the competition better prepared; Freeport was unsettled about Luther's hipness in gaining majority control of his own contract—how had he pulled *that* cursed stunt?—but he was already counting unhatched chickens.

Luther's opinion had changed, also. He was not so much in awe of these dynamiting promoters. He had bluffed once, had made it stick, and realized his muscles were firmer than he had thought.

Shelly changed his mind radically: Luther's brand of What-MakesSammyRun was not innocent ruthlessness. It was calculated. At that moment, what had been vague distaste for his brain child, turned chameleon-like into outright dislike.

As for Jean Friedel . . .

The base of operations had shifted. In her heart of hearts she could not see the difference between grave-robbing and cradle-robbing. All's fair . . .

And so that was how Luther Sellers gained control of the valuable contract of Stag Preston.

Since one admired the other so much, it seemed just naturally the way the old mop flops. Or as Shelly put it in one of his getting-more-frequent introspective moments: *That, friends, is how the old train derails.*

SIX

Phil Moore did things with Luther Sellers that Pygmalion would have admired. It was decided at a policy meeting that they would avoid the Jerry Lee Lewis image (spangled jackets, yellow ochre peg-cuff pants, fifteen pounds of marcelled hair, green lace shirts), while at the same time steering away from the Pat Boone brand of cleanliness. He was consequently inculcated by the mysteries of slim Continental suits, Italian loafers, conservative gray ties, and a manner of walking, talking, *thinking* that retained the minuscule charms of his Kentucky roots, forcefully brought out the humble, disarming manner so psychologically necessary for proper identity, while at the same time reinforcing the animal sexuality of the boy.

They tried names on.

Luther fitted badly inside a charcoal-gray name like Bruce Barton. He glared out hostilely when covered with Alan Prince. The vulgar innuendo of Brick Colter sat on his shoulders jarringly, and Matt Gore almost made it but was eventually discarded because the sleeves were too long.

It was Shelly who came up with Stag Preston.

Natural? Like a run of sevens.

As it was analyzed nine months later in a journal of general semantics: "We cannot by any means overlook the simplest explanation of the priapic Given Name; it is that combination of onomatopoeia and naturalism quickly identified as masculine, forceful, imperative. Stallion, stud, *stag*—each of these conjures the phallic interpretation, sets aside any misconceptions of homosexuality due to the nature of the bearer's style or bearing, and leads the gestalt female attention to the heart of the bearer's presentation. 'Preston' bears the same *hard* quality, in much the same manner employed by Thomas Hardy when he called the hero of *The Mayor of Casterbridge* Michael *Henchard*. Henchard, trenchard. Such awareness, on the part of those responsible for Mr. Preston's public image, of the subliminal potency of the *sound* of certain words, merely indicates yet another of the many reasons for this young man's success."

Joe Costanza and Shelly held long conferences, far into the night, first mapping out the larger areas of promotion, then fine-tuning the program, eventually dwelling with almost pathological attention on the smallest details:

Who should get the first news break about Stag?

(If we give it to Cholly Knickerbocker no one will notice it outside of New York, but we'll have a strong source in Manhattan for future use. But if we plant it with Winchell, not only will it make his column, but he's got that new TV spot, and a mention there—mysteriously tipped as he's made a rep doing it for the past seven hundred years—we'll get a nationwide break. Then there's Kilgallen, or maybe Hedda . . . or a parlay, handing it out in three different regional areas . . . the overlap might not be too bad. But if one tipped to the other's having the same info, we might make an enemy or three . . .)

What label should we record him on?

(If we set up our own company, we lose out on the effective promotion someone like Columbia or Victor might give us. But if we go for one of the big boys, we'll have to cut them in for a taste . . .)

Who gets the first TV look at him?

(If we go the Dick Clark route, then he gets identified as a teen star, and the adults sneer. If we avoid Clark and go the Sullivan or Dinah Shore way, we lose the instant identification of the teenagers. How about . . .)

What product tie-ins should we allow?

(Cereals are out—pre-teens. The T-shirt, charm bracelet, chewing gum bit might be a little too adolescent. If we try to foist off

Stag Preston dinner jackets we'll get laughed at all the way to AfterSix and back. No, best we stay in the sport shirt and after-shave lotion area, with a try for the teens on their own level, but decorous, like very decorous . . .)

Finally, it came time for the pitch.

Shelly made his phone calls—how would the hipster operate so easily, without that wondrous gadget?—and the studio was reserved. A rented studio, a pick-up orchestra, special arrangements commissioned by an unnamed top female exec of a top record company, mastered by a top technician working for one of the smaller jazz labels, and a small group of background singers prepared to drop in *Doo-wah* or *Oo-oo-ooo* when needed.

Out of that session (it was a take on the third try) came Stag Preston's first record, "I Don't Know You Anymore," b/w "Car Hop Angel."

Demo discs were cut off the master and surreptitiously circulated to the four or five most influential A&R men in the trade, with no buildup, merely the word that they had come over from Freeport. They were listened to with careful attention, and tentative feelers came back to the suite in the Sheraton-Astor. Shelly held them off, parlaying interest in the anonymous singer (for there had been no explanatory label on the demos) and promising something very interesting, very soon.

Something very soon was three days later; something very interesting was a personal invitation to the A&R men who had received the demos, to be Colonel Jack Freeport's guests at a high school sock hop in Parma, Ohio.

A chartered plane flew Freeport, Shelly, Joe Costanza, and their guests to Cleveland where three Cadillacs sat panting, prepared for the drive to the suburb of Parma.

The high school was ablaze with lights, and one of Cleveland's leading disc jockeys, Bob Mandle, was waiting. The sock hop was a benefit to raise money for the high school's new library and auditorium. Mandle had been contacted to plan the show, had imported up-and-coming rock'n'roll talent who would work cuffola for the publicity—and Freeport had mildly suggested Stag Preston be made a featured headliner.

He was billed as "A Surprise Mystery Guest" which conjured images of anyone from Frankie Avalon to Lanny Ross, depending on who was conjuring.

The A&R men knew only that they were going to meet the mystery talent Jack Freeport had avoided discussing with them. Shelly could see interest in their faces; arrangements such as these were tantamount to an offer of big gold.

When Mandle led them into the huge gym, Shelly realized Freeport had done more than merely suggest that Mandle feature Stag. (It was a sort of brainwashing that had been effected by the weeks of preparation of their talent; he no longer thought of the boy as Luther; now he was Stag, even in unguarded thoughts.)

A suggestion might have gotten Stag a spot on the bill, but the opulence of the decorations, the almost studiedly melodramatic stage on which the artists would perform—Shelly dredged up memories of Warner Bros. musicals circa 1940—meant the Colonel had shelled out some sugar to swing Mandle to his way of thinking. Some money that had been spent to do the place up the way Freeport thought it should be done up—all the better to showcase you, my dear: a contribution to the library/auditorium fund—one of Mandle's weak spots in these days of public service, now that the payola stink was dulled by the shortness of public memory.

"Seats for you in the front row," Mandle said, grinning, his expression that of a college senior. He waved them to the padded chairs facing the stage. "Show's about to start."

Already the gym was filled. Almost eight hundred boys and girls were jammed into the gym, filling the chairs behind the A&R men, overflowing into the back of the room where they were packed, standing.

Freeport nodded to Mandle, who made a thumb and forefinger

circle, still grinning boyishly. Then he went behind the rigged curtains, and the sounds of guitars tuning, squawking saxophones, a set of traps floated out to key the high school crowd higher.

Shelly leaned over to Freeport. "I'll take a look in on the kid. See how he's doing." Freeport nodded, his eyes straight ahead. This was payoff time for the Colonel, and his stomach was erupting. Shelly withdrew a bottle of capsules from his jacket and pressed it into the older man's hand. Then he rose, excused himself, smiled at Sid Feller of ABC-Paramount, and moved toward the swinging doors to the locker rooms.

The locker rooms had been set up as dressing rooms and Shelly passed down the rows of metal lockers noting the half dozen groups or individual talents Mandle had managed to suck into this benefit.

Luther was alone in the last row.

He was sitting disconsolately on a bench, clad only in socks, shorts, and T-shirt. His hands down between his knees. The expression he wore was one of expectation, not nervousness. Shelly lit a cigarette and stood behind the boy, studying him.

Stag Preston sat there. A shadow, a flicker, a hint of Luther Sellers remained, but now it was Stag Preston who looked out of the dark, hungry eyes. It was someone new, a creature of comment and gold dust and wishful thinking. But it breathed, and it moved, and it was real.

"Scared?" Shelly said, softly. He realized as he said it that he hoped it was true; there had to be a chink in the armor somewhere. But even as Stag Preston's head came up and around, Shelly knew it wasn't true. The hard, wanting gleam was still there, shining dully.

"Hi, Shelly," Stag answered.

"Scared?" he asked again, by rote.

Stag Preston's face twisted in the semblance of a smile. His voice sounded far away, bemused, preoccupied: "No, not scared, just thinkin'."

Shelly sucked on the cigarette. "About what?"

"Oh, about this 'n' that. Thinkin' about Lou'ville and gettin' outta there . . . 'bout what I was, what I'm gonna be."

What are you going to be, Stag; what? Shelly thought.

"You haven't come that far yet," Shelly said.

Stag Preston looked at him sharply. "Oh, man, you don't *know.* You just don't *know!* I've come all the world away. I've made it out, I've busted loose, an' I ain't—I'm *not* goin' to stop till I've got it all. All of it. *You'll* see."

Shelly crushed the cigarette underfoot. Perhaps this was the moment of truth. Perhaps this might be the story Shelly had suspected might be there. He'd wet-nursed this kid for weeks through all the training, all the publicity preparations, but had gotten no closer to him. Maybe this would be the moment when he could work up some warmth for Stag Preston.

"You really want to make it, don't you, kid?"

Stag nodded. There was a softness in his smile now. "Ah sure do, Shelly. Ah never wanted anythin' so much in all my life. You don't know how bad I had it . . . really bad . . . "

Shelly sat down on the bench beside the boy and lit another cigarette. His dark, searching eyes probed Stag Preston's face, looking for some things. For an instant he thought he found them.

"Tell me, will you, Luther? Tell me what you can, how about it? I'd like to know. I mean, we're . . . friends now, as much as business partners. We should know about each other."

The boy toyed with his full lower lip, worrying it with his teeth. Then he pursed his lips and nodded okay. "I s'pose you're right. I never told anyone what it was like, mostly maybe because nobody could do anythin' about it."

Shelly waited. A silence.

Beyond the locker room doors the sound of a combo striking up broke the hush. The show was beginning; but Stag Preston was the smash finale, so they had time—perhaps too much time. Shelly listened.

"I'll tell ya about my father, Shelly. That's the important part. My old man was a gas, Shelly. He was the end, the livin' end. He came outta the oil fields—Burkburnett, Texas, how about that—and joined the Army, spent about eleven years pushin' stripes up his arms. Then he got mustered out at Fort Knox, met my old lady and decided to stay in Lou'ville. Except what he never told my old lady, was that he'd been sick once, overseas some damnplace and they'd put him on narcotics, some kinda junk I don't know, and he'd got hooked. *That* was why he got mustered outta the service. He was a real junkie. Spent ev'ry cent he made packin' in the dust.

"Finally he pulled off a good one . . . got my old lady on the stuff. It's like when one of 'em has it he wants to give it to ev'rybody in sight. So my old lady got turned on, and one day the court just sent me off to the Home, took Pop and my old lady away, and that was it.

"I busted out, made it on my own, and that was when I met the Kemps—" he stopped, remembering his final encounter with Asa Kemp and his wife. It stopped him. He subsided. Finally, he added, "I don't want no pity, no handouts. I can make it on my own; I always have. I can make it, all I need is the chance."

He stared up at Shelly with a mute pleading . . . and still that diamond glint of something else.

Shelly felt pity nonetheless. Father a junkie, mother obviously so helplessly in love with the man she stood still for anything, even to becoming as sick as her mate. The kid a product of orphan or reform homes . . . no love . . . no direction . . . no friends . . . yes, there was room to admire and respect and love Stag Preston. If it was possible to cut away the hungry desire, the fat on his soul, then it might be possible to strike up a rapport with the naked, lonely child that remained.

Shelly put an arm around the boy, squeezed his shoulder. "Take it slow, kid. You're going to crack-'em-out completely tonight." He punched Stag lightly on the biceps and rose to go.

Stag Preston's eyes were moist, and they looked at Shelly with a fierce friendliness. Shelly moved to leave.

"Hey, Shelly . . . ?"

He paused, turned. Stag was still staring at him.

"Thanks, Shelly."

He winked, turned, and walked back out through the swinging doors.

On the stage the TempTones were belting out a song whose lyrics perhaps only Lumumba could decipher. In the front row the A&R men were bored. Sid Feller of ABC-Paramount was the only one making a valiant effort to stay awake; he kept blinking rapidly, opening his eyes very wide every few seconds. Finally, in desperation, he began rubbing at an eye, murmuring, "Damn contact lenses itch," to Joe Goldberg of Prestige Records. Goldberg nodded, stifling a yawn. The Colonel had his eyes closed. Shelly stepped out through the gym's side exit to have another smoke.

Up there, the stars. Down here, another one getting ready to go nova. Shelly Morgenstern lit up, drew deeply, and pondered absolutely nothing at all. Except maybe the inner workings of hatred, and how foolish it was to become part of that mechanism. To hate Stag was folly; he was a kid, simply a kid. He wasn't the ogre Shelly had begun to envision, endowed with the cunning and ruthlessness of an animal. He was a lonely, unhappy kid with a lousy background and a drive to succeed that seemed out of line next to the torpid desires of most people. But he wasn't a monster. Not at all.

Shelly lipped the butt a final time, snapped it away. It hit the gray expanse of the basketball court, showered lovely orange sparks in a wide fan, and was carried away by the ground breeze. Shelly sighed once, deeply, and looked at the stars.

The ethical structure of the universe. How does it apply to you and me . . . you and I . . . Adelaide's Lament . . . a community theatre in Ridgewood, New Jersey . . . a girl in the bushes with a best friend . . . she had to put a cat out for the night while the neigh-bors were away . . . *thoughts*.

He caught himself. Stream of consciousness is all right if your name is James Joyce, but if it's Sheldon Morgenstern, keep them thoughts on Carlene (whom you are keeping, but whom you have not seen since before Louisville), on the Mercedes-Benz (which you are paying on, but haven't driven since before Louisville), on the kid in there who is climbing into his Continental suit, this very moment (a kid who has taken up your time completely, since Louisville). Thoughts. The bane of the working classes.

Shelly sighed again, turned to the gym door, and swung it open. His foot was in the air when the final thought—completely divorced from the others—came through:

Jeanie Friedel.

Bam!

Just like that. He saw again the look Stag Preston had given her at the contract-signing. It had been the glimpse of another face entirely. Someone else's face. The odd and strange and unfamiliar. Then Shelly stepped through into the gym.

For comparison, Mandle had collared the local Cleveland talent, a singer named Bubba Walthers; a kid who had come up with a mild success that Paul Anka had covered after its fourth week on the charts (and had gone over three of a million with it). That had been Bubba Walthers's sole claim to fame; still, he was a local hero. And good comparison for what was to come.

Walthers finished his number, took a smattering of applause that was more reminiscence and lost glory than fervor, and bowed off the stage.

Then Mandle came on again. His face was so well-scrubbed Shelly thought he might have done it with a Brillo pad.

He took the mike in both hands, bending the stand toward him-self, and a tone of such sincerity, such camaraderie suffused the gym that even the A&R men sat a little straighter. Sid Feller said to hell with it, popped the offending contact lens out into the palm of his hand, rubbed his eye till it watered, and proceeded to cleanse it by putting it on his tongue and washing it with saliva. As Mandle went on, the Am-Par A&R man pulled up his eyelid and snapped the invisible hemisphere of optical glass back in. Satisfied, he settled back, an expectant tilt to his head. If there was anything here, he was going to get it on paper; he caught the female executive of one of the other majors staring at him, gauging him. He intended to beat her out. Mandle was still talking.

Whatever it was that Bob Mandle said, in announcement of the mystery guest, Shelly did not hear it; only that all-pervading warmth filling the gym. Mandle snapped his fingers, the combo struck its intro notes—monotonous, infectious, basic—and the curtain swept back to reveal Stag Preston.

"Boys *will* be boys," Sid Feller murmured, sizing up Stag Preston with a cool, promoter's eye.

"Here he is," Mandle pontificated, *"Stag Preston!"*

It was a mixture of disappointed *ah's* and *damn's* from the youthful crowd, intermingled with applause. The great American tradition of applauding *any*thing, by habit, not merit.

Then Stag Preston came on:

Like Gang Busters . . .

Like Attila the Hun . . .

Like Quantrill and all his raiders . . .

Like Stag Preston under full steam and I'm goin' *all* the way and get outta my line of fire because this is *it*, baby, *it* with nitro!

He belted out "Car Hop Angel" with a drive that won the kids immediately. It was a good number, combining all the demanded idiosyncrasies of rockabilly, but with style; a little—not too much—imagination; room for vocal tricks; and enough leering suggestiveness in the phrasing to make the hipper ones titter. He went over. Big. Very big.

When he broke, and slid to one knee for the finish, they came up out of their seats as though electrocuted. They stamped and screamed and demanded more, banging their hands together and whistling, clapping the seats of their wooden chairs, hooting. The A&R men's jaw lines hardened; Sid Feller let a vague smile tilt at the corner of his mouth.

The combo began a soft comp, swaying in on the opening bars of Stag's flip-side record, "I Don't Know You Anymore."

They settled back to silence, bright-eyed, letting him prove himself again.

He sang. Lord, how he sang, Shelly thought, later.

He sang with something more than his gonads. He sang with his . . . what the hell, use it . . . his heart. He sang so that every pimply faced adolescent in that audience knew he was singing about him . . . about her. About the great affair that had just ended. About the tears in the back seat. About the look of youthful desire. About experiments on summer beaches with the others around the fire toasting the marshmallows, unaware. He sang about every sloppy, inept, melodramatic relationship indulged in by every fifteen-, sixteen-, seventeen-year-old there. He had it down pat. He had it all right there, and they took it from his extended hands. They didn't bother to examine it . . . the smell and the sound and the tough touch of it was right.

When Stag Preston finished that number, his success was a foregone conclusion. The A&R men did not stay for the nine more songs he sang, nor for the fifteen encores.

Fifteen encores, and when he left the stage, the name Stag Preston no longer brought *ah* or *damn* to the teenaged lips. It was the beginning of the underground whisper campaign so necessary to a rock'n'roll singer's success. Shelly knew it by heart, knew every inch of the self-devouring tapeworm of mouth-to-mouth promotion. As a small time DJ, before his path and Freeport's had crossed, he had experienced the dynamiting done by flak-merchants. Now he knew what he had to do.

While Stag and the A&R men and Freeport cavorted vocally (Kid, you've got it *knocked*! You are only the greatest!) in the locker room, Shelly sought out The Ringleaders.

Only Shelly thought of them that way. To Dick Clark they were "his regulars," the kids who made up the nucleus of his studio audience . . . the kids who carried the word in phone calls, letters, and mimeographed fansheets to other fanatics all over the country. To Anka or Bobby Rydell they were "the kids," the group from which these teen idols had but recently risen, and to whom they returned for the most easily identifiable praise and the subversive spreading of fame and adoration. To Shelly they were a million unpaid, deadly effective little PR men and women, scuttling around the countryside without pay or prestige—and with so much *power* the mind boggled at the concept. The hard little blonde with the kohl around her eyes who showed up every day on *American Bandstand*; the three Italian boys who boxed in the Golden Gloves and when they weren't working on construction gangs organized fan clubs for half a dozen press agents; the bespectacled, scrawny girl in Bayonne, New Jersey, who spent all her money on a lithographed poop sheet about Elvis Presley, distributed free to anyone who would send her a four-cent stamp; hundreds of them, the ones who held the reins of influence in their adolescent paws. The ones who swayed public opinion without anyone's realizing they were doing it. The ones who fed the gossip to local papers, who wrote letters to TV shows demanding their favorite; the dedicated, lonely, stardust-covered ones who would be appalled at the suggestion of accepting the tens of thousands of dollars to which they were entitled for public relations work that could never be done half so well by twenty-grand-a-year men.

These were the line troopers.

These were the informants, the stringers, the busy bees.

These were the ones Shelly Morgenstern sought out, in that audience, while Stag Preston cinched his future behind the scenes. This was Shelly's job. Sew them up. Make them feel Stag Preston was one of them, was them in fact. So the postcards would go out the next morning or even that night:

Dear Trudi,

    Tonight I heard a great new star. You got to hear him. His name is Stag Preston and he is dreamy. He has only made one record and it isn't out as yet but when you hear it you will flip on account of he really has that beat. His name is Stag Preston and his song is "I Don't Know You Any More" and on the flip side there is "Car Hop Angel" which really is swinging. I just had to write you so you could tell all the kids in San Francisco. That is about all and how are things with you? Are you still seeing Frank or is that off?

Love,
Francine Hasher

And within a few days the record shops would begin to receive calls for Stag's pressing, the radio stations would find they were being besieged for a record they had never heard about, the juke-box gangsters would find there was interest in someone named Stag Preston, and how about maybe we buy a piece of this kid, he smells like he's gonna be a mover.

Then the records would begin to flood out. Whoever did the release would have worked the artists and the photogs and the printing plants overtime to get the flyers and the poop sheets and the labels and the special 45 sleeves ready.

And then . . .

And then . . .

Shelly Morgenstern heard the faraway clicking of an adding machine. All those bucks, all that line, a real fine taste—to pay off the Mercedes, to keep Carlene happy (he put the thought of her long, smooth body out of his mind; not now, I'll tell you when), to get him as far away from the roots and soul of Sheldon Morgenstern as possible.

Mandle had given him a list of half a dozen Ringleaders. He sought them out and drew them aside, playing them like instruments, letting the scent of fame wash over them . . .

"You'll be the first Stag Preston fans in the country. Stag's going to be up there with the biggest of them, and you kids can help. How'd you like that?"

"We get regular letters from Paul Anka when we push *his* records," one sharp-eyed girl remarked.

Shelly grinned becomingly. "Honey, Stag is a *de*mon at writing letters. And he's got a bug for taking pictures all over the place. He'll not only send you letters, but some good pictures, too."

They purred.

"Bob Mandle will be plugging Stag from now on; he thinks he's great, kids, and we need your help, too. Now how about it?"

They didn't sing the "Battle Hymn of the Republic," but they might as well have . . . they were Shelly's gang. He owned them. They were, in the parlance, in his pocket.

If you like carrying grenades with the pins pulled.

SEVEN

Within a month "I Don't Know You Anymore" had passed the million mark. Stag got his first gold record, and not at all oddly, the color reflected back from it by his eyes was also gold. Everything he touched with his vocal cords turned to gold. It was not unusual for a hard-pushed talent to get one big hit, perhaps follow it with a second, not quite as socko, but it was obvious this was not the case with Stag Preston. He was not a flash in anyone's pan. He was a solid property, a talent with something new, something essential, something special. His second record was done by Hollywood songwriter Sammy Fain, the title number from an "A" picture, *The Thundering Land* (with Burl Ives, Robert Mitchum, Sal Mineo, Shirley MacLaine, and a cast of thousands—mostly nonentities). The flick grossed several million, and not a little of its success was due to Stag Preston. His rendition of "The Thundering Land" b/w "The Midas Touch" (a title Shelly considered apropos as all hell) netted him a second gold record. It passed a million and was last seen heading out of sight.

ABC-Paramount had come through with the best deal—or perhaps it was merely that Sid Feller had the sharpest eye for new talent; Shelly suspected that was why he had the cleanest contact lenses in town—and they were packaging him with four-color sleeves on his 45s, with Frank Wess backings and a promotional sweep unlike anything since Kim Novak had been shoved down an unsuspecting populace's throat.

The Brill Building was humming with word of Stag's drawing power. The sheet music operators and the sideline grifters all wanted their taste. The better mousetrap had been built, and Tin Pan Alley was beating a polished Italian loafer path to Colonel Jack Freeport's door.

Inside that door, Shelly Morgenstern, Colonel Jack Freeport, and Stag Preston held court.

The payola (now underground more than ever, discreetly delivered in white legal-size envelopes bought in Woolworth's) spread like a fine slick of oil on troubled waters; and like other troubled waters, they parted to permit Stag Preston's passage through to the Promised Land.

His first album, *Let Me Sing To You*, went onto the Top Ten in its third week and got rave reviews not only from *Cash Box*, *Variety*, and *Billboard*, but Nat Hentoff and Ralph Gleason (the former of *Jazz Review*, the latter of the syndicated column "The Rhythm Section") both found ethnic roots of true blues singing in Stag's presentation, and lauded him openly, thus interesting the jazz audience.

The following month *Down Beat* and *Metronome* each ran an article of analytical discussion anent Stag Preston's emergence as a true jazz singer, his value as the first jazz-oriented pop singer since Mathis had gone bland, and how he was saying things in the jazz idiom. They decided he had "soul."

The fires were being stoked high.

Music Vendor referred to Stag Preston as "the hottest thing since sliced bread."

Shelly caught the Colonel dry-washing his hands like a deranged miser on several occasions. It was Moneysville-on-Thames for one and all.

Stag had begun referring to Freeport as The Man.

Stag's up-tempo version of "Let Me Call You Sweetheart" was pushed like a yak-cart going uphill on every DJ show, jukebox, TV dance program, high school prom or sock hop, every record shop in the country.

Let Me Sing To You passed two million. Stag was now stacking his gold records, biting his golden fingernails, and calling Shelly, "Hey, you."

"Let Me Call You Sweetheart" went into orbit at two million twelve, and Ed Sullivan called for Stag to appear on the "See

America With Ed Sullivan" series, the show emanating from Manhattan. The Colonel, realizing the Big Time came no Bigger than this, made the deal and won Stag a close-out spot on the program. Trendex went out of its mind reporting that an estimated 23.4% of the viewing audience had switched channels to catch the second half of the Sullivan extravaganza, even if they had been elsewhere for the first half.

Arbitron, Pulse, Nielsen, and Hooper clocked similar phenomena and Stag Preston's stock hiccupped into the blue chip strata. Freeport cackled and blushed and clapped his hands in childish glee as he hung up on one agent after another.

"Jackals startin' to suck around real good now, Shelly," he commented. Stag Preston was sewed up, and there was no room for a share-the-wealth policy.

Stag's TV appearances were carefully kept to a minimum. Overexposure was the last disease Freeport wanted Stag to catch. Leukemia, but not overexposure.

There is, however, exposure . . . and exposure.

In the night scene, abruptly, Stag Preston became a familiar sight. Whether it was dinner at The Four Seasons, The Forum of the Twelve Caesars, the Chateaubriand, or The Colony . . . drinks at Sardi's (E and/or W), The Plaza, or The St. Moritz . . . champagne breakfasts at Rumpelmayers and about 1:00 P.M. a drink-breakfast at P.J. Clark's . . . The Blue Angel, Bon Soir, The Living Room . . . the Copa, the Latin Quarter, El Morocco, the Waldorf's Starlight Roof . . . the Jazz Gallery, Five Spot, the Showplace to catch Mingus and his group . . . Lindy's, the Stage Deli . . . wherever it was, wherever the hipsters congregated . . . Stag Preston's face was as much a fixture as the outstretched tip plate (with three quarters thereon) of the hat-check chick.

He found no difficulty in dating. It meant not only a juicy item in the columns to be seen with the scintillant young star, but personally Stag had that indefinable air that marked him unquestionably heterosexual, male, a real guy. There were no rumors—

no matter how malicious the speaker—that Stag was anything but broad-happy. There were, however, a few murmurs that he might be, just a teeny bit, *too* broad-happy. Yet if such rumors were grounded in fact, it seemed to make no difference to the hordes of models, pseudo-models, career girls, pseudo-career girls, visiting starlets, and call girls who made it their business to be seen in his company.

Now that the career-building had settled down somewhat, Shelly found he was able to relax.

The money was coming in nicely. He paid off the balance on the Mercedes, had it rebored and tuned, had the six assorted scrapes and scratches on its gleaming black hide repaired, and took it out on the Taconic for a run. He purposely opened it full-throat and allowed a growler to run him to the curb. He even paid the speeding ticket—with a grin that annoyed not only the prowl cop but the cherubic justice of the peace who charged him. For once, the money didn't matter.

Shelly Morgenstern had hitched his checkbook to a star named Stag Preston.

But like any star—as seen through a cloudy atmosphere—the twinkle was merely an erratic flickering.

At first the flickerings were faint, mere ghosts of what was to come. They were faint, but bothersome for all that. It began to get to Shelly the second night he had returned to staying with Carlene.

It was never hard to go back to Carlene. That was the trouble; it was like getting hooked on junk. The first one or three were easy-come-easy-go. Then a half dozen because it was chuckles. Then another one because it was wanted . . . who wanted? Oh, yeah, I wanted. And who am I?

The answer comes back as down a long, empty corridor—*You are the hooked man, man.*

That was how it was, going back to Carlene.

One of the trappings of seeming affluence, Shelly had "acquired" Carlene almost as though she had been the prize in the

Cracker Jack box. After his first big touch with a television promotion outfit (a lofty term for a *sotto voce* organization who arranged plugs on-screen for payola), he had come into the sphere of influence of Colonel Jack Freeport and one day, almost as though ordered by the stock number, Carlene had appeared in his newly furnished apartment. She had stayed on, had moved in, had lived with Shelly without past or future—only with a non-demanding present.

There was no need for Carlene to demand.

Her existence was demand enough; her face and body were her dues, and she paid them regularly.

It was the ideal, yet the most unbearable, situation for a man of Sheldon Morgenstern's constitution. It was a loveless relationship predicated solely on Shelly's ability to keep her supplied with the delicacies of life, in exchange for which she was always bed-warm and ready, as well as discreet about her transgressions. She was cook, housekeeper, secretary, and bed partner. But that was all. Her similarity to Jeanie Friedel was the spur that drove Shelly's interest between the two women. Each was cold, each was incapable of a true depth of love—whatever *that* meant. Each was compelling by the very withholding of warmth.

And maybe, Shelly had simplified it on several occasions, to himself, *I'm just a sucker for that type of broad.*

There was considerable merit in the concept.

But periodically Shelly would decide he wanted a more realistic, a less surrealistic, life. At those times he would not even consider sending Carlene away, but would move himself either to Freeport's suite in the Sheraton-Astor or would take a room in some 42nd Street fleabag.

But he always came back.

It had to be that way. She had come into his life unbidden, and by demanding only silently, bound him with his own desire.

I'm a prisoner of my crotch, Shelly would unfailingly, unhappily muse, in the cab on the way back to the apartment and Carlene.

He had thought just that, for the hundredth time, in the cab returning after Stag's career had gotten smoothly running. He had avoided going back—though the thinking could not be avoided—but it was months, and now like the hooked man he was, he was returning.

That night she bound him ever more tightly with loins and lips and liquid stillness. It may not have been the most perfect of all lives, but it was undeniably Shelly's and he was stuck with it.

When he opened the door, he knew another man (*men?*) had been there. Not too recently—there was always somebody, a bellboy, a doorman, a flak-man on his staff that Carlene had gotten to, who would tip her when he was getting ready to trek back—but someone had been there. The smell of Mixture 79 pipe tobacco was faint but detectable.

She was in the kitchen, her long, perfect legs encased in sheath slacks that fraction of an inch too tight to produce a desire to grab her by her cheeks and pull her up against him. They were white with black piping and they were topped by a silk blouse cut on full lines. Carlene was shy in the chest and though it really never occurred to anyone who was stopped by her almost Grecian-symmetrical beauty, and her height, it was a constant pique to her. Hence, the baggy blouse. Her black hair came down in a pageboy, a smooth, sloping fall that caught the kitchen light from overhead and toyed with it, much as she toyed with him. Her eyes were hidden, but Shelly saw them nonetheless. They were green. As green as something utterly unromantic.

Choose one: an unset emerald, slightly flawed
green slime on a condemned pond
a snake's skin
dollar bills old, wrinkled, being sent
    back to the mint to be burned
the color on the base of old toy soldiers.

She looked up suddenly, as he stood in the kitchen doorway,

and he was struck by the green of her eyes. They were none of the things he had considered them. They were green, very green, terribly commandingly green, extra deep, and faintly moist. (Was it from the onions a-peeling in the sink, or the mist of a woman secreted behind the iris?)

"Welcome home," he said.

"You look tired," she replied.

"What's been happening?" he said.

"Not a thing. Want a drink?" she replied.

"Not now, thanks anyhow. Any mail?" he said.

"Nothing but a few bills. I paid the current ones; you've got a letter from your tailor, whatshisname," she replied.

"Breidbart," he said, "Jack Breidbart."

"That's right. Him," she replied.

"Do not pass go; do not collect $200," he said, turning.

This time, she did not reply.

He ate dinner with her in silence, wrote out checks to cover the bills, considered *TV Guide*, and finally gave himself up to it.

They were in bed, straining, feinting, playing at mutual passions, when the phone rang.

"Damn!" he snorted, against her shoulder.

"So don't answer it," she said in the tone of a woman who is polishing her nails while talking to you, "let it ring."

It rang. It rang again. On the seventh, he hoisted off and snatched at it.

"What the hell do you want at this hour, schmuck!" he bellowed into the mouthpiece, and slammed it back onto the cradle. He fell onto his back as she rolled away from him, and for a long moment stared sightlessly at the ceiling somewhere above in the darkness. It was no good, no damned earthly good. But he had to have it; to the man who has nothing, nothing with substance is something.

The phone rang again.

This time he clapped it to his ear before the first ring had faded away.

He was about to use The Words when a woman's voice crashed against his anger. "Shelly! Shelly, for Chrissake help me!"

Jean Friedel.

"What's the matter? What the hell's wrong?"

"I'm up at the suite. He's got me locked in the bedroom . . . Jeezus, he'll break through that muthering door in a minute, Shelly, get over here!"

Only it was not that ordered, not nearly that coherent. There were breaks and sobs and frightened whimpers.

"Who? Who'll break in? Where's the Colonel; what the hell is happening, Jeanie, answer me, stop mumbling!"

"Stag, the kid. He's . . . he had too much to drink, Jeezus, he doesn't want to just make love, Shelly, he wants to, Jeezus, *I don't know what*. Please . . . get over here, will you!"

The sound of her frenzy screeched galactically past the receiver. Carlene sat up and turned on the headboard lamp; the sheet was clutched over her bosom. "What's the matter?"

He covered the mouthpiece. "The kid's got one of the hotel secretaries cornered in the suite. Freeport isn't there, I suppose. She wants me to come over." A shriek erupted from the phone.

"He's breaking down the, *Jeezus,* Shelly, *please!*"

"I'll be right over . . . keep him out somehow," he yelled, and cradled the receiver. He was out of bed and pulling on his trousers from where they had fallen on the floor, without bothering about underwear. His shirt, the jacket, and he was streaking from the apartment.

By the time he had reached the lobby, Carlene had called the doorman and a cab was waiting. "The Sheraton-Astor," Shelly squawked. He fished in his wallet and brought out a bill. Without looking at its denomination he said, "This is for the baby if you bust your ass making it over there," and was thrown back against the seat cushions as the cab careened away from the curb in a rocking U-turn.

It might be too late.

The gravy train might have already been derailed.

Oh, that bitchette! Oh, like *wow*!

Who cared if she had the ass stripped off her, who gave a bloody! Just keep that kid's rep intact. *Floor it, Jim!*

Go!

EIGHT

Shelly was out of the elevator almost before the doors had slid completely open. The suite was silent. It looked as though Quantrill had herded his raiders through mounted on rhinoceroses. The drapes were torn, tables had been overturned, one Italian marble coffee table had been broken in half as though someone had dropped an anvil on it. A stain of wet ran down the wall and on the floor beneath the stain, a shattered vase and flowers lay in a pool of moisture. Every door was open, a bookshelf had been pulled down, the telephone was off its hook and a pair of legs protruded from around the curve of the sectional sofa. Shelly's face went dry and tight.

It was all over. The show boat had gone 'round the bend for the final performance. It was enough to make a grown man shatter and bawl—hundreds of thousands of bucks flying South for the duration. Shelly leaned over the sofa, prepared to see Jean Friedel's throat blue with finger impressions, the eyes wide and staring nowhere, the body twisted where she had fallen. He stared at her for a long moment, swallowing hard, before he realized he was not seeing what he was seeing.

Stag Preston was lying unconscious at the side of the sofa.

"I hit him with a bottle of after-shave lotion," Jean Friedel said, coming in from the bedroom. She stepped over the remains of a straight chair that had been used to club open the door. "Wrecked hell out of the bottle." She held it up; it had been shattered at the base of its two-foot stem. Shelly realized the pervasive smell of strong men's scent hung in the suite.

"*Jeezus* epileptic *Kee*rist, baby, you have just jobbed my meal ticket!" Shelly climbed over the back of the sofa and plopped down, his feet on Stag Preston's stomach. He lit a cigarette and stared down woefully at the unconscious singer. "*Kee*rist!"

"Don't cry, little man," Jean said, dropping the neck of the bottle on the rug. She came toward him, sat down with her bare feet on Preston's thigh. "He'll survive. He'll probably want a few of those little Bufferin B's zonking around in his system, but he'll survive." She yawned, moving her head in a short arc as a tired driver might do it after a night turnpiking it behind the wheel. "Who do I have to assassinate to get a drink?"

Shelly puffed out his cheeks and rose. The bar was a shelf in the kitchen. "What's your reward, Joan of Arc?"

"Has he got branch water in there?"

Shelly rummaged and came up with a half-filled bottle. "Bourbon and branch?"

"Just fine." He heard the record player click the beginning of its cycle. As he mixed, the saccharine tones of a Jackie Gleason record lofted through the suite.

When he brought her the glass, she was back on the sofa, legs stretched out before her. "None for you?"

He handed over the bourbon. "That's all I'd need; on top of all the adrenaline I'd have a beautiful case of Seventy-Day Sour Stomach. By the way, thanks a bunch, Rapunzel."

"For what?" She quirked an eyebrow, then sipped daintily.

"For alarming my ulcers. My specialist'll love you for it; might even give you a little taste for piecework above and beyond." He lit a cigarette, his hands shaking slightly. Beside him, the girl smiled thinly.

"Shelly, would you mind dousing some of the light?"

He turned and examined her expression. There seemed to be no ridicule there, no taunting; she had said it very matter-of-factly.

"What is this, prelude to a seduction?" he asked. "The beautiful barefoot seductress, the Jackie Gleason background, and now, 'Shelly, would you mind plunging us into darkness?' Come on, Jeanie, don't tell me I look good to you suddenly?"

She gave him a peculiar smile over the lip of the glass. "Well, it's not that. Maybe I'm just seeing you differently for the first time."

"What in the hell is *that* supposed to mean?"

She let loose the same peculiar smile. "You must have left your apartment in a hurry . . . your fly is open."

He started, looked down, saw it was so, and felt himself turning red all the way down to the exposed area. "Oh, *Jeezus!*" he blurted, leaping and zipping. She was lying back against the arm of the sectional now, laughter coming in short, sharp buffets. He continued to blush, grew angry, flustered, bemused, amused, and convulsed, all in the space of a few seconds.

When their mutual laughter subsided, he was slumped against her, and the scent of perfume on her neck overrode the smell of after-shave lotion in the air.

Without realizing, they flowed. Their mouths touched and the drink bounced once on the carpet, spilling in a dark, living stain. "The light . . . get the light . . . " she murmured against his tongue, muffled and desperate. He didn't listen till she had jacked her knee into his side. "Get the light, damn you!"

It was one of those scenes out of a Mack Sennett comedy. Shelly running zigzag about the suite, flipping switches. When he returned to the sofa, he knew she was naked, even before he touched her.

She had done a workmanlike job on Stag. He dozed with child-like abandon till well after the third round.

"Later," he said, later, "they lay looking into the smoke spirals, wondering at the nature of the evil bond that now bound them."

"Lovely," she commented, drawing on her cigarette. "Frances Parkinson Keyes?"

"Aimee Semple McPherson," he replied. "If you believe."

She nudged him. "Move over, I'm half on the floor."

"This is so sudden, Miss Friedel." He slid sidewise. "You know," he said, "you've got a very hip looking—"

"Forget it, de Sade," she said cutting him off. Figuratively. "Or I'll get dressed." He had the abruptly distressing thought that nakedness offended her . . . lights off . . . quick puffs on the cigarettes casting ruby highlights across her breasts . . . it was a spooky bit. He shrugged mentally, eloquently.

They lay together—though, oddly, not really together, more like two weary travelers off the same road, seeking a moment's respite before struggling on—not speaking for a short while. Then:

"Okay: I've played your little game. Now why me, why tonight?" he asked coldly.

She did not answer for a time, then said, around the cigarette, "I don't want to destroy your manhood, my lover, but if The Tin Woodman of Oz had walked through that door I'd have stripped the can off him. Your boy Stagorooney does a good job with tooth and claw. Pity he got carried away; we could have made such beautiful music together."

"Nasty break," Shelly replied sarcastically. "Sorry he punked out on you while the fires were banked. But what the hell . . ."

She sat up, began fumbling in the dark for her clothes. He listened to the rustling for a while, then said, "What's a guy have to do to make your scene?"

She gave him a long pause, again.

"He has to be set." There was no banter in her tone now. She turned to him, and he could see her face, hard and tight in the feeble glow of the cigarette. "Look, Shelly," she said, as though about to state a credo, "I'm a girl with lots of wants. I never had it, and I want it. I want everything there is to want. And I want it to be so much that if I don't want it . . . it shouldn't be worth having. If that sounds shallow, then sue me, sue me, what can you do me."

"Guys like me are supposed to talk about 'The Long View' at times like this," he said, reaching out to touch her.

She pulled away. "Stop it. You're the kind of guy I should make a beeline for, every time."

"So? I'm available: parties, luncheons, bar mitzvahs, orgies, gas station openings, supermarket closings . . ."

"I know, I know." She stopped him. "You've used that shtick

before. I'm telling you something, Shelly, and you're clowning with me. This may be the only time you'll ever hear the truth out of me, so grab it while you can."

He subsided, realizing she was leveling. "Go on. Tell me."

"Oh, what the hell. Why bother? I'm a poor little girl from Kalamazoo, Michigan, who found at the tender age of fifteen that she couldn't keep her pants on. So before too many in big K had sampled the wares I decided to get out and sell it; I've always contended charity begins at home.

"Up till now I've been a scuffler, and I'm sick of it, Shelly. Really fed to the teeth with guys on the make and rent overdue. So now I play it for all it's worth. You just happened to get caught in the backlash tonight. Chalk it up to nymphomania."

She stood up and smoothed the skirt across her thighs. "Come on, lover, cheer it up. We all have our little illnesses. I'm not so bad, you know. I might be hot for the wet towel scene, or whips, or even coat hangers. I've had some friends with real kinky habits."

He wanted to say something gentle. Something that would penetrate the crust of scorn and cynicism she had burned around herself. But they weren't operating on that level. Sentimentality was for Kalamazoo or Pittsburgh (where his father still sat *dovening*; still studying the Talmud late at night). Sentimentality was for the suckers who'd settle for nine-to-five and two weeks paid in the Catskills. It wasn't for the hungry ones. He had understood Jean Friedel even before she'd spoken to him like this . . . his desire for her had been something subliminal, something dreamlike . . . a villa at Cap Ferrat, a gold-plated Rolls, a night in bed with Loren, Lollobrigida, and Bardot, with Monroe for a chaser. A dream. A wish out of a fairy tale.

"We'd better wake up Primo Carnera," Shelly said, reaching for his pants. It took a bottle of smelling salts and three cups of coffee to do the job.

Stag Preston, had his picture been flashed coast-to-coast, might easily have lost his followers had they seen the Val-Packs under his eyes. "Don't blink or you'll bleed to death, Beany," Shelly advised him. The singer sat on the floor, head in hands, moaning.

"Why don't you record that," Jean Friedel said, coming in from the kitchen with a fresh pot of coffee. "It's got that whatchacallit— *beat*!"

"Why don't you go fuck yourself, sister," he snarled. "You ever lift your paw to me again, I'll cream ya!" He tried to rise, slumped back again. "Ohh, my head, suh!"

"Lay off him, Grushenka," Shelly said grinning.

Stag looked up. "Who?"

"Forget it," Shelly said. "Have some more coffee."

"I don't want any more. Where's The Man?"

"Take the coffee and shut up. You'd better hope the Colonel doesn't breeze in here while you're off your pony. He'll have you back picking boll weevils out of your pompadour."

"Like hell he will. Forty fuckin' percent, I got, Big Brother Sheldon. Forty big P."

Shelly raised his eyes to heaven.

"I'm going home," Jean said suddenly. "Shelly, will you drive me?"

"I came by cab, but I'll ride up with you. You're still on 97th, aren't you?" She nodded. Shelly caught the glance Stag threw at them, from the corner of his eye. He hoped the boy would avoid complicating matters at this juncture.

"Go to bed, kid," Shelly said. "We've got a heavy one tomorrow." He turned toward the door. Jean had her shoes in her hand and was almost to the elevator doors. "I'll take Jean home."

"Have fun," the kid said. Sullen. Annoyed. Sick.

Shelly shrugged, and reached the doors just as they sighed open. On the way down he said nothing to Jean Friedel, and in the cab the conversation was sparse.

"He didn't like that," she said.

"I know. Nuts to him." He moved to take her hand. Surprised, he found she did not resist. "Jeanie . . . " he started.

"Forget it, Shelly. I'm the girl with the cast-iron heart, remember?" There might have been a softness in her face. There was a softness in her voice.

Manhattan late at night was a pearl. It shone and it rested and it lived all at once. Cabs with dome lights warm and softly orange cruised past, hissing on the streets freshly wet from the sanitation sprayers. Mailboxes hunkered on street corners waiting for young men in trench coats to post last-minute letters. It was a time to go someplace; a time to have someone nearby. A time when loneliness seemed a sin, and even false acquaintances had merit, were treasured. From this hour of the waning day, the dawning next, phony love affairs were born. But in the back seat of the cab Shelly had no such misimpressions. He was holding a hand, –30–, finis, end of report. This was a ship that had passed him several times in the night, and might again. But there was no breeches buoy to carry one across to the other's vessel.

"Where *was* the Colonel tonight?" Shelly asked.

"Don't *you* know? I thought you kept the tabs up to date?"

Shelly lit a cigarette with one hand, still holding her with the other. He snapped the match against the striker as a truck driver might. "Well, he was supposed to make some dinner at the Overseas Press Club and then a premiere at the De Mille. But he should have been back by now. Oh well . . . he's a big boy; he can take care of himself."

She didn't reply, and when they pulled up in front of her building she urged him to stay in the cab. "Don't bother, Shelly. I'm beat. Thanks. For tonight. For being you. See you around the campii."

Then she was gone. He told the driver to wait a moment, watching the street-facing window of her fourth floor apartment. The light had been on. A hunch; a mere trickle of an inkling.

When enough time had passed for her to get upstairs, he told the cabbie to wait and left the cab. He walked across the street, into the building, and found the doorman. It was surprising in a city where once you slipped into your burrow in the wall and thought you were secret, how much doormen, bellboys, and elevator operators knew.

It only took a fiver. Information goes at a very low rate in certain social strata.

Yes, Miss Friedel had a visitor. No, he had arrived a little earlier. Yes, he had a full head of white hair. Indeed yes, he almost looked like an ambassador, or a celebrity, like a patriarch, like a middle-aged playboy.

Perhaps?

Yes, indeed.

He looked like he might have been an officer; even a Colonel.

Shelly got back into his cab and gave his home address. Carlene was waiting. The cup that chills.

She was lying awake, smoking, when he came into the bedroom. "Joe Costanza called about five minutes ago. He left a number, wants you to call back immediately. He said it was an emergency. Something about the kid."

"Whaaat? I just left him at the hotel. He was plowed out of his mind."

She shrugged, proffered a piece of paper with a number. Shelly bit his lip and dialed the number. "Hello, is Joe Costan—Joe, that you? Where the hell am I calling? The Blue *Angel*? He's WHAT! Are you putting me *on*? Oh, for God's sake!

"Well, the hell with him. I hope he gets his ribs broken . . . no, I don't mean that. Get him out of there. That guy's a born trouble-maker and he'll kill Stag if he gets mad enough. What? No, I'm not coming down. I've done my Gandhi for the evening.

"He's all yours, baby. Just get him out of there, drunk or sober, and up to the suite. Get him to bed. We've got a date at the recording studio tomorrow.

"I don't give a scrim *what* he's doing or *who* he's feeling up. I don't care what Kilgallen or Winchell or anydamnbody says. Get him out of there, and don't bug me any more tonight. I'm beat bushed whacked-out finished. I've had the Boy Wonder for one night. And so saying, I retire.

"Good and *night!*" He slammed the receiver, fell back on the pillow without removing his clothes, and was asleep in a matter of moments, his mouth open, snoring.

Beside him, Carlene smoked for a time, her mouth thin, cruel, undemanding. Then she snubbed the last butt, turned off the light, and slid down beneath the covers.

Her last act before dropping off was to turn away from the man beside her.

Her legs were crossed.

NINE

"Let's forget our friendship, Shelly. This is a business meeting. We have a cursed problem on our hands, and someone has *got*, I say *got*, to solve it."

Freeport paced the bedroom anxiously. He went from the breakfast table on wheels—steeped in odors of kippers, English muffins, oatmeal, and shirred eggs—to the window; from the window to the huge bed; from the bed to the chair in which Shelly sat pinned by a glance. And all the time prowling.

"I've got a million dollars tied up in this boy, Shelly. He's been paying off, but the overhead, well, you know what that's like. I can't afford to risk it. Something will have to be done to curb his, er, activities."

Sheldon Morgenstern spread his hands like a pair of diving doves. "What can I tell you, Colonel? I've tried to keep the kid straight, but he's some kind of a nut. He wanders around late at night like the Werewolf of London. After that scene up here I thought he was stacked away for the night, next thing I knew he was—"

Freeport rattled a newspaper snatched quickly from a stack on the bed. "—he was brawling in a nightclub with a paunchy ex-movie star whose finest examples of histrionic ability have been in pubs and gin mills, the past five years. You've made every column in the city . . ."

" . . . well, publicity can't *hurt* hi—"

"—*hurt* him! Shelly, I'm surprised that you would try that fast talk on me. We both know this is the worst sort of press he could get. Look at this." He folded the paper lengthwise as subway riders do, stabbing at an item circled in red grease pencil with an angry thrust. "They're calling him 'Stud Service Preston!' That is impossible, Shelly, impossible! I won't tolerate it!"

Shelly felt his head swimming. He was suddenly not only his brother's keeper, but regulator of public morals, suppressor of secrets, and nanny to the hottest toddler in or out of perambulators. He raised his hands in mute forestalling, hoping to ward off the Colonel's next words.

"Shelly, I'd like to tell you something.

"You may have been wondering at these long distance calls I've been getting from Atlanta the past two weeks. Well, they're from an intermediary who has been trying to move a little land purchase for me. I'm almost in the final stages of negotiation to buy back all the land my family owned in Georgia. I'm going to rebuild a home that was sacked and burned at the time of Atlanta, my boy; it is a dream I've held for many years. The estate of Freeport will grow again. Now you own a good piece of Stag Preston yourself, Shelly, and I know you feel very much a part of this project, but if my own plans are put in jeopardy, I'm afraid I'll have to take steps to remedy matters. There *are* ways, you know."

Shelly knew. He felt unhappy. Very unhappy.

"So let me summarize, Shelly. If you can't do something swift and decisive about curbing this cursed infant's bad habits . . . I'll have to seek out someone who can.

"Is there any area of our conversation that remains muddy?"

Shelly shook his head, mollified, subdued, cowed. The conversation was clear as an unrippled pool. He knew precisely what the Colonel meant. There were men who could be hired who charged by the broken limb. One hundred dollars for an arm. One fifty for an arm and leg combination. Two hundred and fifty for a broken back. With prices on request for special services peculiar to the client.

He stood up. "Colonel, say no more. As of this moment, I am the Jiminy Cricket of the hip set. I will stick so close to Huck Finn that he will have to send through an interoffice memo if he wants to use the bathroom."

The Colonel winced at the indelicate reference, but smiled immediately thereafter, clapping Shelly on the back, adroitly steering him toward the door. "Good, good, my boy. I knew all it would take was a little close talk on our parts. We're doing fine, Shelly, just fine."

And he was outside.

It was the same sort of bum's rush the Colonel had given outsiders, or people on the staff who were on their way out. The image of Needleman—somewhere out there hustling again—came to him. Was there a power grab in the offing? Shelly began casting about for ways and means to shore up his position.

Then again, he caught himself, *I'm in fairly swinging shape if I can keep the Creature From the Stork Club out of trouble.*

It sounded a good deal easier than it was destined to be. As Shelly found out twice within the space of a week and a half.

His first mistake was in taking Stag up to his apartment. His second mistake was leaving the singer with Carlene while he changed out of the charcoal brown business suit into a tux. His third mistake was in not leaving the bedroom door open to overhear their conversation.

They were slated to attend a banquet of pop music publishers, and Stag—who had kept the lamps going all the night before in the watering holes—had not bothered to change out of his Continental tuxedo. He had worn it all the next day, and though he looked rumpled, the animal grace of him canceled the taint of *deshabille*. But Shelly had to change, and so Stag Preston met Carlene for the first time.

"Listen, Carlene, fix Stag a drink, will you? I'll be out in a couple of minutes." It was not that Shelly was unaware of Stag Preston's proclivities toward new women, nor even that he thought Carlene's fidelity was a thing of cohesion and permanency.

It was simply that he was rushed, harried, and harassed. He went into the bedroom to change.

Stag Preston's eyes fastened on the long legs and the hidden planes of the face, and for a bright instant the eyes glowed golden.

"Shelly never told me he had a girl," Stag whispered.

Carlene moved with sinuous caution beneath his glance, stepping around to the small bar, forcing the muscles of her buttocks and legs to strain against the sleek Pantinos. It was the ritual mating dance of the creatures in Jungle York.

"That's a polite way to put it, Mr. Preston."

"Put what?"

"May I fix you something, Mr. Preston?" She dodged the obvious answer.

He followed her and nudged in between the bar stools. "Oh, how about a Scotch old fashioned, on the rocks?" He stared pointedly at the baggy folds of her Bohemian overblouse, trying to ascertain the size of her chest.

"J & B all right?" She offered the bottle.

"Swing," he said negligently, falling into a self-assured groove as he realized she was fencing. There was interest here.

For a quiver he considered the ethics of shafting his buddy Shelly. The quiver passed.

"So you're Shelly's girl," he said, without tie to the rest of the conversation; the point dropped, talked around, and suddenly picked up again, reiteration, throwing the other off-guard through frankness.

"It depends what you mean by 'Shelly's girl,' I suppose."

"I guess it means you're on tap when he needs you."

"A girl might be annoyed to be just 'on tap.'"

"Hot and cold running tap?"

"That isn't too funny, Mr. Preston."

"Hot and cold running Stag."

"Mr. Preston."

"*Stag!* You don't have to get nasty about it. I'm only being friendly. Extending a little good cheer to my friend's girl."

"Hot or cold, Mr. Preston?"

"Depends on the receptacle."

Her carefully plucked eyebrows rose. "They've taught you big words, too. I thought all you knew were words for your songs; the ones with one syllable."

Stag's jaw jumped. He could play the dodge-and-sway game only so long. He was used to getting his way. This one was coming on snappish. He reached across as she offered him the freshly mixed drink, and fastened to her wrist. The glass dropped from her hand and tipped onto the bar top, spilling. He pulled her half across the counter, till her dark, remote face was up next to his own.

"What's your story, bitch?"

She stared back at him. She had experienced it all during her peregrinations. This approach was not new. But the boy was. There was money here; more money than Shelly would ever know, because the same things she saw in her mirror each morning, she saw in his face.

"You bore me, Mr. Preston. Please let go of my wrist. Or I'll have to call Shelly."

He pulled her further toward him. The bar top cut painfully into her stomach. "You keep chewin' on me, bitch, I'm gonna climb your frame."

She sneered. "That seems to be your only interest, Mr. Preston. You're an animal, you know."

He reached across with the other hand and wrapped it in her hair. He was standing as tall as he could, pulling her up by wrist and hair, painfully, when Shelly came out of the bedroom, half-dressed, on his way to the bathroom.

Stag did not see him. Carlene saw him out of the corner of her eye. Shelly saw it all.

"Animal, huh? You never saw how much of an animal I can be, bitch. I got an animal's—"

"You've got an animal's mouth, Stag," Shelly said coldly, from the doorway. "Get your goddam hands off her before I tear your windpipe out!"

Stag did not loosen his hold, but his head turned, and at first a quip formed on his lips; then he saw the white, corded expression on Shelly's face. Then he let Carlene drop. She plopped back behind the bar with a gasp.

"Get out of here; go wait in the lobby," Shelly said, pointing a trembling finger at him.

Stag started to argue, started to mouth inanities about fun & games. "Get out of here, you little bastard, before I crack your skull for you."

He moved away from the bar, but he wasn't finished. He was Stag Preston and he didn't go quietly.

"S'long, bitch," he said to Carlene, ignoring Shelly. "Don't forget us animals; we get around to makin' it sooner than you'd think."

Shelly moved toward him, threateningly, and Stag paced himself enough to make the door before the shorter man reached him— without actually running.

As Stag opened the door, Carlene said, very gently, "Goodbye, Mr. Preston. Come again."

He looked at her as the door closed. It was not a look of enmity. The rank, raw glance of the mating beasts smoldered there.

The door closed and Carlene began mixing another drink. Shelly began to feel like Frank Buck.

Three nights later, the Colonel's talk still painfully reverberating in his memory, Shelly found himself with Stag, two chorus girls out of *Carnival!*, and a half-dozen assorted nameless hanger-on nonentities down front at the Bon Soir. Stag had particularly wanted to make the scene that night.

"A zonky-lookin' com-eed-ee-an," Stag had said.

When it came to the patois of the Broadway hipsters that Stag had recently adopted, Shelly was of the express opinion that a little vocabulary was a dangerous thing.

The "zonky com-eed-ee-an" turned out to be a nationally famous cabaret performer, no longer a spring chicken, who was breaking in a new act. Stag sat through the first show, his ears turned off to the mildly blue (while attempting to be Sahlishly controversial/contemporary/sociological) material, but his eyes corked open on the woman in her stranglingly tight, blue-sequined gown. With every breath, the decolletage dipped and so did Stag's eyes. Shelly felt, however, that as long as he kept Stag off the bottle, the boy would behave himself. What did itch at his peculiarity center, however, was that Stag made frequent trips to the men's room.

The first six times, Shelly (ah, glorious naiveté!) assumed it was the debilitating effects of the ginger ales Stag had been swilling. But when the singer returned from his seventh sojourn, wobbling, as it were, through the ranks and files, Shelly realized the kid had either been nipping from a flask secreted on his person, or from a cache deposited with the black attendant in the washroom.

Stag slumped heavily into his seat, instantly returning his hand to its former position somewhere beneath the skirt of the tender *Carnival!* showgirl. She made not a sound; or as Shelly put it to himself: *not a mumblin' word.*

When the second show began, Stag sat up very straight, twisting at his tux's bow tie, crookeding, rather than straightening it.

When the comedienne made her entrance in an amber spot, this time in a flame-red velvet gown that flared mambo style at her trim calves, Stag literally began to drool. His palms were wet and red from applauding. She smiled down at him with the phony stage affection packaged and sold to performers in gross lots. Stag flipped.

Halfway through her routine (accompanied as it was by sporadic paradiddles by the drummer in time to the performer's bumps and punctuating grinds), Stag leaped up, took two steps and three obscene phrases toward her, and encountered a solid right to the cheek.

The slap was heard 'round the room.

"Sit down, tot," she snarled, "I stopped picking green apples like you when I was thirteen."

The laughter was heard 'round the room.

Stag, infuriated, went for her and managed to wrap a hand in the dress.

The rip was heard 'round the room.

Shelly, ghost-white and furious, tore Stag away from the stage, pushed and hurled him back out of the club, the comedienne cursing foully from her naked vantage point in the amber spot. The next day the columnists took a swinging shot at Stag Preston.

The shot was heard 'round the world.

"I'm telling you, Colonel, it doesn't mean a thing. They can say anydamnthing they want in the columns, it only makes for good copy on the kid. Okay, so he's a problem, but I'm telling you it's only the success that's going to his head. He'll get over it." Shelly was sweating.

"This is it, Sheldon," the Colonel said, from his chair. He was deep in the chair. Neptune about to open the waters and engulf those audacious enough to defile his realm.

"Look, Colonel. The kid's strongest source of publicity is the whispering campaign these teenagers have got. As long as the underground loves him, the hell with what the big-mouth columnists say. I'm telling you it's worked this way before and it'll work this way again. The kid is solid, and no little incident like that one last night can hurt him. Now I'm assuring you, Colonel, that blah and blah and blah blah blah . . . "

Long, and hard, and far into the night.

It finally quelled the savage thrust of Freeport's anger. The waves broke on the rocks and crags of Sheldon Morgenstern's quick thinking. The Colonel subsided, but it was the uneasy rest of a dyspeptic giant threatening to break slumber and seven-league stomp the principality.

Which was all prelude and prologue to The Affair of the Road Show Romance.

Lyric and refrain by Stag Preston, last of the red-hot papas.

Stag was practicing dropping putts into a simulated fairway cup in the exact center of his bedroom. He was using a specially made iron with his name in gold on the shank. One more of the many big-time habits the singer had taken up with his sudden success. He kept his head down, knees locked, and followed through sharply, sending the red dot on the golf ball rolling over and over.

He missed the shot by a good three feet.

Then he looked up at Shelly.

"I don't dig, Shelly baby. Why we goin' outta the Big Apple?"

Shelly perched on the arm of a chair, rolling the cigarette between tongue and lip. "Forget the hip patter, Stag. Talk to me in native English."

Stag made a placating gesture. Awkwardly, still holding the putting iron. He replaced it in the hand-tooled leather caddy bag and moved over to Shelly. "Gimme a cigarette."

"Forget it," Shelly said. "You've got only one thing to sell, Tiger, and that's your voice. Now what's your problem?"

The boy turned and opened one of the sliding doors to a full-length wardrobe. He considered the sleeves of several sports jackets. "You like this one, Shelly?" he asked, withdrawing a Scotch plaid, Continental cut.

"I'm nuts for it. Now what's on your mind?"

"Well, I just don't understand why I have to go on this road tour. Weren't you supposed to fix up a date for me at The Palace? I mean, I've wanted to play there for a long time; I think we're ready for it." He let his full lower lip sag petulantly.

"Well, I'll tell you, Sol Hurok; the Colonel's running this particular show, and he's a little perturbed about you slipping and sliding into every gin mill on the Great White Way. He is also, may I point out, bugged by the nickname 'Stud Service Stag' which the funny boys over at Lindy's have handed you. In short, clown, he wants you out of the way for a while, so he can bribe the powers that be into letting your case slide. And it won't do you any harm to make a little goodwill tour into the provinces. So it's the road show scene for you."

Stag considered the publicity man for a long moment. Then— seemingly out of context—he said, "You know somethin', Shelly, you got to learn to talk to me with respect."

Shelly's mouth dropped open. The cigarette clung to his lip. "Whaaat?"

Stag tried to explain, but his self-consciousness showed through. "Well, I mean, I *am* a star, Shelly, and you talk to me like I was still some snotty kid outta Lou'ville. It doesn't sound right when anybody's listenin'."

In the months that Stag had been away from Louisville, months in which he had sopped up Manhattan customs and glamour, he had steadfastly attempted to lose his Low Southern inflections and vocal mannerisms. For the most part he had succeeded though grammatical errors were still an unnoticed, frequent happening. But when he was being himself, just a little of the old Luther showing, he slipped back and the twang was there, the slur was evident, the rattles, bobbles, and roller-coaster last syllables protruded. At those times he made a studied, conscious effort to get back to the hip, slick New Yorkese he admired so much, and the effort only made his origins more apparent, embarrassing him. It happened now as he tried to put Shelly in his place.

Shelly pursed his lips around the cigarette in the mock-frustrated facial expression only the Semite can muster properly. Talking to an unseen conversationalist, looking over Stag's right shoulder as though such a person stood there, he nodded his head softly in further realization of that peculiar expression. "He's a star, right? He's a big man in the metropolitan scene, is that right? We bring him up out of the mud and he's in desperate need of respect. How about that? You hear what he said? He says: *Shelly, you talk to me like I was a newcomer and you been around for ages.* Did you hear that?" Then, shifting tone and nuance as only exponents of that particular Yiddish mien can, he said to Stag, "Listen, buddy-boy, as long as you keep swilling and wenching, you're going to get talked to like you were an incompetent. Because, frankly, that's what the Colonel and myself are beginning to think you are."

"Aw, now, Shelly . . . "

"Aw, now, Shelly, my ass, tot! *That* is the reason we are going out of town. We are going to let you cool off a little, let our boy talk to Lyons and Winchell and Marie Torre and the rest and try to get you back in their good graces. That scene with the ha-ha girl the other night was the capper. They want to stuff you and display you on Times Square right alongside the giant wastebasket that says 'Put Your *Dreck* Here.' And in case you haven't picked it up yet, *dreck* is an old Irish word for garbage. We kikes stole it along with the Holy Grail, just after we spot-welded J.C. to the cross.

"All this bad press is bound to hurt us unless we can get you out in the grass-roots scene and let the kids see you're still the same, sweet teenaged Stag Preston they all know and adore. Do I make my point, Lochinvar?"

Somewhat mollified, Stag turned and walked out of the room, escaping the blunt unkindness of Shelly's words. When the flak-merchant came out of the bedroom, into the huge living room of the suite, Stag was staring out the window, down into Times Square. The Colonel had had French doors built onto the tall windows, opening onto a small balcony. It was seldom used, save in the summertime when even the air conditioning in the suite was unable to make the inhabitants comfortable. The tiny breeze brought in off the balcony was humid, soot-laden, and slow-moving, but its emotional, therapeutic value was limitless.

Now Stag stared out through the French doors, across the little balcony, and down to the cavorting gnats bumping and rushing and strolling in Kandinsky patterns. "I guess you're right, Shelly." He said it very softly, and once more Shelly felt that whatever cock-eyed compulsions corrupted this boy from time to time, he was, essentially, a pretty good, a highly swinging kid.

"Listen, Stag," he said, reassuringly, walking to him and winding an arm around his shoulders, "don't let it bug you. This trip will be fine. You'll be headlining a bill with some pretty big people, you'll get to see parts of the country you haven't played, we'll make a pile, and there's bound to be some good-looking tail all along the route. So cool it, howzabout?"

Stag turned and, gradually, the smile over which millions of women had dream-sex fantasies, boyish, clean-cut, God-what-a-doll—broke out. Then they had a drink together.

Later in the day, Stag had half a dozen more. Assorted.

Have *you* ever tried a Pink Squirrel mixed with a Singapore Sling?

Joe Costanza brought him back to the suite, upside down, across one of Joe's big, Sicilian shoulders. He deposited him at Shelly's feet and said:

"I started pushing a hack in this town when I was sixteen. My old man died on the street, some kind of a kidney thing, I believe they called it nephritis. They called an ambulance and took him to Bellevue. In those days they didn't have as advanced methods as today. He died on the way, or maybe he was dead when they found him; I don't know. You ever see Bellevue, Shelly? It's a big, ugly, depressing, red brick thing . . . looks like it was made for the dead, not for the living. I had to go down and identify him. That was my junior year in high school, my last year, the way it turned out. I had to go lie about my age and get a hack license. I pushed a taxi in New York for fifteen years, summer and winter . . . hell, I remember back when they only had three doors on cabs, so the driver could carry big trunks up in the front seat; it got cold in the winter. Then I get a break; I get into the promotion racket and my sister can stop teaching school, get married, settle down in Jackson Heights; things start to swing for me; my wife and my kids stop postponing meals, and I got time to take up bowling, learn how to ski . . . you know I went out to Squaw Valley on my vacation last year? I'm a pretty fair skier. I've got loot in the Manufacturer's Trust on the corner of 43rd and Fifth Avenue; I got a car; my wife has a car; my kids have cars, and I've even been known to smile at people who push too hard in the revolving doors of this great New York hotel."

Shelly stared at him, bewildered.

"Hello," Joe Costanza said, his big square face hardly crossed by any emotion at all.

Shelly said, slowly, "I know the entire, dull story of your *bourgeois* life. Why me?"

Joe Costanza pointed at the prostrate form of the great Stag Preston. "I like my life the way it's built. This kid is going to knock out the pilings from under; unless you open a can of whup-ass on him, Shelly. I hear the road to the poorhouse is paved with bad actors. Did you ever drink a Pink Squirrel mixed with a Singapore Sling?"

Shelly winced at the thought.

Costanza slapped his hat back onto his balding head and turned to go. At the door he paused, smiled benignly, insipidly, helplessly, and said, "*Ciao!*" Then he was gone.

Shelly put Stag to bed and completed inking the itinerary for the start of the road tour the next day. Later, he thought about it, and decided that his first impression was correct. A Pink Squirrel mixed with a Singapore Sling *was* mondo hideous.

He shuddered, left a note he had written to the Colonel on the desk, turned off the lights, and went home to Carlene.

She thought it was pretty bad, too.

TEN

There is a kind of girl who is seen at certain (right) bars, at jazz nightclubs of the Birdland variety, at cabana clubs, who dances the merengue with the proper hip movements, whose person is all one, the same person. A type.

It is difficult to describe this type, this person—so many of this person.

A description needs specifics—and all the specifics of this person are nebulosities. Unless you know what to look for, unless you can sense them (as the poet said: *sniffing strange*), see the aura that surrounds them, you will have no idea of the subjects in question.

The girls are easier to spot than the men. The men generally have casual Peter Gunn haircuts or pomaded pompadoured hair; they usually wear Continental clothes (like the little Italian messenger boys on Madison Avenue) or they wear the one-button rolls. They come in many shapes and shingles, but they aren't too important here. *The* girls . . . the Girl . . . *this* girl.

This girl has fine legs that look tight and good in her straight, tight skirt. No matter whether this girl is one hundred percent Italian or two hundred percent Yiddish, her profile is strictly Irish. Clean-cut. Sultry. Desirable. Empty. Surface-seeing. Easy to covet, these girls, this girl is too easy to covet. This girl's hair is soft, glowing and probably (today) in an artichoke. She taps her hands when she hears the music. She applauds at the wrong place, before the number is finished, when an unimportant, saying-nothing soloist has pyrotechnicked.

She is the girl the conga player eyes from the bandstand.

She is a hipster.

There is a great deal of difference between a truly "hip" person (that indefinable *awareness* of what is right, what is current, what is lasting; beyond sophistication, beyond class, it is the essence of being "with it") and a hipster.

A hipster is a pseudo. The good-looking girl from Fond du Lac, Wisconsin, who feels stifled (for the wrong reasons) in Fond du Lac, Wisconsin, and emigrates to Chicago. Look for the girl two months later in the bars on Chicago's Rush Street. Look for her just off Times Square; on L.A.'s Strip. You know her. The sleek, well-fed, looks-to-be-good-in-the-hay chick who crosses her legs too high. The chick who gets her meals bought, who has to worry about paying only for her extensive clothing needs and the rent.

Often, it's only the clothes.

This is the girl who thinks Don Ho is a jazz singer, who goes to Birdland to hear Herbie Mann's Afro-Jazz Sextet because he plays the kind of jazz you might (if you were a hipster) cha-cha to. This is the girl who wears charm bracelets that jingle.

This is the empty woman, without her own standards, with a Hollywood conception of reality, the girl who talks during the sax man's solo.

See then, a cultural phenomenon. A leech personality, singularly devoid of purpose, of substantiality. The shadow-people.

The hipsters. The people Sheldon Morgenstern knew well.

And the people Stag Preston knew well. The ones who infested his life in the great cities where he worked and preyed. But these were not the ones who came to the Stag Preston concerts. Mashed Potato Falls, Kansas, had its share of girls, to be sure, but they were wide-eyed and their mouths hung open, exposing the wads of chewing gum.

Yet they were broads.

Chicks.

Stuff.

And Stag Preston—who longed for the sleek, well-fed gloss of his New York hipsters—was forced to make do with what was on hand and underfoot.

It had taken Shelly a long time to recognize the hipster for what he or she is. It had taken him too long, perhaps, but when he did, he realized that the greater portion of his life, all the things he had valued as "with it" were only dross. That was when he first began thinking about the way out. When he realized, sensed, tagged, identified the phonies who did not act like the phonies. The hipsters. A set to which he belonged, blood and bones. A set he abruptly knew was not so much his any longer. He was growing away.

From them.

The hipsters.

Stag Preston's friends. Not his worshippers (as the kids at the concerts were his subjects), but his friends.

They never saw these people at the concerts Stag gave. They never saw them, because they were the ones who only went to the "hip" places, and a rock'n'roll show was certainly (Jeezus, are you *kidding*?) not hip. Instead, Shelly and Stag came into contact with the grass roots, the vacuous adolescents who were too much in love with an image to recognize the stain that by now showed clearly in Stag's handsome, arrogantly casual demeanor.

The tour ran a month. In Philadelphia at the Stanley Theatre they had a near-riot in which three girls and a scrawny youth of indeterminate sex were trampled. That was the first stop of the twenty-city tour. From Philly (and a side trip to Chester, Pennsylvania, to put in a brief, uneventful appearance at a charity show for a new school bus) they moved on—the entire company of no/some/& lots of talent acts—to the Steel Pier in Atlantic City. It was the biggest smash show since Frankie Avalon had broken it up at the Pier the year before. An old woman from Connecticut hit the water. She was rescued. The newspapers picked it up, any-how: that was how Shelly made his money. Rub-a-dub-dub!

Then Boston, Buffalo (Stag enjoyed the zoo and rock garden), Indianapolis, Des Moines, and Cleveland. In Cleveland Stag staged a triumphal return engagement at the high school where he had

had his first important exposure. They also did three shows at the Palace Theatre.

Then in rapid succession came the Fox in Detroit, the Woods Theatre in Chicago (and appearances on Marty Faye's TV show, Dan Sorkin's radio show, and a spread with Hefner at the *Playboy* offices), a barn-like hall in Milwaukee whose overlong title blissfully slipped from Shelly's memory, K.C., St. Louis, Omaha, Dallas, Houston, Salt Lake City (where Stag threatened to drive a friend's sports car across the Bonneville Salt Flats at 150 mph and was restrained only by force), and Reno. When they reached Las Vegas, where Stag was initially booked at the Sands (while the rest of the company, on half-salary, lolled, languished, and lost their loot at the faro tables), Freeport was waiting.

He took precisely sixty-eight seconds to commend Stag on the wonderful job he had been doing, patted the boy on the shoulder, took the cigarette away from him, and ushered Shelly into the elevator, leaving the star surrounded by his acolytes, four girls from the Sands chorus line, and the baggage.

On the way up, Shelly gently extricated Stag's ex-smoke from the Colonel's fingers and finished the butt. "What's happening?" Shelly asked. "How come you're here?"

The Colonel delivered a withering glance signifying: *Don't you know better than to talk in the elevator in front of an elevator girl who's probably getting paid to remember what cursed bigmouths like you haven't sense enough to keep to yourself till you're safely behind closed doors?*

It was quite the glance, all things considered.

Shelly shut up, staring soulfully at the butt end of the cigarette. When they reached the Colonel's suite, he unlocked the door and preceded Shelly into the room, up to his ankles in the pile rug. They breaststroked across the room to the bar and Shelly maneuvered behind the counter. "Want a Julep, Colonel?" Freeport shook his head.

"I'll take a Pimm's Cup. This dry, cursed weather."

To Shelly the cliché of a Southern colonel (albeit an expatriated one with a dream of rebuilding the Yankee-burned ancestral plantation) drinking Mint Juleps was almost too cornball for consideration; but the potency of Freeport's personality simmered in his very hewing to the stereotypical impression of Suth'rin aristocracy. That way, when he pulled off a snakelike Manhattan maneuver, it was unexpected, and usually successful.

But he was right; in Vegas, dry and warm Vegas, the Julep was about as appealing as sulphur water.

Pimm's Cup, indeed. He mixed it, strong, cool, tall.

Then he mixed a Rob Roy for himself.

The vermouth was distantly introduced to the Scotch, much as a commoner would be introduced to royalty. They nodded at each other, and each went his way.

Shelly moved from behind the bar and settled on the soap-colored sofa. The Colonel remained perched on the bar stool.

"Shelly," the Colonel said, scrutinizing the drink in his hand.

"I'm ready," Shelly said.

"We are about to launch our little satellite into his orbit." He paused dramatically, then added, "Last night I received a call from Hollywood. Charlie. He seems to be interested in Stag for the motion pictures."

Shelly's Rob Roy paused on its way to his mouth and he let loose a whoop of delight. "That's *great*! Contracts?"

Freeport held up a staying hand. "Apparently Milt called him from Hollywood, and Charlie flew out there for a conference. They want us out there as soon as we can make it."

"Well, we've only got three more stops on this tour—San Diego, San Francisco, and L.A. Why don't we cancel out the last three and fly right into L.A. tonight?"

The Colonel was shaking his head.

"I don't think so, Shelly. I don't think we should jump. There have been other offers, you know."

Shelly agreed. "Maybe you're right."

The Colonel nodded. "After I got the call, I called one of Universal's press agents, a girl named Billie Sanders. We talked for a while and finally met for a cup of coffee at The Brasserie."

"How's her son?" Shelly asked.

"Does she have a son? I don't know her that well."

Shelly nodded. "Yeah, a nice kid. His name's Kenny. I worked with Billie on a promotion for *Operation Petticoat* while you were in Europe year before last; she's a good kid."

The Colonel dismissed the opinion hurriedly. "Well, in any event, I talked to her for a while and tried to ascertain whether there had been any murmurings in the Universal organization. She hadn't heard anything definite, but *her* superior, a Herman Kass, had alerted everyone on their field representative staff to be ready for something big."

Shelly sipped and asked, "So?"

"So," Freeport said slowly drawing his conclusion, "I believe they're anxious for our Stag Preston to join the organization, and by canceling, by leaping at them, we may lose a bargaining position. No, Shelly, I firmly believe we should let the tour end when and where we had planned it, and *then* strike."

Shelly thought about it for a long moment, then nodded. "I believe, Colonel, sir, that were they to cast for the life of Machiavelli, you would be a definite shoo-in. I bow." He did so.

They toasted each other silently.

Meanwhile, back at the Sands . . .

Stag's apparent good behavior for the preceding month and three-quarters was not entirely due to Shelly's watchdog attentions. It was due to the one-night-stand nature of the tour. It was hard to screw a moving target. Stag was here and gone in a flash, just like The Flash, except without the winged doughboy helmet. Here, then quickly gone: he couldn't make the contacts and preliminary make-out advances. Not only that, but with the performances, publicity appearances on radio, TV, in department stores, high schools, luncheons—by the end of the eighteen-hour day, the boy was more than glad to drop onto the rack and stack up Zs.

Yet Stag Preston had tasted of the fruit of success, had, in fact, bitten deeply of that passionfruit, and like the hophead, wanted his regular supply. Being unable to get at the hordes of luscious young admirers who leered, lusted, and drooled over the footlights, Stag's attentions—as well as his thoughts—turned inward.

There were now ten other acts with the show. Most of them were one-hit record attractions whose name value was (as Shelly phrased it) from Nilsville, but who beefed up the poster listings.

One of the acts was Trudy Quillan, a pneumatic sixteen-year-old who had cut a disc on "Mood for Sorrow" and sold a quarter of a million copies of same. She had joined the tour in St. Louis and had been fourth on the bill. She was a strikingly attractive girl with an ample bust, good legs, dark black hair, and high cheek-bones. Her life in Florissant, Missouri, had been devoid of charm or significance until she had begun singing around town with a rock'n'roll trio. Friends had told her, "Amy," (for her name was not really Trudy Quillan), "why don't you go on into St. Looie and make one of them demonstration records. You got a *won*derful voice, child."

So Amy/Trudy had gone into St. Louis and she had, indeed, cut a demo. It was heard by a scout for a local waxworks who tentatively pressed it. The song was a currently popular R&B dirge and she sang it badly. But the wife of the man who had tentatively pressed it (singularly lacking in taste, but not in enthusiasm) enjoyed it and demanded—suggested?—enjoined?—that Trudy be given something else to sing.

The scout had found a down-in-the-socks composer of rhythm and blues opera and had commissioned him, with the promise of a bottle of Jack Daniels, to do a song for the young girl. That had been "Mood for Sorrow" and it was the only record on the Firefly label that ever got off the ground . . . even as high as a firefly.

Trudy had, in a moderate way, arrived. Arrived sufficiently, at any rate, to be booked onto Stag's tour. And booked onto Stag's tour inevitably entailed being booked onto Stag's roving eye.

Trudy was an easy place for any eye to settle. Stag's had settled on her the day she joined the troupe. Unlike most girls on road tours who invariably travel with a "stage mother," Trudy was an orphan who had lived with an aunt and uncle in Florissant, and so came to the show unchaperoned.

Which was very much like staking out a young lamb for sacrifice.

Back in Florissant, there had been few idols with whom Trudy could identify. There had been Elizabeth Taylor, and there had been Leslie Caron (because Trudy's features were out of the same general pixie mold), and on the other side of the sexes there had been Nick Adams and Rock Hudson and Elvis and Fabian and, of course, Stag Preston.

What would be your reaction, coming face to face with:

(If you are a dancer) Eglevsky . . .

(If you are a writer) Shakespeare . . .

(If you are a lover) (male) Cleopatra . . .

(female) Don Juan . . .

(If you are a philosopher) Solomon . . .

(If you are a physician) Hippocrates . . .

(If you are religious) God . . . ?

Then you have a close approximation of how Trudy Quillan felt when Stag Preston made his first tentative gestures in her direction. You have an idea, also, of how Tamerlane took over the civilized world. With a gung and a ho!

At the same moment Colonel Jack Freeport was dripping the sweet honey of future wealth on Shelly Morgenstern, elsewhere in Las Vegas, Stag Preston was making merry.

Or to be more specific, Trudy.

Naked, Trudy Quillan was even more appealing than clothed. At sixteen her young, hard body was as voluptuously developed as that of a nineteen-year-old's; her dark eyes wide, trusting, capable of being filled to moistness with passion newly found and, most of all, love.

The object of her love, Stag Preston, was staring down at her naked form with horror, disbelief, and anger. "You are *what*?" he was saying, as the Colonel and Shelly planned his future.

"I'm gonna have a baby," Trudy said again, not quite understanding how her lover man could fail to understand the meaning of the word *pregnant*.

It meant swelling all up with a little child and going to the hospital and then Stag and Trudy would be Momma and Poppa and even if she had never had a Momma and a Poppa, as far back as she could remember, at least her baby would have a Momma and a Poppa and wouldn't that just be marvy!

"*Jeezus Chrah*st!" Stag howled in pain, falling back suddenly into his Kentucky speech-patterns. "Oh, this is just *swell*!" He hit the side of his hand and turned away from her, leaving her ready young body waiting, empty.

Stag turned away and stared at the air conditioner for some time. Trudy lay silently on the bed, watching him. She was confused; his attitude had altered so abruptly from anxiousness and energy as he was about to join her, that she could not understand him now.

Stag cursed foully, softly, effectively.

"Well, you can just forget about it," he said, spinning on her. "Just forget it altogether!"

Trudy stared up without speaking. He didn't mean . . .

"I got a—"

"Don't say it—"

"—career to protect and I ain't—"

"—please don't say it, Stag—"

"—goin' to louse it up marryin' no damn—"

"—I LOVE YOU! Don't you say that to me . . . I didn't do it . . . *you* did it, now you better—"

"—well, just kiss off kid because this is *it*! Now g'wan, you enjoyed it as much as me, so g'wan, get out of here, and don't plan to give me no trouble, because I've got influence."

Trudy leaped up and dressed with supple, quick movements. Somehow, the sight of her in full skirt, shirtwaist, and flats did not equate with her announcement of imminent motherhood. She closed the door behind her softly, but firmly.

Twenty minutes later, the manager who owned ninety-nine and forty-four one-hundredths percent of pure Trudy Quillan, an ex-fight manager named Horace Golightly, banged—without announcement—on the door to Freeport's suite.

Horace Golightly was a misnomer. Horace could no more Golightly than the Budweiser Clydesdales at full tilt.

When Shelly opened the door, Golightly stomped through—a short man inclined toward velvet vests and Tyrolean hats—and brought up short before Freeport. The Colonel was still perched atop the bar stool, sipping at his Pimm's Cup. His face was a battleground of uncertain emotions. He was undecided whether to be annoyed at Golightly's appearance, pleased at least superficially by a business acquaintance's attentions, or overflowing with joy because of private good news.

He fell back on the time-honored demeanor of the Southern gentry:

Open hostility.

"Sir, what are you doing?"

Golightly skimmed the Tyrolean hat with its alpenstock feather onto the marble-topped end table and took up a heroic stance before the Colonel. "I'm here to see justice done, Colonel, *that's* what I'm doing here!" His voice seemed to come from the bottom of a sealed barrel, hollow, resounding, but entirely wooden.

Freeport set down the drink with a snap of the wrist. He slid off the stool and approached Golightly. The manager moved back a pace. "What exactly, sir, are you blathering about?"

"Justice, Colonel, that's all. Just a little common, decent justice, the kind one man expects from a fellow man, the kind—"

"*Golightly!*" Shelly said, cutting off the rotund manager's ramblings, "get your mouth out of gear and just tell us what you're gibbering about!"

"Stag Preston, Mr. Morgenstern. *That* is what I'm talking about." Shelly looked up at the ceiling with exasperation. He mumbled something to himself that sounded vaguely like *The man is deranged!* and rotated his hands in a go-on-and-make-your-point gesture. Golightly summarized quickly: "I've stood back and watched that boy of yours carry on pretty shockingly, and haven't said anything, because it wasn't my business, but when he gets one of my clients in trouble and refuses to marry her, then I figure it's about time I sa—"

"Aaaah!" Shelly shrieked, clutching his head. "No! No, you're putting me on, Golightly, you're making a giggle, that's it, that's what it is, tell me that's what it is!" He reached out and grasped Golightly by his lapels, dragging him forward. "Talk, you greasy little gozler . . . talk, and talk straight!"

"Trudy Quillan . . . Trudy . . . he's got her, he's got her in a family w-w-way . . . stop shaking me!"

Shelly released the lapels and slumped back against the wall, stunned. "You're kidding."

The Colonel, for the first time since Shelly had known him, seemed inwardly disheveled. "Mr. Golightly, this is not funny. If this is some sort of prank, sir . . . if you're trying to get that girl a more formidable place on the tour . . . if you're trying to hold us up for . . . "

Shelly cut him off, without a glance. "Golightly, this is on the level? You're not kidding?"

The manager related the story as Trudy Quillan had told him, then launched into a fierce diatribe against young boys with too much activity in their sex glands, too much money, too big an estimate of themselves, and too much success. Shelly did not listen. His mind was whirling. After trying to keep Stag out of trouble, and deluding himself that he had done precisely that . . . *this!*

"Well, it's a simple matter, Shelly," the Colonel said. "If this is true, and—" he aimed a finger at Golightly, "we intend to have our physician assure us it is as you represent it, sir, then we merely make a settlement on this young girl, this—what's her name, Shelly?"

"Trudy Quillan," Shelly said in a small voice.

"Yes, Trudy Quillan. We make a settlement on her, let her have done what must be done, and we're through with it. It's a cursed business, of course, but nothing serious. Every hot-blooded young man gets at least one girl in trouble before he's married. Ha ha."

Shelly heard the hollow laugh and answered it with one of his own. "Yeah. Ha ha. But not every prominent, talented, apple-cheeked, red-blooded All-American boy, free white and over puberty knocks up a Black girl.

"Chew on *that* one awhile!"

ELEVEN

Clichés begin to stink after they've lain around for a few years, and there is no more redolent cliché in the listings than, "He turned white with shock."

Yet that was precisely what happened when Shelly pointedly informed his employer that the girl Stag Preston had knocked up, Trudy Quillan, was in point of fact, a lovely young subscriber to the Negro persuasion. Freeport *did* turn white. He turned ashen. He went dead sheet white. His complexion matched his great shock of snowy hair. Someone pulled a plug out of his rump and drained the blood from his face. In short, damn the clichés and full speed ahead, he turned white with shock.

Shelly watched as his own personal God fell apart. It was something to see; a definite facial and metaphysical *altering* of Freeport's appearance. More than merely his substance: his reality. The Colonel took a faltering step backward, found the bar stool with his searching fingers, and plumped onto the edge of the seat. The Pimm's Cup might have helped, but it was unnoticed by Freeport's elbow. The room had abruptly gone darker, to Shelly, with Freeport's blue eyes that peculiar almost-albino white that seemed lifeless.

"A *Nig*rah . . . "

As though someone had just told him all fifty-dollar bills were counterfeit. As though he had opened his wallet to examine the sheaf of fifty-dollar bills therein and had found not Ulysses S. Grant staring up at him, but a winking jester, an epileptic leper, motley, insipid, rotting, leering. Then he would turn and say, "Counterfeit . . . " the way he had said, "A *Nig*rah . . . "

Golightly looked to Shelly for an explanation. "Didn't he . . . ?" Shelly shook his head.

"Uh-uh. He didn't know." They both watched the Colonel. It was an unpleasant but fascinating thing to watch—a man's face shriveling and changing and changing again. Emotions played like heat lightning across Freeport's countenance, finally settling into a semblance of normalcy.

Normal to anyone but Shelly, who had worked under Freeport long enough to recognize the restrained fury the man was trying to conceal. Freeport was a man who felt he could get more by speaking softly, by operating gently, until that final instant when the hound catches the hare and snaps its neck with one twist and bite. Now he was like that. Calm to the eye of Golightly, seething to the more practiced eye of Shelly.

"I want the boy up here," the Colonel said gently.

Shelly moved to the house phone, waited, spoke into it softly. Before he was finished, Freeport was speaking to Golightly. The manager seemed disinclined to argue, and as Shelly hung the receiver he heard Freeport saying, "just go to your room and wait for my call. Keep that girl with you. If she speaks to *anyone*, sir, I'll hold you directly responsible."

Golightly mumbled something slight but appropriate, retrieved his Tyrolean hat, and made a hasty exit. Then the Colonel turned to Shelly. The face dissolved from its posture of composure and the fire that licked at Freeport's brain sent visible shoots of red into his cheeks. "This time, Shelly, that rotten boy has gone too far." Then he cursed.

In all the years Sheldon Morgenstern had worked for Freeport, he had never heard the man swear. It was a mark of character, something you could hang your identification on: Colonel Jack Freeport never used foul language. He had taken on awkward speaking habits to avoid swearing, referring to something as "cursed" or "rotten" before he would offer up even a mild damn. Now, he cursed.

Foully. In a torrent that Shelly never thought possible from anyone playing the role of aristocracy as heavily as Freeport played it.

And when Freeport was silent, Shelly knew twinkling words would not mend this rift. Stag had stepped over the line. The Colonel had been piqued by Stag's amour, was even more annoyed by his carelessness. But with a *Nig*rah . . .

It was more than shocking; it was a personal affront.

The knocker clanged twice and Shelly stepped around the Colonel to answer the door.

Stag bowled through, a wide, slap-happy grin on his face; the charm that turned millions of women on was now coruscating around him like a halo.

"Hey! The Man and my favorite personal bodyguard, Sheld—"

His bubbling friendliness was cut short as the Colonel took a short two-step and met the oncoming singer with his fist. He drew back and punched Stag Preston full in the mouth. The boy's rapid advance and the force of the older man's blow combined to spin Stag sidewise, blood pouring from his torn lip. He stumbled, caught himself on a pedestal table, tripped over it, and crashed to the floor, whimpering in pain.

Shelly stood transfixed as Freeport moved with the grace of the trained boxer, dipping, grasping Stag by his jacket front and bodily jerking him erect. He stood paralyzed the way any by-stander must stand paralyzed in the face of sudden, unexpected violence. Violence on the TV screen never takes anyone by surprise, because that is the home of sudden movement, senseless violence . . . but life is filled with side-steppings, avoidances of conflict, and the abrupt clash of two people shocks, stiffens, frightens.

The Colonel held Stag away from him—now Shelly knew the Colonel's muscled back and shoulders were not merely for the young chippies—one-handed, the other hand a pendulum, flat and hard and back and forth that cracked against the boy's face with systematic, agonizing, open-handed blows. He was not pulling his punches. He was not using his fist to break bone and shatter carti-lage, so his property would be unable to perform . . . he was not that insane with fury, but he was racking the boy.

Stag's eyes began to glaze as the fifteenth, sixteenth, seventeenth blows tick-tocked against his skin. His head slipped to the side, escape! The Colonel grasped him by the hair, dragging his face close. Then he spat in Stag's face!

"Little scud!" he cursed him, teeth clenched, lips drawn back till the skin about his mouth went pale. He shook Stag furiously; but the boy was half-conscious. Terror and pain had combined to drain away all the arrogance and shine from Stag Preston.

The Colonel, impelled by his anger, released Stag's hair and drew back for another full-fist smash, driven past the hounds of sense by the very fury of his actions. Then Shelly moved. Abruptly galvanized, he ran across the room, wrapping his arm about the Colonel's.

Freeport bellowed like a beast, trying to wrench loose, with his other hand shaking Stag till the boy's eyes closed and he went limp. Shelly dragged back on the Colonel, adroitly twisting his wrist, pulling it up behind the bigger man's back.

No one spoke, and the jagged rasp of breath in and out of Freeport was a steam engine gone berserk. Finally Shelly applied so much leverage that the pain filtered through to Freeport and the big man began to cast off fury. It was very much like the final percolating of a coffee pot, with rapid exhalations and madness in the eyes, then tapering with longer periods of breath-catching silence, then a final upsurge of insanity, and all at once the Colonel was restored.

"Let me go, Shelly. Please let go of my arm; you're hurting my arm." Shelly gently disengaged himself.

The Colonel shook out Stag as though he were a drip-dry shirt, and cast him away. Stag bumbled once and collapsed in a heap on the carpet. Shelly still could not reconcile what he had seen with the portraits of these people built up in the past. Freeport—the quiet, deadly gentleman more adept at screwing the opposition than at clouting them; Stag—almost six feet of young hotblood, well-built, full of arrogance and self-importance.

Now here they were: Freeport a madman, as easily able to break a man in half as he was to destroy him financially. Stag a taffy-limbed, spastic bundle of dirty clothes unable to stand or speak or see straight.

The façades had been ripped away.

This was the true face of the creatures that prowled Jungle York.

Shelly elbowed past the Colonel, stooped to one knee, and lifted Stag's shoulders. The boy was semiconscious, barely able to draw breath. "Colonel, help me get him on the sofa, he may have a concussion."

Freeport came to them and bent from the knees, jacking the singer into his arms with a fluid movement. Without help he carried Stag to the big sofa and dumped him there. Then he went into the bathroom and Shelly could hear water running in the sink.

It had been an eventful, a revealing, five minutes.

In the bedroom, Shelly could hear the Colonel moving around, a drawer opening, then closing. A few minutes later Freeport emerged from the bedroom. He had changed his shirt, and it had taken time that Shelly had not realized was passing. A cigarette Shelly could not remember having lit was half-smoked between his lips. He felt confused and weary.

The Colonel pulled a chair up alongside the sofa and sat down, staring intently, searchingly at Stag Preston. The pale blue eyes swiveled up to Shelly. "Get some water from the bathroom, Shelly. I want him fully awake."

With half the glass of water *on* the boy, and the other half *in* him, Stag came around sufficiently to register fear at the Colonel's face so close to his own. *He looks the way he looked that night in the Dixie Hotel in Louisville*, Shelly mused, watching. *Tight, scared, ready to eat the whole damned world before it can eat him.*

Stag was Luther Sellers once more.

And Colonel Jack Freeport was himself again. The voice was controlled, the great mane of white hair had been recombed, the gloves had assiduously been pulled back on, and the cuffs shot. Freeport leaned forward.

"If I knew what to say, precisely, to avoid what we have just come through, boy, I'd say it. But I don't know what to say." He waited.

Stag did not reply; he merely stared with malevolence. Freeport pursed his heavy lips and clasped his hands on his knees. "That girl's manager came to see us. You knew that was why I sent for you, didn't you? Answer me, boy, or I'll have to slap you around again."

Stag sneered and an unpleasant half-smile came to the corner of his mouth. "I knew. So what? That's your problem; that's why you got thirty percent of my contract—to take care of me."

"Listen, Stag—" Shelly interrupted.

Freeport stopped him with a vague hand movement. "No, this is the time the boy and I have our talk, get matters right between us."

"Stop callin' me 'boy'! You know my name."

The bright pyrite sheen of arrogance was coming back over Stag Preston's face. He had been too long exposed to the deadly radiations of success, and it only took a booster to bring him back to his previous level of unbearableness.

"You listen to me now, *boy*." He spoke slowly and with menacing care, each word prose. "You listen to me very carefully, because I am not going to mince words. Your flagrant transgressions were difficult enough to bear, as they came one after another. We have managed to pull you free each time, at considerable expense to ourselves, but this time you have endangered the entire operation. That girl you got pregnant—"

"She ain't a broad, for Chrissakes, she's a *nigger*!" Stag started up, and caught the Colonel's palm across his jaw. He fell back, the fear showing through for an instant; then it was washed, laved, drowned over with hatred.

Freeport's voice was still soft, commanding. "That is just it, you unfortunate simpleton. She is a Nigrah, a member of a lower race, a person with black skin, and for that reason you could destroy us inside twenty-four hours. Not only yourself—for that would be little loss—but the entire structure of my holdings which, unfortunately, I have come to build around you. We are on the verge of a very important motion picture deal, involving your dubious services, and this would stamp finis to it. The end; instantly.

"Do I make myself clear?"

At the mention of movie contracts, Stag had tuned in more carefully. His ears almost went up in attention. He stared at Freeport, then swung his glance to Shelly for confirmation.

He got none. Shelly sat frozen in silence behind a lapis lazuli gaze. Freeport's words about Trudy Quillan had been painful to him. He remembered all the little times he had side-stepped prejudice himself . . . all the words in school yards, all the jobs he had not gotten, all the restricted cabana clubs in Florida . . . and he was, oddly, hurt. Inside himself, he had never categorized Freeport that way, despite the man's heritage, despite his obvious feelings about certain groups. Freeport had been above it, because he was a businessman too sharp to allow mere prejudice to stand in his way, because he was a member of the hip set that Shelly identified with, who might not like an individual, but who would never condemn a group *in toto*.

But Freeport *was* a bigot. A silent, perpetual bigot, as deadly as any other, though not as offensively obvious as—for instance—the Kemps had been that day in the bicycle shop. But he cared not a damn that Trudy Quillan was in pain. All he cared about was that her skin was black. It suddenly made a difference to Shelly.

The rot was even here, where he thought he was above it. The bigger they get doesn't necessarily mean the less blighted they become. Stag looked at Trudy as a piece of tail, that was disgusting enough; he saw her as some sort of breed animal. But Freeport actually hated the girl because of race. She was more than an inconvenience—a white girl pregnant would have been that to him— she was an object of open hatred.

Stag found no confirmation in Shelly's face.

It was as though Shelly had been tuned out.

"So this time, boy, we're going to let you get out of the scrape yourself. I have no idea how much this Nigrah's manager will take, but whatever it is, the money will come from you, for a change. Not us." Freeport got up, pushed the chair back, and walked to the door.

"I'm going to talk to the girl and Golightly. Keep him here, Shelly. I shall be back shortly." He opened the door, paused for another look of absolute contempt at his talented Stag Preston, then walked out, pulling the door firmly closed behind him.

Shelly and Stag sat in silence.

The boy began rubbing his face, still crimson from the Colonel's attentions. Blood had dried in a thin, arterial line down his chin. He tried to sit up on the sofa. Shelly shoved him back.

The boy glared at Shelly for a moment, then began chuckling. "C'mon, Shel-baby, don't put me on the way The Man did. I was just rompin' a little."

Shelly hunched forward slightly. He put his face as close to Stag's as the Colonel had. "You want to know something, Stag?"

"What?"

"You stink, kid. You stink on ice!"

Stag Preston leaped up. The words had been delivered by a mongoose about to strike its cobra. Such hatred. Such open loathing. Such realization of who and what Stag Preston really was. Not what he *thought* he was, but what he was really made of.

The singer stalked to the other side of the room, hands thrust deep into his pockets. He spun on Shelly and whatever innocence might have acted there was now gone.

"Who the hell you think you are? Who the hell you think you're talkin' to, guy? Maybe you don't remember, but I'm the guy that's been makin' your pile for you, so you could ball that Carlene, so you could wear three-hundred-buck suits . . . so don't get all smartass with me!"

Shelly stared. Blankly.

"If you think I'm such an s.o.b. why you been pushin' me? What's made you hang around here so long for? I'll tell you why . . . because it's loot, and you like a lot of that stuff, *that's* why, you hypocritical bastard."

"You mispronounced hypocritical," Shelly murmured.

"Go do it to yourself, you leech! You been suckin' thirty percent of my skin the longest while, and now you got the gall to come up and lean on me because I done took down a little dark meat. I guess you've poked the same place . . . what makes me such a criminal?"

Shelly stood up and approached the boy. It was obvious Stag could take him, even half-coordinated as he was from the Colonel's beating. "I'll tell you why, you little hard-on. Because she isn't a girl to you, she's some kind of black plaything and it's all right if she has a *litter* of pickaninnies, because the Great God Stag Preston needed a place to dump his load, and whatthehell, she's only a jungle bunny, anyhow. That's why you stink, you little bastard!

"All that guff you fed me about your old man and the dope and your mother and the orphanages . . . I figured any slob who went through that deserved a lot of breaks, but brother, you've used up all your turns. You can turn in your soul now, fella. You smell bad." He turned to walk away and felt the hand on his shoulder only an instant before he was spun, and the fist drove into his stomach.

It was the only blow.

Shelly doubled, all air exhaling, and tumbled over onto the carpet, on his side. Stag stared down at him, then brought back one Italian loafer and kicked him solidly in the groin.

Pain groped for Shelly, found him, and for a moment he was certain he would faint. Above him he heard Stag mouthing words. "You high-talkin' sonofabitch!" Stag snarled, "I'd tell you *any* damn thing to keep you on my side. That was crap just like *you're* crap.

"My old man was like any other old man, and my old lady was too dumb to stop me from robbin' her purse when I needed the dough to get away. I'd do anydamnthing to get away from them self-made, pious assholes, and you'd better know I'll do the same to stay where I am. You just ain't sharp enough, Shel-baby, to know when someone's snowin' the ass off you."

The pain receded. There were greater pains. Shelly felt, all at once, like crying.

"And now that I'm big time, sucker, you can shove it. And if you don't like it, you can sell your thirty percent and get the fuck away from me."

Shelly stared up at the boy. He saw very clearly the face of the boy, not as he had deluded himself into thinking it looked, but as it really was. The face of the . . . the . . . *creature* he had helped create. He was stung and bled dry by his naiveté in actually believing what he had wanted to believe—that there were any sparks of decency in the boy. All at once he knew how Einstein must have felt, or Victor Frankenstein, or the obscure Chinese who had first invented gunpowder. He knew what it was to feel responsible for turning loose something hideous.

Check out? Forget the boy? Let him shift for himself? That was no longer possible. He was responsible. He had molded Stag out of inert matter, and now it was his job to stay handy, to mitigate the evil Stag could turn loose on others.

(And somewhere in him, the Sheldon Morgenstern who had himself prowled and eaten in Jungle York reminded him:

Your investment is at stake.

Carlene will leave you.

You've grown accustomed to the good life.

What will you do on your own . . . you aren't a hotshot kid any more.

You aren't your brother's keeper.

But it was a voice from someone else, someone dying, who had occupied this Sheldon Morgenstern's body with him. A voice from a life before Stag Preston had knocked him down and made him see the truth, unglossed with greed. He heard that voice.)

But he just lay there, watching the boy's retreating back. Stag stopped at the door and turned. Everyone was making exit speeches these days.

"Take care of yourself, Shelly. See you later. I got a date with one of these Sands chorus girls. Get back to ya later, sweetheart."

Then he was gone, and Shelly lay there enjoying his pain and his penance.

TWELVE

Trudy Quillan had not been as young and simple as she had looked. Or perhaps it was simply that contact with Stag had hardened her. She would not accept Freeport's first two offers of settlement in Stag's name. She jacked them ten thousand dollars higher, gave ten percent to Golightly (who gladly signed the release Freeport's lawyers drew up), and went off to Pennsylvania by jet to find the Good Doctor there who would scrape and cleanse her.

Shelly did his work as he was expected to do it, and no mention of the affair was even breathed to the Hedda/Louella/Sheilah set. The matter faded, from everyone's mind but Shelly's, who had noticed something:

Stag had had difficulty raising the money to pay Trudy Quillan and Golightly. His spending had been catching up with him, and while it was nothing that serious, a few more peccadilloes and Stag might be working for a small salary from his stockholders.

After the Sands engagement they made short work of San Diego, San Francisco and waded through a hard four days in Los Angeles, aware constantly that they were being watched by the Eyes of Movie Town. Freeport grew pensive, distant, cautious. Stag grew more arrogant, skittish, as he was discovered by the night-flying wastrels of the area, and smug toward Shelly, who did his work, kept his own counsel, and took to drinking Mexican hot chocolate in espresso houses along the Strip.

The status remained quo.

Waiting.

When the time finally came for talks with Universal, Freeport went into them—Shelly saw it—the way Roosevelt went to Yalta. Banks of lawyers, accountants, statisticians, recorders, and secretaries followed the Colonel, Stag (who insisted on being present), and Shelly into the offices of Milt Rackmil, head of Universal. It took three days, and in that time thirty-five butcher's pads of scratch paper were consumed, fifty-nine pencils were worn to nubs, eight hundred and nine cigarettes, cigars, pipes, and hookahs were smoked, one tape recorder blew a fuse, three gallons of coffee and other assorted beverages passed down throats, innumerable suspicious glances were cast, and not one curse word was used.

When the smoke cleared, everyone was happy. Both sides thought they had pulled a *grand coup* on the other. What neither side realized was that there had been *three* sides in the affair. Theirs, ours, and

Stag's.

During the third week of shooting, Ruth Kemp's letter came for Stag. The months of preparation for the filming of *Rockabilly* had been so crammed with early risings and late takes that the time had passed without Shelly's noticing it. Stag had been effectively put out of commission insofar as night life was concerned by the very rigors of his schedule. A week of screen tests (which, not having been taken *before* the contractual talks, led Shelly to believe Universal's spotters had been watching Stag for some time, and *knew* he had a well-developed stage presence), a week of costumes, makeup, sittings before the publicity cameras, interviews with the hennaed harridans from the fan magazines, "deportment talks" with the high brass, all these (and back through the gauntlet again) combined to whisk the time away, and dull both Stag's and Shelly's interest in extracurricular endeavors.

As though magically, a script appeared, and Shelly stood in awe of Stag as the boy disappeared for three days, no one knew where though nails were chewed to the quicks, and returned with a solid working memory of the entire screenplay. Everyone was amazed at his quick study, and a memo came down from Olympus praising him.

Stag said nothing, acted as though he had been getting "into" scripts all his life.

Shelly appeared on the set daily, appeared at the reading rooms, showed up at walk-through and blocking sessions, and soon knew the script himself. He was of the (silent) opinion that *Rockabilly* would not give the producers of *Black Orpheus* or *Paths of Glory* any heartaches. Avant-garde, it wasn't. Chopped liver, it wasn't, either, but only by the barest margin.

The screenwriter assigned to the project had made a sizeable income and a residence in Coldwater Canyon on the strength of forty-eight "B" melodramas alternately extolling the merits of various gangsters and life in The Big City. It was competent hackwork. From the outset, it was obvious the sole redeeming facet of *Rockabilly* was its star, young and scintillant Stag Preston. The director, the producer, the Senior Toady, everyone agreed they had something hot here. Whatever Stag had on stage, in person, it was not lost on the screen. And by the studious application of shadow to the face (much in the same manner Joan Crawford had been shadowed), the hardness of Stag's features was diminished. The cruel set of the mouth was retained; the masses liked their gods with a touch of what they thought was strength.

Which brought forcibly home to Shelly how little anyone really was able to differentiate between strength and cruelty. He had only recently ingested the knowledge himself.

But Stag worked. Lord, how he worked!

Then, in the third week, with shooting ahead of schedule, the letter came from Louisville. It had been forwarded by Joe Costanza from the New York offices, the name familiar to him, but to no one else in the office.

After all, who had ever heard of Luther Sellers?

Shelly shuffled the letter out of the morning's stack; he stared for a time at the return address and Luther's name in Ruth Kemp's handwriting (he assumed); a carefully worked script that struck his memory as resembling the cards his first-grade teacher had put on the blackboard illustrating how the letters of the alphabet were written. He considered opening it and reading the contents; he also considered burning the letter and flushing the ashes down the toilet, but thought better of it; if it was something that might touch Stag, then it might ameliorate the current tense situation. If it was bad news, then the little bastard deserved to suffer. If that was inhumanly possible.

He took the mail over at the noon break. The boy was having lunch with Leslie Parrish, his costar, in the studio commissary; when Stag saw his publicity man, the curling sneer appeared unbidden. "Well, if it isn't my man, Shelly. Whatcha got for me, guy?"

Shelly handed him the letter.

Stag's grin melted away like mist on the moors as he read the return address. He fingered the short, squat envelope for a moment, then ripped it open carelessly. He unfolded the two sheets of note paper, a pink self-conscious shade that somehow seemed proper, coming from Ruth Kemp. He excused himself from the girl and she smiled briefly, politely, at Shelly before addressing herself to the pineapple and cottage cheese salad.

Stag read the letter, a tiny nerve in his jaw tripping. When he had read both sheets, he refolded them, put them back in the envelope, and tore the entire packet neatly in half. "So?" he said, turning an innocent expression on Shelly.

He handed the pieces to the older man and turned back to Leslie Parrish, his steak sandwich, and his own world.

"So nothing," Shelly answered, shrugging.

"So I'll see you around." Stag dismissed him without turning around. Leslie Parrish smiled briefly, politely. She looked uncomfortable.

Alone in Stag's dressing room, Shelly fitted the pieces of the letter together. Once assembled, they read

Dear Luther,

Both myself and Mr. Kemp are very happy for the way you have

been making such a success of yourself. Things here have not been so good as with you.

Asa has been very sick, and to be truthful the doctors do not see much hope.

The truth is that Asa is very sick and I don't know how to put it down properly, but we are all afraid he will die.

Luther, Asa keeps asking for you and if you can see your way clear to doing it for him, he loves you so, we have your old room all made up and it would only be for a couple of days. Do you think you can make it? He wants to see you so much Luther and it would make him so happy. I know we have no right to ask this of you as the last time we spoke it was not on the best of terms but this you can see is something that is breaking my heart. I am all alone Luther and as you know Asa and I have been hard pressed to make ends meet so every cent I have will have to go to make Asa comfortable for what ever time he has left—and after. I cannot write any more Luther except to beg you please to come to Asa now when he wants to see you so much.

You know you are like a son to him. Please.

> *With love,*
> *Ruth Kemp*

Shelly read it over again. The jagged tear lines where Stag had ripped the letter only made it easier to read. There were smudges on the paper, and small wrinkled spots where Ruth Kemp might have cried. He pictured little Asa Kemp, lying in a big bed, alone, prepared to go, not too unhappy about it, except he wanted to see the boy he had taken in, and wondering what his wife would do now that he could not run the bicycle shop. It was every man's inevitable finis, and Shelly could not work up too much sympathy, yet the callousness of the boy ignoring the letter made him queasy. Was such utter disregard for human emotions possible? Or did Stag feel a demand, a drag, from his past? Was all his callousness merely affectation, a bulwark against a return to the days and memories Stag hated and feared so much? Abruptly, Shelly remembered Stag's words on the plane as they had left Louisville that first time:

Goodbye, you sonofabitch poor, goodbye.

How much fear could one mortal shell contain? Didn't it reach a surface tension where it domed up and spilled over? Or was it like "hitting bottom"? No bottom, really, just falling and falling deeper and deeper, and never hitting the bottom that did not exist. Was it like that? Was fear like cancer? Could it rot someone out like a tree stump, like a rotten tooth, like rust on a piece of iron? Could it eat away all decency and leave something not quite human?

If it could, then Stag Preston was a prime example of the disease. "And somebody'd better get up a telethon for him," Shelly concluded aloud.

He neatly whisked up the pieced-together letter and dropped it into the wastebasket.

That afternoon, on the set, Stag ran through a scene of deep emotion, with a quaver of sincerity and hopelessness in his voice that Shelly grudgingly admitted sounded honest as hell, without a drop of phoniness or "acting" in it. At one point Stag dropped out of character and politely, in a dulcet tone, asked the director if the phrase shouldn't be put *thus*, rather than *so*, as the script offered it. The director snapped for his script girl, who came running, the place marked with a silver fingertip, and she stared over his shoulder as the page was studied. Shelly shivered inwardly as the director looked up with respect in his expression.

"Go ahead, Stag, try it that way; I think it'll play."

Stag read the line—no, that wasn't right: he lived the emotion of the line—in his personal manner, and it added, it dragged from the prosaic script a nuance Shelly had missed completely when reading it.

Around the set smiles and nods of admiration came and went . . . leaving behind them another glowing facet of the legend.

Shelly went out and got very drunk. That night he found himself lying naked in a heap of four girls with unpleasant body odors, unclipped and straight hair, and fingernails bitten down to the quicks. When he extricated himself, smelling musky and like the aftermath of something he had never known existed—dirty sex—he put on his clothes and staggered out of the Venice Beach bohemian pad. How he had gotten there he never knew. His car was nowhere in sight. He was broke, save for twenty-four cents caught in the turned-around lining of his left pants pocket.

He used a dime of the money to call Carlene collect. There was no answer at the apartment. He managed to get a cab that drove him back to the bungalow he rented; and the owner, recognizing his tenant, paid the cabbie, put it on Shelly's bill, and half-carried the exotic-smelling publicity man to the proper bed. He undressed him to his shorts, slipped Shelly between the cool sheets, and shut off the lights on his way out.

But Shelly was not asleep.

Drugged by dissipation, gagged by remorse and the itch of new ethics, sour stomached with the realization that Life Is Not A Fountain, and bewildered by the disappearance of the creature who had been Sheldon (I Want Mine) Morgenstern. But not asleep.

Never asleep.

Cerberus standing guard to ensure no one's entering the gate of Stag Preston's evil.

Ever-faithful, hammered out of his nut, grin as big as all outdoors Sheldon Morgenstern, whose Poppa said a *kaddish* for a dead son gone to Hell in Hollywood. But not asleep.

For several hours he lay there, staring at the play of lights on the ceiling from night-running trucks grinding past on the highway. Staring at lights, with his hands crossed against his chest as though he were laid out with lilies, smelling the embalmer's formaldehyde.

THIRTEEN

Rockabilly was completed and in the cans ten days ahead of schedule. The Gods Upstairs threw a cast party at which Stag was gifted with a solid gold cigarette case and lighter, his first name tastefully spelled out in rubies on the face of it. Leslie Parrish kissed the boy several times, but for the most part smiled briefly, politely. The director made a short speech about how they had accomplished more in *Rockabilly* than they had set out to do, chiefly because of their friend the star, Stag Preston; the producer ventured a darkling hint about Academy Awards, and the hint was chased by impressed *oooh's* and *aaah's*. Stag found it necessary only to smile and bow and wink knowingly during the proceedings—until he was able to break away to ball an extra, a short girl with pixie black hair named Marcie, from Joplin, Missouri.

The film was sneak previewed in five locations simultaneously: The State Theatre in Kalamazoo, Michigan; The Varsity Theatre in Evanston, Illinois; The Boyd Theatre in Philadelphia; Radio City Theatre in Minneapolis; The Esquire Theatre in Stockton, California. There had been some talk of letting word slip at The Manor in San Mateo, California—word that Stag's first picture would be screened there—but the studio decided not to rig the results with a horde of teenaged admirers. The sneaks went off as scheduled and when the cards had been returned, no one doubted they had a star and a money maker.

Even the most critical moviegoer—in this case a "Cinema Reviewer" for a college newspaper visiting a girlfriend in Stockton—hailed Stag as (quote) That seldom-seen phenomenon, the personality that endears, excites, and visually leaps off the screen (unquote).

Then followed two weeks of tour cross-country, banging the tympani for *Rockabilly* (which oddly enough, was getting the sort of puff that removed the picture from the category of "teenage rock'n'roll ditties" and lent it serious attention).

Stag was heavily exposed: via TV interviews, in fan magazine pieces, at women's luncheons, across the high school circuit, during record shop appearances and benefits, and he appeared, with fanfare, as a feature of half-time ceremonies at the Dartmouth-Harvard game. It was to his credit that the catcalls from Ivy Leaguers too sophisticated to accept Stag as anything more than an adolescent idol—were sparse and drowned under by applause and "gimme a locomotive!"

When the night of the premiere arrived, the De Mille Theatre was the brightest jewel in all Times Square. Father Duffy's statue winced and averted its eyes; too much neon, too many cerulean minks, too much voltage in the air.

The beaverboard portraits of Stag that rose seventy-three feet above the De Mille marquee showed the boy in an artist's conception that was a cross between Horatius at the bridge and The Little Dutch Boy Who Stuck His Finger In The Dike.

Stag arrived with his co-star on his arm. Miss Parrish smiled briefly, politely, and was borne inside after the radio interviews.

One hundred and fifty-eight minutes later, as the audience poured out onto Times Square, Stag, Shelly, Freeport, Joe Costanza, and an amorphous mass of hangers-on found they had left America and were residing in Valhalla.

Stag Preston was a hit. Not just a success, for that was a status that both Shelly and Freeport had known ... but a hit ... an unqualified smash ... a state where everything touched turned to U-235. There was the *feeling*, a sort of tension in the air, a very noticeable difference in the way people looked and the way the lights blinked, and the way everything had a crystal ring in its tone. There was no contesting it, because it couldn't be defined by science or emotion or any other yardstick. It was like God or Goodness or the odor of a bakery. It was success, and the top of the anthill, so why think about it, why not just swing with it? It was there; you could sense it even before the columnists told you you'd been right. And the amorphous mass grew as the bandwagoners arrived.

They made it to Freeport's suite—Shelly noted with momentary uncertainty that Carlene was present—and sat waiting out the graveyard shift . . . the first papers with reviews of *Rockabilly*. There was too much nervous laughter, too many handshakes and assurances that "you got it made, kid." It was a leech throng, satiated with its own need for luxury and surroundings of achievement. Shelly despised them intensely, seeing them now as an outsider, realizing he had been umbilically joined to them, might still be, but was in the process of cutting the cord.

Carlene made of herself a remote island on the other side of the room for most of the evening, chattering with whoever paddled into her lagoon. They felt no need to talk to each other; he knew which bed she would occupy that night. It was very much like the relationship of a couple married thirty years.

Finally, the newspapers arrived.

A rush was made for the entertainment sections, and the business of absorbing, shifting, and reading another began. In twenty minutes, with shrieks across the room of, "*Jeezus on toast*, do you *see* what Crowther said?" and whoops of elation, the verdict had come down from the pundits.

A composite might have read like so:

> After the current spate of greasy-haired, wailing, no-talent teenagers who have given us a surfeit of insipidness, the announcement of The Current Conqueror's appearance on film did not stir this reviewer. However, last night at the De Mille Theatre, Stag Preston made his acting debut in a bit of persiflage titled Rockabilly *and the result was just short of incredible.*
>
> After dispensing with the banal plot (poor boy from Down South makes the Big Time and loses his Soul), the songs gauged

to pre-puberty intellects, and the rather pedestrian performances of the supporting cast, we are left only with Mr. Preston and his talent.

Happily, this is more than enough.

Stag Preston is definitely not another squawker-turned-actor. He has a remarkable grasp of matters thespic, a very sure comedic touch, and a personality that at once commands and repels. This critic views Mr. Preston as a troubling shadowy resonance of that vitality and je ne sais quoi, that salt-lick of anti-social renegade behavior only briefly glimpsed, yet deified, in James Dean. But there is much more than the surly restlessness of a Dean in Preston. The singer has a driving personality dichotomously self-destructive yet vastly appealing. His manner with essentially carbon-copied dialogue from endless "B" movies is miraculous; nuances, subtleties, depths we usually only see in the best imported films.

Even when singing, in an area of music long lost to maturity and any depth of perception, Stag Preston manages to capture a sensitivity that marks him a performer of rare gifts. This is Stag Preston's show, from first to last, and he runs it with assurance, skill, and verve.

As they say in the trade, he plays like a baby doll. Give this one 3$\frac{1}{2}$ stars, and cover any side bets about Oscar nominations.

That might have been a composite review. And, in point of fact, with the exception of the final paragraph, one columnist wrote it just that way. Stag was a hit.

Rockabilly was a hit.

"My Sad Dog Heart"—the ballad Stag sang in the picture—was a hit.

Shelly paid himself a stock dividend—the Mercedes was re-bored. Again.

Stag bought his own music publishing company, and spent whatever profits the enterprise might make in the next eighty years on a free-for-all party that caromed between The Plaza, The Stork Club, a rented mansion on Long Island, and a villa in Coldwater Canyon, on the San-Fernando-Valley-side-of-the-hill, California.

The party went on for five days, and Stag was forced to turn over half the bills to Freeport's Hollywood accountants for payment. Freeport had them paid, but noted the total expenditure in a little green-leather notebook he had begun carrying in his jacket pocket.

Stag began going on the town with a group of smaller-name contract players and starlets, a few bogus-titled European expatriates, a wealthy playboy with a penchant for sports cars and heavy drinking, and various easy lays attracted to the neon glitter set. They soon became known as "The Ginchy Set." Shelly tried to keep a close rein on Stag, but when he was surrounded by his devotees in "The Ginchy Set" it was virtually impossible.

One night they left Googie's after a wild round of hot fudge sundaes, went off into the Hollywood Hills in their identical Dual-Ghias (or Porsche Speedsters, for those who wanted "in" but hadn't yet built the marquee-name to afford the more exotic vehicle), and only four escaped when Stag and the others were arrested for holding a "chickie-run" against an electrified fence.

Shelly was able to get Stag out of jail after only three hours of incarceration, but it seemed no warning to the singer. Three nights later Shelly was again called to bail Stag out. The boy and three starlets had been arrested driving through the center of Los Angeles; this had not upset Shelly until he had learned the charge was Indecent Exposure, abetted by minor charges of Inciting to Riot, Insulting an Officer of the Law, Assaulting an Officer of the Law, Running a Stop Light, Driving on the Wrong Side of the Road, Reckless Driving, and $1906 damage to the plate glass windows and showcases of the gift shop into which Stag had piled the Dual-Ghia.

Trial was set for the 18th of the following month.

Before it came to a jury, Freeport had had charges dismissed. That cost money. The figures went down in the small green-leather notebook.

Finally, it came to a head. It had to end, and Shelly knew Freeport would see it end this way and no other; he had worked for him for too long to expect anything else. It happened, however, a bit more messily than Shelly would have imagined.

Porter Hackett was glib. However few charms he possessed—aside from the sheaf of bills omnipresent in his wallet at all times—glibness was his most endearing.

Two memorable things were said of Porter Hackett. The first was that he could sell sandboxes to Bedouins, and the second was that he had rubber pockets so he could steal soup. The first was improbable, and the second he had discarded early in life as being improper for a cultured con man.

Porter Hackett was thirty-two years old, looked twenty-six, had been run out of every major city on the Eastern seaboard, and was steadily working his way inland when he was added to the entourage of a wealthy but aging ex-actress who was having nymphomaniacal difficulties with her menopause.

This daughter of Eve, in an attempt to scuttle the demands of the flesh, imported Porter Hackett and several other young studs to her Beverly Hills home and settled down to alternate rounds of gimlet-drinking and erotic acrobatics.

She, inevitably, collapsed and died of plumbing difficulties, leaving equally divided shares of her estate to the quintet of young rakes—Porter Hackett included—who had serviced her. Financially afloat at last, Porter Hackett began to live as he had always wanted to live. As a man about town.

Shelly, using the untranslatable vernacular of his people, would have termed it living like a *mensch*, like a somebody, like with class, with moxie.

Since Porter Hackett was *not* a *mensch*, he substituted glibness and money.

In a short time he became a familiar in the haunts along L.A.'s Strip, at cocktail parties in Beverly Hills, in the Polo Lounge of the

Beverly Hills Hotel. He was one of those familiar names linked with the barely famous in Skolsky's column. Or the fan magazines.

And eventually, he became a member of "The Ginchy Set" of Stag Preston.

"It's going to be a quiet little party, Stag." Porter Hackett grinned across the car seat at his passenger. "It's just a few guys and a few broads. We'll have us a ball."

Stag allowed a slow leer to foam up on his face. He was not easily duped; he knew Porter Hackett was a leech; he knew Porter was running through the money he had been left by a wealthy old aunt (rumor had it she might have been whacked by Porter) and needed famous or influential friends to keep him going. But Porter knew all the wettest people, and he had a memorably weird way of making fun out of boredom. Stag allowed Porter Hackett to fawn over him, seeming to allow Porter to use him, as long as the returns were worthwhile.

Tonight, for instance, Porter had picked him up at the Bel-Air and had even stalled off Shelly, who had wondered where they were going and whether it might be worthwhile to tag along, to insure his investment. Porter had applied the grease; and though Shelly had been aware he was being conned, after ten minutes of Porter Hackett's verbal gymnastics it seemed the lesser of two evils: pretending they weren't potential seismic temblors, just happily letting them trot off like The Rover Boys, with big bucks and hellfire festering in their pockets.

And now they were on their way out to one of Porter's obscure hangouts, where a weird group would do weird things. That was the value of Hollywood to Stag. The strange scenes to be made. For a boy from Louisville who had been everywhere, done everything, it was only the strange scene that brought on the kicks now.

Stag glanced across and was disturbed by something in Porter Hackett's face (something other than Porter's nose, which he genuinely loathed); whatever it was, it was gone in an instant. But during that instant he saw something more than the puffy features, watery blue eyes, grotesque schnozz, and overfed good looks of little Porter Hackett. Perhaps it had been a satanic gleam of crimson along the fleshy cheeks—like two rosy poisoned apples—reflected off the dash lights. Perhaps it had been an involuntary tightening of the muscles serving Porter's full, sensuous mouth. Perhaps it had been a gleam of stealth in the otherwise inoffensive blue eyes. Whatever "tell" it had been, whatever tic of body language or facial insight . . . it unsettled, disturbed him. With success and almost regal treatment by the highest and lowliest alike, Stag had acquired a deeper, more sophisticated sense of distrust—of everyone—than that which had festered in him when he had been more provincial and socially maladroit. He knew more people now, knew more *kinds* of people now . . . and was more suspicious. Of everyone. And though he put up with Porter Hackett (for whatever value in return there might be) he knew the guy was a fuckin' parasite, no way to be trusted. Still . . .

They had stopped at several bars along the Sunset Strip—including Dino's, remarking as always that 77 was not only not the office of private detectives, it wasn't there at all—and Stag was feeling a bit smashed.

He knew he was bugged, but not why. The night, perhaps. The tension he had felt ever since Ruth Kemp had written that letter . . . sometimes he thought about old Asa. He hadn't been a bad guy, but he was always whining, always pushing, always trying to suck up to Stag by trying to do for him. It made the boy shiver to think back. They were dark, fleeting thoughts. He ignored them, turned his mind back to Porter Hackett, who is also a pretty good guy, even though he's a sneaky bastard, and I can't trust the sonofabitch as far as I could drop-kick him, but old Porter-Worter isn't smart enough to give me any real aggravation unless I let him do it to me, and since I don't want him to do it to me, he can't. That's what. And I don't care if Porter the Sporter borrows a few Cs from me from time to time, I mean what the hell, he's all the time fixing me up with action, so who am I to complain. I mean, it's more than that bastard Morgenslop'll do for me. I'm gonna have to lay it down to *him*. When I want him to fetch me a broad, toot-toot, then he's gotta *do* it. Otherwise I'll have 'im blackballed in the trade, that's what I'll toot-toot do. And that Carlene of his, that's another scene. Toot-toot.

"Hey, Stag-baby." Porter Hackett pulled the emergency brake forward and clicked off the lights. "We is here. Dis de blace."

Stag looked up and for a moment it was as if everything swam under a film of fleshy plastic. Like the oily skim on the gefilte fish Shelly had tried to get him to eat one afternoon at the Stage Delicatessen back in New York. Everything had twin shapes, superimposed one on another, and he had to blink to realize he was not deranged, but only momentarily fogged by moisture in his eyes, and by the smoggy night, and by the peculiar blue spots playing across the front of the huge Moorish mansion.

He opened the door on his side and stepped out.

The house was built along the lines of a decaying castle, rotting as it settled, like a bad tooth. It was massive, dark, and altogether bizarre, bathed in deep blue by the strategically placed spot on the great front lawn.

"You're kidding, of course," Stag said to Porter.

The shorter man laughed—a bit too violently considering the depth of humor in Stag's words. Stag gave him a bemused and disgusted sidewise glance. "You know, sometimes you really are a drag, Porter."

Again, Porter Hackett laughed. It was his bit. His shtick. He couldn't afford *not* to laugh. They walked toward the front door of the house. From within, Stag could hear the squeal of female voices, a shatter of crystalline hysterical laughter. A bit of a dream shattering.

He grinned down at Porter Hackett.

"We're gonna have us a time, Porter-boy!" He threw an arm

across the shorter man's shoulders. "Yes*indeed*sir, we gonna have us a *bawl* tonight, sweetie!"

Porter Hackett had an entirely different meaning as he looked up into a cashier's check for one hundred thousand dollars and grinned. "You can *bet* on that, baby!"

Glib. That was Porter Hackett.

Somewhere Stag could hear the musical, lulling whirr of a movie camera grinding. But he was too busy to concentrate on it. He was all addled and muddled and befuddled and warm with pleasure. He was stretched out on top of just about the ginchiest chick he'd ever seen. A loose-mouthed doll, with hair all blonde and combed close to the head and pulled down into a braid off one side of her small, exquisite head. The girl had a name—Stag was sure of that— but he didn't know it. Her eyes were very small and he could see the blue smoke in them, if he peered close.

But they were drawn down and half-closed with passion, and opened only a fraction each time Stag thrust down into her.

He could hear sounds. They were fine sounds. Cool sounds. The girl was making them, over and over, and he liked the sounds, trying to match them. Someone said, "Move the mike in a little, ah, that's got it; *sweet*!" But Stag paid no attention. The girl was smooth and warm all over and he had this heavy thing on his back and it was himself, pressing down into the blonde girl. He loved her, he really loved her, she was so warm and all.

A while or so later, or so he thought, a while later, he was with another girl . . . she had very black hair and it was all loose and he put his hands through it and draped it over his face so he was hidden in a little hut of nice silky black, but someone said, "Get his face outta there, we gotta see it, for Arnie to . . . that's got it, now keep him faced around like . . . ah, yeah . . . swing!"

So Stag swingadingding and the weight on his back wasn't himself anymore, it was guess who! The blonde again and all three of them were there having a wonderful time and there were smooth things to touch and little hard things to touch and every-body was swinging warm and swinging wild.

Stag had a wonderful time.

Until he was back outside with a sour stomach and a buzz of Christmas tree lights that bubbled inside his head, getting into Porter's car once more, and one of the girls who was in the car said, "What'll we call it, huh, honey?"

So Stag listened because this was 'mport'nt, wasn't it. And he heard Porter, his sweetie *bubbie* glib Porter Hackett answer with a twinkle in his voice, "Well, this is his magnum opus, this's his finest effort to date, and we got a name for it."

And the girl asked again, annoyed, and a little tipsy herself, "So whaddaya gonna *call* it . . . c'mon!"

Porter laughed in the back of Stag's head, and answered simply:

"We're going to call it *STAG!*"

It fit.

FOURTEEN

Porter Hackett waited only long enough to have half a dozen prints made of the film and an equal number of tape recordings cut off the master, to be synchronized with the film. He did not have long to wait, for in the rumpus room of the huge Moorish-style mansion there was a completely outfitted darkroom. A fully outlined processing setup. A fully developed facility for producing dozens and dozens of "art films" to be sold and distributed throughout the country.

For smokers. For stag dinners. For office parties. For private collectors. For fraternity rush parties.

For blackmail.

When Porter and his two-hundred-and-twenty-pound sidekick tried to get the money from Stag, he laughed them out of the scene. Stag Preston knew almost all there was to know about handling himself on the stage; he even knew a considerable amount in the field of human reactions, taken singly or taken as a gestalt in the shape of an audience. He did not know about the fickle turning of public opinion . . . that emotional mob rule without reason, such a mixture of love and lust and sin and hate . . . that admiration so easily turned to vitriol. Hate/love. The cliché held. They weren't a thin line apart—they were the same.

Shelly knew it.

Freeport knew it.

They saw the film and blanched. There had been smoker movies, and there had been smoker movies, but this . . . this . . . it was aptly titled *Stag*!

Their money-making child star, clean-cut and continental Stag Preston had performed every obscenity in de Sade's scrapbook with a few melodramatic touches of his own, reminiscent of his earthy, all-too-human style before more legitimate cameras. Someone had to pay the ransom for the films.

Over the barrel and into the woods, without a paddle to break over Stag Preston's head.

They negotiated. The price went up for dallying. Two hundred thousand dollars. Stag suddenly found he was not as affluent as he had imagined. Advances had been drawn on his records, more than would allow any further; his payments on the Universal contract were tied up with the accountants and the tax people—they had been spaced out over a period of years to allow him the best possible break, though he was in the 91 percent tax bracket; and he was into Freeport for a staggering sum.

"Aw, to hell with it!" Stag said, folding his arms, stubbornly staring out the window. "Let them show the damned thing. Let them run it in every theatre in the world, see if I give a damn!" He was a three-year-old, railing idiotically at the adult world.

Shelly stood over him, trying (he knew not why) to explain the seriousness of it all. "What's the matter with you? You got holes in your head to let the stupidity run out? Bigger names than you have been ruined by less than this. Are you clowning, or what?"

Stag snarled, "Who? Who ever got ruined? You tell me one: just name me one!"

Shelly threw up his hands. "This isn't Monroe on a nude calendar. Or Mitchum smoking a little grass. Wasn't anything wrong with that. This is pornography, smut, filth, screwing, you simpleton! It can get you blackballed by every PTA and American Legion post in the country. The Legion of Decency will be all over you like piranha fish. The NODL will excommunicate anybody who even reads the marquees on your film, you stupe! The record company will dump you. Universal wouldn't touch you if you were gilded. Kid, you'll be back in the slums of Louisville so fast you won't know which way the truck went!"

Stag bit his lower lip. His tone was less domineering, less imperious. But still Stag. "Aw, c'mon, you're just trying to scare me. Who ever *really* got burned by a scandal?"

Shelly named a few.

"Fatty Arbuckle, Alan Freed, Charlie Chaplin, Dalton Trumbo, Gale Sondergaard, Howard da Silva, William Talman, Lila Leeds . . . hell, do I have to run through the *Who's Who* for you? Some make it back, okay, but most of them get hung good and proper. And don't think you're that big that you can risk it, sonny-boy. Are you willing to take the chance?"

Stag bit his lip again. His eyes narrowed. He wanted to strike out. But at which face could he throw the punch? "That bastard Hackett! I'll get him . . . I'll get the sonofa—"

"Listen, just bag that punchout shit for the moment. You've got a problem, and don't forget it. Try to *focus*! He's got god knows how many prints of that film, and you'll be dead in a week if they get out . . . or what if the *Confidential* stringers get wind of it?"

Stag flailed his arms to windmill clear the very sound of Shelly's voice from the air. "Lemme alone, willya, fer chrissake; I can't even *think* any more. I don't know what the hell to do! I haven't got that kind of money, and you know it!

"You and The Man have been makin' it all off me." He was suddenly snarling, belligerent. "I've been workin' my ass off and you two are raking in the bread. Why should *I* have to pay the freight?"

Shelly aimed a finger at him. There was no sympathy as he said, "Why? Because you've blown every cent you've made; you've acted like king of the hill and clipped the Colonel and me for every penny you could mooch, just to pay off your stupid debts. Now this one is *yours*, Sunny Jim.

"Either you pay it or get started washing your socks for the long hike back to Louisville. Because *you* know and *I* know the Colonel will dump you like a bucket'a garbage if this thing breaks. And I've about had it up to *here* with you already so don't count on any more support from me!"

Shelly was surprised at how easy it had been to tell Stag the truth. Whatever friendship or empathy he had felt for the boy was now sickened, dying. He still harbored a pang of uneasiness as a shadow of fear crossed Stag's face, but that pang subsided as the old arrogance once more seeped back into Stag's expression.

"They wouldn't *dare* blackball me. I've got a contract." His mouth curled in a tight return to former assurance.

Shelly shook his head wearily. "Boy, I'll bet you believe in leprechauns and the Easter Bunny, too, don't you? Sure you've got a contract, you simp, and your contract's got some fine print called a morals clause! And in case you haven't figured it out yet, that little film you made the other night is what the studio would term 'offensive to the average citizen's morality.'"

"Aw, hell!"

"Aw, hell, my backstrap, Stag! Listen, you think I'm trying to scare you, and maybe I am, but if I am it's because I like my share of what you make and I'm not happy about the idea of going back to flacking for a living."

Stag threw a hand at Shelly, and a snarl. "What's the matter, partner, you afraid you'll have to go back to work at an honest job? You've been making a pretty buck off me . . . you're as bad as me, blowing your dough on that pad of yours, and Carlene . . . "

He caught himself.

Shelly's jaw muscles worked. That was a part of his life he didn't talk about. But Stag had come into contact with that part a little too often. He ignored the matter, for the moment; obfuscation and sidetracking would only make logical arguments murkier.

"You really think you're big enough to buck it, don't you? You really think you're a hero, that your hotshot teenagers'll stick with you. Are you in for a surprise! The crowd is like a . . . like a weather vane, or like a pet panther. As long as it gets meat, it won't bite your hand. You miss one meal, or sneak in a red herring instead of ground round and watch how fast it goes after your throat!"

"I don't believe that. It's different with me. They love me . . . I've got 'em right in the palm of my—"

"Bullshit! They have no mind . . . it's a mob. Don't tell me there's any reason in a mob like that. Otherwise there wouldn't have been riots at the University of Georgia when those two Negro kids wanted in . . . there wouldn't be any lynch mobs or strike riots or—"

"What's that got to do with me? What the hell are you talking about?"

"Oh, forget it. I wouldn't expect you to understand." Shelly remembered Trudy Quillan. "Especially not you. But listen, did you ever hear of Dashiell Hammett?"

"No. What's he got to do with—"

"Ever hear of *The Maltese Falcon* or *Red Harvest* or *The Glass Key*? No, forget it, I wouldn't expect you to have—did you ever hear of *The Thin Man*?"

Stag nodded slowly. "Wasn't there some TV show like that?"

Shelly agreed with a nod. "Yeah, right. Well, the character, the Thin Man, was dreamed up by a writer named Dashiell Hammett."

"So?" Stag was bored, but still concerned by the problem at hand.

"I'm trying to make a point, so listen: Hammett was a big writer in this town. He had it locked. But he got mixed up with some stupid political affiliations and they crucified him . . . "

"What was he, a Commie? He deserved it, they all oughta be strung up by the b—"

"Yeah, sure. That was the kind of pudding-brained thinking that got Hammett slaughtered. He was the biggest, Stag; he had a reputation that couldn't be touched, maybe the finest detective-story writer we've ever had. And do you know what this rotten town did to him . . . he died about six months ago in New York, and no one had heard of him in years. Hell, I thought he was long dead; it was a shock when I heard he was still alive . . . or had been.

That's what this town'll do to you if this thing gets out. They'll run over you like a Mack truck.

"You want to lose everything?"

Stag had listened. Finally, he nodded. "Okay, tell the Colonel I'll go along with it."

Why had Shelly worked so hard to convince Stag he should pay off the owners of the film? Why had Stag balked? It was all tied up with Stag's deflated bankroll and the debts Freeport had been marking down in the little green-leather notebook.

Stag was broke.

Freeport would pay the tariff.

But Stag had to sell a block of his controlling interest in himself. To Freeport.

The Colonel had laid it out to Shelly simply. Either get Stag to agree, or start looking for a new line of work. Ruin was an easy mistress to acquire in Shelly's line, and he had no reason to refuse. So he told Stag about Dashiell Hammett. At length.

Until Stag said, "Okay, tell the Colonel I'll go along with it."

That was the point at which Stag Preston began his long, untidy trip to the garbage dump.

The film had been destroyed; Freeport had talked at length to Porter Hackett, alone, and whatever it was the Colonel had said to him, Porter Hackett turned over all prints. There would be no further demands. Freeport had a way about himself in these matters.

But now Stag worked for Freeport and Shelly. Bits of his share began to chip away. A new matched pair of turquoise Rolls-Royces for the twin showgirls Stag was balling, a few bribes to keep Stag out of court on old charges incurred while running with "The Ginchy Set," minor expenditures for partying, wardrobe, appearances. It all added up. But so much was coming in . . . who cared?

Certainly not Stag Preston.

There followed a dispute between two major TV networks as to which would sign Stag for exclusive appearances (out of which only Shelly and Freeport emerged the victors, with sky-high advances and residuals for the partners), a series of successful club appearances, two more gold records, and the emergence on the nation's lips of the words **STAG** and **PRESTON**. Householdly speaking, saturation-wise, Stag Preston was the hottest thing since the walking man. He became a commonplace subject for magazine cartoons, comedians' jokes, minutiae in realistically written *New Yorker* and *Evergreen Review* short stories, and arguments between parents and their wild daughters.

At which point of the graph-climb, Stag Preston was booked triumphantly into The Palace.

Enter the physical presence of the Past—in the form of Ruth Kemp, widow.

And holla! to thee, O Spirit of Christmas Wasted. Swing!

With that disregard for coincidence it seems to favor, Fate stopped the breath of Asa Kemp within the same hour Stag Preston was exhaling his own breath in the opening song of his triumphant Palace engagement.

That was the first day of Stag's reign. He had done away with all phony, disingenuous pretense to the pop throne by taking over the show completely. The audience—saturated with his teenaged supplicants—burst into revolt at the merest suggestion that a secondary act might interfere with the glimpsing of their demigod. The revolution was quelled by the paying-off of the other talent and Stag's ascension to the stage, to the throne. A one-man show, starring a twenty-two-year-old teenager.

Two days later, as Shelly stood in the wings, watching his meal ticket, he felt a presence behind him. Stag was settling into a natural rhythm of performance, seemingly putting everything he had into each show; yet Shelly was able to discern a subliminal holding back, a concealment. Stag had been that way ever since Freeport had gained controlling interest in the contract. It was as though the boy sensed his soul was not entirely his own any longer, and he must never give everything to a show, for he had to hang on to a bit for plotting . . . for getting revenge . . . for regaining his control of himself. It was a silent, soft war raging. Shelly was able to sense that the boy was holding back, not exhausting himself. The reviews had been fabulous, however, almost as enthusiastic as they had been for the film, now being held over at neighborhood theatres after a healthy run on Times Square. The crowds were so large at The Palace, in fact, that Stag was doing a "fire escape" performance after each show, to empty the theatre for new patrons.

But it was not peaceful, not a moment of it.

Stag had taken to eyeing the young girls in his audiences, and had even gone so far as to take one up to the suite in the Sheraton-Astor. Freeport had warned him to be careful. (Shelly dwelled bitterly on the fact that Freeport now had controlling interest and could afford to let Stag find solace in other directions. It spoke ill of the Colonel's ethics. Shelly found himself frequently nipping from a bottle of Pepto-Bismol. He considered putting an end to the chain smoking which had, in the time since he had met Stag Preston, progressed from one, through two and three, to four packs a day. He considered it, and dismissed the idea. *Everyone's entitled to go to hell his own way,* he reasoned, and lit up.)

His reveries were jaggedly broken as he realized someone was standing very close to him; someone he should turn around and see. He stayed where he was, watching Stag. The compulsion raged within him, but he continued to stare out toward the lone figure in the spotlight.

"Mr. Morgenstern?" someone said behind him.

He knew that voice. Knew it before it spoke.

He stared fixedly at Stag for another moment, wishing he had never met the boy, wishing he had become what his orthodox parents had wanted, wishing he was serving another miserable stretch in the Army. Anything but being here. He knew what Ruth Kemp would say; nothing else could bring her to New York. Shelly turned around.

She looked the same. Fat little women seldom alter too much. They only get fatter. Perhaps a few more character lines among the older residents, perhaps a bit more sag to the dark pouches beneath the eyes. But essentially the same, physically.

And even so, Shelly knew she was alone.

Asa Kemp had died. It showed. She was no longer half or more than half of that entity that had been Ruth and Asa Kemp. She was alone now. A woman without a husband, a widow, one of God's most pitiable creatures.

"They told me who you were," she said. "I didn't remember you from that time I met you, until I saw your face." She was very humble. It went with the hideous black dress she wore, the white gloves, the little hat perched ridiculously on her bun-tied hair.

Shelly remembered her. He remembered an unrecognized slur she had thrown. But was he entitled to harbor that grudge now? Here? It seemed so petty. Even prejudice became asinine and childish in the face of death, loss, loneliness, emptiness.

"Hello, Mrs. Kemp."

She tried to frame a smile, but it came off jerkily, spastically. She pressed her lips together, bringing dimples, and lowered her eyelashes momentarily. It wasn't quite a smile but it bespoke understanding, sympathy for what he was not saying as sensed by her, and returned. It was an altogether winning expression.

"I've come to ask Luther something." Shelly said nothing; so she went on. "It was Asa's last wish almost. He wanted Luther to sing the hymns at the funeral. They're holding Asa at Refton's till I get back. D'you think he'll come, Mr. Morgenstern?"

Shelly felt a constriction in his throat.

"I don't know, Mrs. Kemp, I really don't."

He silently hoped her altogether winning expression could be dredged up on a moment's notice. He had a feeling she might need it. He turned back to the stage.

Stag went on singing.

FIFTEEN

He ended with "Sister Boo-Boo," an upbeat number Ross Bagdasarian had written for him. Bagdasarian, under his *nom de plume* of David Seville, had done an instrumental version of it, recorded with The Chipmunks, and converted it for Stag. Stag had recorded it, but it had not yet been released; it was being tested at The Palace. Now, as he came off, paying no heed to those waiting to praise him, he grabbed the towel from an outstretched hand and buried his perspiring face in it. "You can call 'em and tell 'em they can go ahead and let 'Sister Boo-Boo' loose, Shelly. They eat it up every time."

He rubbed briskly at his auburn hair, mussing it out of all semblance to the posters outside. Still his face was buried in the towel, and he continued speaking. "It ought to go real good; they got it echo chambered with Costa leading the—"

His face emerged from the towel, bright and pink and the dark, penetrating eyes staring directly at Ruth Kemp. Shelly tried to say something, to bridge the momentary gap, but nothing came. Stag looked at her, fiercely for an instant as the remainder of his triumphant mood washed away, then with self-consciousness as he knew who she was, why she was here. It stood out on her like her sorrow. He needed no perceptivity to see it.

"Hello, Luther. How are you; I saw you; you were real fine . . . how are you?" She tried to get it all in, the months he had been gone, her feelings, a rapport, something that would morally intimidate him before she asked, ensure success for her mission.

He tried to be jocular. He gave a wry grin and a sidewise bobble of the head, the way two buddies who had had a schoolyard fight might embarrassingly grin as they are forced to shake hands and make up. It didn't take. He handed the towel back to the shadow who had proffered it. "Hi. Uh, how's Asa?" He needn't have asked. It showed in every dark line of her face. His words came with too much hipness, too much flip nonchalance, as though it was small talk. How do you like the weather? Are you having a good time your first trip to New York? Did you like my latest record? Is your husband dead yet?

She answered him with her eyes.

Shelly saw mist in her eyes. He was sure she would not cry. That wasn't Ruth Kemp, however else she might debase herself before the boy her husband had befriended.

But she answered him with her eyes.

"Well, uh, you gotta excuse me." He tried brushing past her, while the group watched, sensing something between the boy and the woman. "I—uh—, I've got this, uh, show to do off the fire 'scape, I said I, uh, told them I'd be—goddammit! Shelly, get her outta here!"

He tried to get past.

She did not move.

Shelly felt a hand on his sleeve and caught sight of Jean Friedel with a briefcase under her arm. She leaned toward him, whispering, "I came over with some papers for you to sign from the Colonel. What's, what's going on?"

Shelly nudged her quiet, and turned his attention back to Stag and Ruth Kemp.

She had not moved. The boy had backed up when she would not let him pass. Now he stood uncertainly, nervously, trying to gauge the texture of the situation, inherently aware he had to get away, but also aware of the emotional charge in the air.

"Luther, Asa passed on two days ago. He didn't know what was going on too well toward the end, but he asked for you. He was all ... all doped up by the doctors, Luther ... but he asked me to come see you, to get you to ... to ... "

She turned away. He was staring at her as though she was speaking some incomprehensible dialect; he was not going to help her say it. She almost gave up. At the turning-instant, that quarter-beat in which decisions are made, she turned back.

"He died, Luther. He died, the kindest man I ever knew." She was not hysterical, not even pleading; it was a deep pulling at each word to get the full meaning across. "My husband, Luther. He died of a broken heart, do you know that? He died of what everyone did to him; he was a good man and he never wanted to let people down, and that's all anyone ever did to him. Let him down, don't you see?"

Stag stared around the wings impatiently. "So what's that got to do with me?"

"He asked me to come see you, Luther. He wanted you to sing the hymns at his service. He didn't know what was going on most of the time—he was in so much pain they had him all doped up—but he said that to me when I saw him the—the last time . . . before . . . "

"Stag." Shelly cut in firmly. "We can catch a late plane after the last show; I'll talk to the Colonel, he'll arrange with the theatre to fill in for a day, we can be back in time to—"

Stag waved him to silence. The Lord of the Manor waved his serf to silence. "We aren't goin' anywhere." He looked straight at Ruth Kemp, and there was no more nervousness now. Up till this moment it had been inconvenience and an awkward situation. Now his position in life was being threatened, however momentarily. "Sorry, I've got a show to do. I've got a cont—"

"It was Asa's last wish, Luther, that you sing."

Stag Preston's face lost its theatrical comfort. The naturally cruel set of the mouth reappeared, the hollows in the cheeks deepened. "*Pack it in.* I've got a show to do. I don't owe you a goddam thing; you and Asa had it from me, all you wanted when I was snot-poor. Now I'm out of all that. I ain't, I'm *not* going back to it; not even for a day. So g'wan, blow! Beat it, split, and let me work, will you?"

No one spoke. Jean Friedel's hand tightened spasmodically on Shelly's arm. Even the sound of The Palace, emptying and re-filling, faded back to surface noise, as though the scene itself was waiting, listening.

Ruth Kemp began speaking. It was a great boulder rumbling down a hill, beginning far off softly and louder and louder till it became an avalanche. It was a dynamo hurling itself to life, spinning sibilantly at first then whining at top-point efficiency till the sound mounted up and up and glass shattered.

"Look at you. Look at what you are. You aren't anything to be proud of. You think you've gotten away from being poor, because you wear silk clothes. But you're lower than ever. You have no heart, no soul. Look around you, see these people? They're as foul as you. They don't care what you do as long as they can make the money. But we *know* you back home. We hear what you do.

"You're an animal, Luther. You were always an animal, but we needed something to love, we wanted to be hurt, and you were always ready to hurt us. But you're not human . . . you're too selfish for that. You won't live long . . . you *can't* live long.

"God won't allow it. He'll find you out soon enough."

She said more, but it wasn't necessary. She belabored her point as those who live outside one-line put-down New York always do. But she had made her point.

She named him for all to see.

An abomination in the eyes of God and Man.

She stripped him of all the sham and glitter-pretense he wore onstage. He was, undeniably, an animal.

Ruth Kemp left, finally, without tears.

Tears in the dust of drained emotions.

Jean Friedel wanted to say something, now that they had left the theatre and were in the dim rear of the cocktail lounge. She wanted to say something pertinent, now that the steam-bath heat of back-stage was gone and the air-conditioned stillness of the lounge surrounded them. She felt the need to declare herself in regard to what she had witnessed, now that Stag was somewhere else and her hand was wrapped around a martini. She wanted desperately to remove the sight of pain and loathing in Shelly's eyes but she could not. With that peculiar insight women possess, she knew she should be still. Not a word. Not a sound. No confusion; no inserting herself as another factor in his thinking. It would only annoy him, infuriate him, muddle his thoughts. So she sat very quietly, smoking and sipping from her glass, realizing that for the first time Sheldon Morgenstern meant a very small something to her; he looked good to her; she wanted to *do* for him . . . something, anything that might clarify this attraction she felt. It was not love, she had no doubts about that—her declaration so long ago about their relationship still held—but there was a bond between them. The bond of two people who have glimpsed degradation and Hell together and who can reminisce about it. Not love, but something a lifetime deeper. Recognition. Empathy. The honest emotion of need and the unsullied desire to help. Jean Friedel felt more like a woman, less like a pornographically oriented machine, than she had in a great while.

But she sat very still and watched, waiting for a flicker of light in Shelly's face. A flicker that would signal his emergence from thoughts that even *looked* dark and swirling from where she sat, outside his mind. Cut off, but so aware of what he was doing inside himself that it was painful to her.

She sucked in her underlip and reached out with her mind for him. He was nowhere to be found. Out of touch, out of sight, out of mind, deep within himself.

What can do this to a man like him? she thought. *He's not the kind who breaks up; he's too much the laugher, too flip. But perhaps that's the kind who hurt worst. What has he been going through with Stag to get this way . . . such hurt? Such very much hurt. What is he thinking?*

Thoughts:

Dear God, what have I done? What have we all done? I'm as bad as he is. *I've lied for him; I've covered all his tracks . . . and for what, for what? So he could get bigger, too big to destroy. She was right, he isn't human. No one with a heart could have turned her down, no matter how she's bigoted. But she never hurt him . . . the both of them, she and Asa Kemp, all they ever gave him was affection and help. What sort of mentality has he got? What kind of mind turns down a request like that? Nothing can write it off; I can't say he's afraid to go back to poverty, because he's beaten that already. It doesn't figure. It's like trying to figure the thought-processes of an infant, or a cat. It's alien, terrible—what have I done?*

Thoughts. By Sheldon Morgenstern. Flagellant.

Then finally, a rationale. A means through the maze.

The labyrinth develops a pattern, and an emergence into some sort of sanity. Shelly said to himself:

I've got to get out. I've been as bad as he, and for what? I've got a car and a woman who isn't a woman and no soul of my own.

He lit a cigarette, alone there on the plain of his thoughts, with the wind of remorse whistling in and out, lifting his hair lightly, then dying down, allowing the heat off those plains to bake out his thoughts.

I've got to get out. It's been so long, too long, too hard the way I've done it. Poppa. You knew, didn't you? You knew, Pop. You wanted me to be something I could never be, but you knew. You wanted me to stay away from this life with its substitutes.

Substitute hipness for emotions, substitute sharp clothes and possessions for work that matters, that keeps a guy clean, substitute cigarettes for muscles. Bad, it's all bad. The people I dig, the places I go, the whole scene. It stinks. It's like a pool of swamp water somebody dumped old factory chemicals into, and one day a monster comes out of the slime. That's what the kid is. He's a slime-thing I created with Freeport and the hip scene. He's a product, that's all. He's no damn good, but he's only what we made him. And how good can I be if I can stand still for a creation like that?

No good, that's how good. No earthly good.

I've got to get free.

Then Joe Costanza walked up to the table. He stared down at Shelly for a while, wondering just how a man's eyes could go watery and glazed like that. Then he turned to Jeanie Friedel, and she shrugged softly, worry there, and bit her underlip again. She was out of touch, and so was Joe Costanza. Shelly's cigarette hung unnoticed in his mouth, the ash dangling . . . then a crevice in the gray matter . . . and it tumbled scattering all over his jacket, the table, and into his drink.

Costanza said, very softly, "Shelly?"

No answer. How deep a man must go, sometimes, to see himself and the leech world that feeds off him.

"Shel? Hey, Shelly?"

A rustle, a shift, and the eyes returned, bringing with them reason and the man. Back from himself. Shivering.

Shelly's eyes focused and he looked at Jean without realizing Joe Costanza was there; then, as her mood and the level of her eyes indicated something was different, he moved his head slightly and caught sight of his assistant. "Uh. Oh, yeah, Joe." Weary. Very weary. A long trip. An unpleasant ride. "What's the matter, Joe?"

Costanza spoke gently, as though realizing he was dealing with a tired voyager (an invalid?), "There was a call for you, Shelly. Carlene at your place. She asked for you, and said it was important. I think she wants you to come home for something. I figured you'd be in the nearest bar."

He was sorry he had added the last.

But it went over Shelly's head.

"Thanks, Joe." Absently. Very absently. There were greater problems than Carlene, the woman who was not a woman. "I'll call her."

Costanza left, and Shelly excused himself for a moment.

When he reached her, all she said, coolly, was, "Would you come up for a minute; I'd like to tell you something."

He said he would cab over, and hung up.

Jean sat waiting, her glass almost empty. "Your cigarette's out."

He threw the dead butt into the ashtray and asked, "Will you wait here? It'll only take me a half hour or so. I don't know what's up, but I'd like to talk to someone. Carlene won't do. Will you wait?"

She nodded. "I'll have a couple more. Take your time. I'll be here when you get back." She didn't smile. It wasn't the time.

Shelly left the bar, blinking into the sun, and caught a cab on 47th Street.

When he got to the building he realized his mind had been dead all through the cab ride. Safety valve. Don't blow the fuses. Automatic switch-off, cut-in circuits, save the total mechanism, don't burn out.

When he unlocked the door, he knew instantly what Carlene had to tell him. The bags were packed, the matching set of steel-gray Samsonite plane luggage. Packed, by the door. She was dressed in a severe navy blue suit with a small white pillbox hat squarely on the top of her head. She sat with her legs crossed, smoking, the apartment very clean, all the ashtrays save the one she used as clean as when she had come to Shelly.

He closed the door and walked across to the chair facing the sofa, where she sat. He put himself lightly into the chair, and waited for her to speak. He knew it, so why not let her present it in her own way?

"I've got to be going, Shelly," she said. Oddly, she was nervous about it, hesitant, as though she was doing something she was ashamed of relating. But that was out of character for her.

How could a toaster apologize for popping up the toast?

How could a gumball machine say I'm sorry for issuing a gumball and a penny prize?

How could an IBM cluck regrets at its encoding processes?

She was leaving, as he knew she would one day, and she was departing from her giving-without-giving character by being ashamed (was that what it was?) in front of him.

Shelly sighed a sigh of finality. It was over, this part of it, and he didn't care. He had come to terms with himself in the bar. He knew who he was, at last; and that meant recognition, nomenclature, for everything and everyone around him. He knew what she was, and he could not muster up honest regret that she was going.

"Okay, I suppose that takes care of it. Do you need anything? Need any money?" He made a tentative move to his wallet. She stopped him with a half-completed motion.

"No . . . no, I'm all right. I—I just wanted you to know I had to leave, I had to go, Shelly. It didn't seem right to just pick up and move out without saying something."

There was no more. They didn't say *Well, take care of yourself* or *Let me hear from you*, or even *It's been interesting*. It was all said imperceptibly by her embarrassment, and his silence, his acquiescence. He understood and so did she.

He had a suspicion where she was going, into whose home and whose arms she was placing herself. Even that didn't matter; in fact, it was fitting and proper.

Then she left, and Shelly smoked a cigarette.

It was just another facet of the life that had equipped and aimed him for the creation of something like a Stag Preston. Her leaving was the severing of another link with the hip, clipster past he had come to despise in the past few months, so flamingly the last few hours.

He made a conclusion about the animals in Jungle York:

It's true. Animals can sniff each other out. Best of all the human animals. They always seek their own kind. A jackal knows another jackal by the little signs, the smells. And when an animal has mistaken a changeling for one of its own kind, it bolts away when it recognizes the shift away from that kind of beast. When an animal changes, its mates and friends slink away. Don't be near the sinking sinner. It can be contagious, this reverting.

She must have smelled it on me the last few months. The loss of hipness. It was enough to drive her away. I've lost my hunting, my prowling, and my hunting prowling partners.

What was it the poet said: sniffing strange. That has to be it. They go away.

There must be some hope for me. I must be getting well, if they bolt away. I must be getting well.

Then he put out the cigarette, put out the lights, closed the door to the apartment, and took a long walk halfway to the lounge where Jean Friedel waited, promising nothing.

He took a cab the rest of the way, received a great deal from her, and even gave a bit of himself, for the first time in so long he could not remember the last time it had happened. And he spent the night at a married friend's house, sleeping on a sofa the man and his wife had fixed. It was not entirely a good night's sleep, and he smoked too many cigarettes, but the next morning was clear, very clear, and he felt as though he might like to take a walk in the morning air.

Nor did the orange juice taste bitter.

Sixteen

So he told it. He told it all to himself, in a matter of moments as he walked the little redhead through the wings and up the metal stairs to Stag's dressing room. He thought about Louisville and Asa Kemp, about that first appearance at the Kentucky State Fair, about the look in Stag's eyes as they had flown away from Louisville. Shelly even remembered what Stag had said.

He had remembered it all, in that moment. Four full years of it. The creating of a talent, the sneak preview in Cleveland where the A&R men had sensed the talent building in the boy once known as Luther. The first gold record, the rush of success, the drinking and girl trouble, the night he had been slapped by the comedienne (what had happened to her? she'd cut one comedy album and then phffft!). Shelly had brought it all back in an instant of vacant thought; the tour, Trudy Quillan, and the beating the Colonel had given Stag; the revelation that Stag had lied about his childhood and the gradual realization on Shelly's part that he had been rotting for many years. The movie deal, the blackmail after Stag had drunkenly made his pornoflick, Stag's selling off the chunks of his contract, and finally Asa Kemp's death, the scene with Ruth Kemp, and Carlene's leaving. It had all seemed so fast. Too fast.

Was it possible?

Could it have been?

Four years?

Yes, that's what it had been. Four full years, in which Sheldon Morgenstern had become a cipher. He had had no life of his own. His every moment had been devoted to Stag Preston. His sex had been CarleneSex, which was none at all. That had been a draining process, not a giving process. Now she lived with Stag, in an apartment the singer had rented and furnished (under Jean Friedel's grudging supervision; Paul McCobb, Knoll, and Saarinen did not happen to be Stag's taste; he ran more to Kresge, Woolworth, and Lamston, so he had dragooned Jean into doing it for him.) Lots of luck to them both. The cobra and the tiger lie down together.

It was a torrent of memory, in that walking time between the alley and Stag's dressing room. It was all the silt of incidents deposited abruptly in the delta of his mind. He had it all, all of it, captured there, each bit of time and space prismed and imprisoned as though on a slide, about to go under the microscope.

Even the taking of this girl, this abundantly built teenager, to Stag's dressing room. That had been part of the memory, slipping into the past even as it happened. For it seemed to have happened a dozen other times . . . and, in point of fact, had happened a dozen times since Stag had come to The Palace . . .

When Stag had come offstage that first time, the day after Ruth Kemp had gone back to Louisville, he had made his initial request. "There's a girl in the fifth row down there, Shelly. She's got black hair in a pixie cut. I motioned to her to come around back after the show. Get her up to the dressing room, will you?"

Shelly had carefully removed the cigarette from his lips, his eyes narrowing; it was all he had been able to do to keep his fist from balling and driving straight into the kid's mouth. Very quietly he answered, "I'm a stockholder, Stag, not your pimp. If you want to get her, go get her yourself."

Then Stag had made some penetrating comments about how easy it would be to drop a mention to Winchell or Lyons or Killgallen—oh, *very* delicately—outlining the switch in residence of Carlene. It certainly wouldn't *kill* anyone, but what a helluva lot of snickers and glances askance it could cause in Lindy's or The Stage Delicatessen. That sort of business could rob a guy of his manhood, *muy pronto.*

It had been that, partially, no mean threat in a world predicated on how many times a night you could make the scene with a chick. But it had been more. It had been the awkward feeling that his presence might keep Stag from even greater evils. An egocentric thought, Shelly knew, but one that continued to intrude. Stag had been his creation, and thus was his responsibility. It would be too easy to check out now, letting the kid run loose. He had to stay close by and absorb some of the driving shock of the kid's rampages. He had to get in the way of the pneumatic drill.

So, illogically or not, Shelly had become Stag Preston's procurer. All these thoughts, four years' worth of them, as the little redhead followed Shelly up the gunmetal-gray stairs to her idol's dressing room.

Shelly knocked on the door, but he knew Stag could not hear it. Stag was out on the fire escape, doing another number, giving his "papoose" show that rode on the back of the regular performance in the theatre, helping to empty the seats for a new audience in two hours when he went on again.

Shelly opened the door and hustled the redhead before him. She stood transfixed, staring at God within a few feet of her, his back turned, one foot up on the rowel of the fire escape enabling him to brace his guitar. He was playing "Light a Fire" and comping behind it with broad chords and slides:

> "Light a fire in my heart,
> I want to burn for you.
> Don't need matches, just your kisses,
> I want to burn for you.
> *I got a* (whump!)
> *Fever of love* (whump!)
> *Smolderin' for you* (whump!) *so*
> Light that fire in my heart,
> I wanna wanna wanna burn for you!"

———

It was a gutty, almost burley bump-&-grind treatment with every *whump!* accented by a thrust and counter-thrust of hips. Down in the alley behind the theatre, the horde went wild, and behind him, in the dressing room, the little redhead did her own private flip.

Just as Stag finished, bowed for the inevitable mad applause from below, and launched into "Warm Baby" (indistinguishable from "Light a Fire" save for the placement of *whump!)* the phone rang. Shelly ground out the most current cigarette in a coffee cup on the dressing table and put the receiver to his ear. "Yeah?"

"Shelly? Jeanie."

"Hi. What's happening?"

"Stag finished the first show?"

Shelly looked out onto the fire escape. "Yeah, I guess you'd call it that. He's feeding the *animals* a few scraps off the fire escape now."

"I've got some contracts here from Sid Feller; he wants your signature and Stag's. It looks like ABC-Paramount's going to release a two-record Commemorative Set of his gold records, or some ridiculous thing. Will you be there for a while?"

Shelly moved against the wall, shielding his mouth, watching the redhead to make certain she could not hear. "The Marquis de Sade has a new case study going on at the moment," he said.

"He's still putting the make on those kids, oh Shelly!"

"Listen, what can I do . . . ?" He shrugged helplessly.

"Oh, Shelly, can't you do *some*thing? Did you get her up there for him again?" He did not answer. She spoke again. "Did you, Shelly?" Still no answer. Shame rode silently along the wire. Finally: "Oh, *Shelly!*"

He snapped at her. "Lay off me! It's a living, isn't it?"

Her answer was brief: "Is it?"

The tone of his answer had not been the New Shelly. It had been an Old Gimme-Gimme Shelly. "I guess you're right," he said. "But at least with me around he can't take 'em on the rug against their will."

Stag finished "Warm Baby" at that moment, and took his applause.

"Should I bring the contracts over?" Jean Friedel asked.

"Yeah, I suppose. C'mon over, we'll wait."

A third voice broke into the conversation: "Who's coming over? Who're we waiting for?" Stag had come in off the fire escape, seen the girl, and heard Shelly's end of the conversation. Now he had again taken control; a few words and he was in charge.

"Hold it a minute, Jeanie . . . hey . . . oh hell, she hung up, Stag. It was Jean. She has some contracts, she's on her way over. I told her we'd wait."

Stag looked over the girl critically. Her skin was a honey-tan, and her body was firm, tight, built the way teenaged girls had never been built when Shelly had been that age and the girls wore colored bobby sox and pennies in their loafers. Stag liked what he saw. He didn't want to wait for Jean and the contracts, lose any of the two hours he had.

Today was quickie day. Every day was quickie day.

The original Stag Preston was hungry, and felt no need to wait for his dinner. "I don't feel like waiting. I'm going up to the hotel for a rest." He turned to the little redhead with the ponytail and the large chest. "Hi, I'm Stag Preston, who're you?" The smile was straight out of the Crocodile That Swallowed Captain Hook.

She colored and answered softly, "I'm Marlene. I'm President of the Secaucus Stag Preston Fan Club." She beamed.

Stag turned to Shelly with a questioning glance.

"New Jersey," Shelly explained.

Ohhh, Stag made a wide head-movement back to Marlene. "Oh, sure, of course! Secaucus, New *Jersey.* Great town, very pretty."

Shelly died a little inside as Stag called an industrial town more marshland-and-stink than habitation a "great town." It was customary when riding the tollways past Secaucus to place thumb and forefinger over nose, and pray. But the busty redhead swallowed the schmaltz and continued beaming.

As Stag studied his prey, deciding what gambit would be least taxing to get the chick up to the hotel room, Shelly studied Stag. In the clean sunlight coming off the fire escape he was quite a different image from the one thrown against nightclub dims or onstage spots. He was no longer the young and vital Stag of Louisville days, or that night in Cleveland when ABC-Paramount Records had first seen him. *He drinks too much now,* Shelly thought, cataloging what he could see in the planes and lines of Stag's face. *He's running in company too fast and worthless. And no one can tell him anything. He won't last past forty; the gaff'll kill him.*

A voice deep inside added, *If we're lucky.*

Yet Shelly realized Stag's popularity had not waned. If anything, it had grown, by the mystic underground communication system of the teenagers who loved him. Teenagers just like sexy little Marlene here. A girl who was going to be main course on Stag's next meal.

"Well, listen . . . uh, Marlene? Marlene. Listen, I'm a little beat, you can understand." She nodded on schedule. "And I've got to go up to my hotel for about an hour or so, but since I've met you I'd like to give you a souvenir, a memento you know, somethin' personal of mine to keep. How'd you like that?"

Ding ding ding!

Shelly's eyes rolled up in his head at that one. Had Marlene been anything but a precocious teenager, brought up on the saliva of confession magazines, toothpaste ads that guaranteed her charm *as well as protection,* and a distorted Hollywood view of life in our times, she would have laughed the crude proposal back into Stag's teeth. But all her sex had been on the sofa in the rec room while Mom and Dad watched the big TV upstairs, or in the rear seat of a compact car while the drive-in movie raged above, so she turned crimson again and nodded agreement.

"Great," Stag said enthusiastically. "Shelly, you stick here and wait for Jeanie with the contracts. I'll just walk Marlene over to the —"

"I'm coming along."

Stag's face suddenly went to stone. "I said you could *wait, here,* Shelly. I'll walk Marlene over to the —"

"I'm coming."

His jaw muscles jumped, and his mouth worked, but he did not repeat himself. More words and it would become apparent that there was something not quite proper in what Stag had suggested, or it might even (Heaven forbid!) convey the impression that Stag was not sovereign of all he surveyed. "Okay, sure, Shel," Stag agreed with the bite of the asp in his voice.

Shelly wrote a note to Jean Friedel asking her to leave the contracts. It was obvious to Shelly that had Jean not called to say she was coming over, Stag would not have bothered taking the girl to the hotel, he would have made his play here in the dressing room.

They left by the stage entrance and as they emerged from the fire door, Marlene gave a squeal and ran to her friends still clustered and waiting. Stag bolted to the waiting taxi; Shelly lagged— without spoken instructions—for the girl.

"Listen, listen, hey, I'm goin' over to Stag's hotel for a souvenir. Listen, you come on along and wait outside downstairs and I'll get him to wave to you," Marlene burbled. "I'll get him to step to the window with me an' an' an' Trudy, hey, you take a pictchuh of us willya, huh?" Her words were excited, tripping, confused in pleasure.

Trudy—the fat girl with pimples—nodded furiously that if Marlene could get Stag to step up to the window and lean out, or onto the balcony or whatever the hotel had, she would be nutty insane wild craaaazy to take a pictchuh!

So Marlene waved, joined Shelly, and got into the cab for the three block ride over to the Sheraton-Astor, the Colonel's big suite, and Marlene's souvenir from her idol, Stag Preston.

Oh pretty baby, thought Stag Preston, *am I gonna give you a souvenir.* Fa-jooomp!

Marlene squealed when she saw the opulence of the suite. The Colonel was out and the place was silent; vulgarly garish in the full sunlight of day, a suite designed for dusk-to-dark-to-dawn living but uncomfortably blaring in the light of day.

Shelly mixed himself a drink, waiting for Stag to make his play, and settled into a chair near the door.

Stag suggested to Marlene she might use one of the bathrooms to powder her nose, in the event of a picture being taken, and when the redhead had swirled into the bedroom the singer advanced on Shelly.

"Hey, listen, guy, what the hell *is* this?"

"Statutory rape, Stag."

"Say, listen, get your finger outta my eye, baby. This kid has a set on her like a cow. Don't tell me she don't know what it's all about. If she had as many stickin' outta her as she's had in her, she'd look like a pincushion."

Shelly sipped at his Scotch. "What's the matter, Stag, isn't Carlene keeping you happy these days? You got to take off after every good-looking piece that comes in range?"

"Now, listen, Shelly . . . nothing's going to happen to her. I promise you. Just grab a quick feel. Hell, I've only got—" he consulted his wristwatch, "—another forty minutes before I have to be back at The Palace. I promise not to make the kid do anything she doesn't want to do. But who the hell are you to stop her if she wants to neck with Stag Preston for a while. Probably the biggest thrill of her life."

Shelly thought about it for a moment. Actually, the girl was as hip as any chick her age, with her looks and build, would be. If he went in the next room Stag wouldn't try anything. He'd hear any noise. And so what if Stag did feel her up a little? She'd blush and carry the tale back to the Secaucus Fan Club like a banner:

You know what happened when he hugged me? I mean Stag Preston! He put his hand right here and he was smilin' all the time, you wouldn't expect it almost in public but he was so strong, y'know, and when he kissed me I mean he Frenched *me and all, y'know, oh God it was the wildest and—*

It wouldn't do any harm, not if there was someone handy in the next room in case Stag got out of hand. And it would keep the animal at bay a little longer, till he could take it out on Carlene. That was safest, letting him release his hungers on a paid—no, stop thinking like that, she used to live with you, stop thinking of her with recriminations, she's no more a paid whore than . . . just stop thinking that way. Stop!

"Okay, Stag. You can play your game, but I'm right next door in the bedroom. I hear one peep out of that girl and I'll be here in a second. So keep it above the belt, baby." He got up, carried his drink into the bedroom, and closed the door. He did not hear Stag place the chair under the knob and force it tight, effectively locking the door.

When Marlene came out of the bathroom her face was radiant. Stag was sitting on the sofa, and he smiled his best lithographed poster smile. "C'mon over and sit down, Marlene."

A quick scurry of alarm passed her features, and then she shook it off as she was enveloped by the glamour of the suite, the nearness of Stag Preston. She sat down beside him. His arm went over the back of the sofa. Again the scurrying of frightened feelings. Then he talked to her. Slowly, cajolingly, interestingly, getting nearer.

When he leaned down and kissed her, she was startled at first, not because he had done it, but because Stag Preston, after all, *Stag Preston* was also human. In a moment, though, she reacted, and it was pleasant. She cooperated.

Right up to the moment he tried to slide his hand inside the front of her peasant blouse. Then she heard the alarm bells and tried to remove his hand. But Stag Preston was not a fumbling adolescent in a movie house balcony. He was Stag Preston, the king of the rock'n'roll singers, a voice in his time, a figure to be contended with—and what was more, he *knew* how teenagers thought. He *knew* this chick wanted some kicks, he *knew* she was only trying to put him off so he wouldn't think she was a tramp, he *knew* there wasn't a girl built like her in this day and age who hadn't gotten it somewhere along the line. He *knew,* because he'd seen them, every day, the little chippies dancing on the TV rock'n'roll shows. He'd seen them flipping their bodies at him. He *knew* how depraved kids were today.

After all, wasn't *he* a kid, and wasn't *he* the same way?

Which was what bothered him about the way this Marlene was fighting. She wasn't making noise . . . a grunt or a gasp or two, like that, but mostly silently, mostly real intensely trying to pry his hand off her tit. She had him by the wrist, and she strained, her face white with terror—too melodramatic, as far as Stag was concerned. She was putting it on. She was only giving him a hard time, and after all the easy lays he'd had, that only made Marlene more interesting. A little fight always helped to juice a guy up.

He struggled with her.

For a moment there was only the sound of her grunts of exertion, soft *uh's* and half murmured *please's* as she wrestled with him on the sofa. Then she got her face away from his, her breath pulling deeply, rasping. "P-please, *please,* Sta—Mr. Preston . . . d-don't, uh, p-puh-please . . . "

"Aw, now *sheet,* chick! Don't put me on like that . . . uh . . . god-*damn* it, take it easy, stop *pullin'* like that, it's gonna be nice . . . come *on* dammit! Knock that crap off!"

He shoved her heavily, annoyed at the way it was going, and that did it. Marlene was not a virgin; Stag had been correct, she *had* known boys. But they had done it in clandestine ways, in fur-tive places, and she was a virgin in attitude. It was the 1961 code of ethics. Give it away but only after you've convinced your con-science that you love the guy, that he loves you, that it's wonder-ful, not quick and sloppy. But Stag was pushing it; the thinking had not been right—the attitude had not been given enough time to switch. She was capable of being made . . . but not this way. She wavered, and would have relented, soon, but he forced her.

She went back over the line.

It was as though she had never been touched before.

The virgin screamed.

Then she jammed her thumb into Stag's eye. Her peasant blouse ripped down the front as Stag lurched away, his hand still caught in the thin fabric. It ripped down with a harsh sound and revealed the pink and black lace brassiere she wore. Half-aroused and half-infuriated Stag came back at her, one hand at his eye, the other groping for the girl.

She tried to pull the ripped blouse across her chest, and it only accentuated her body the more. *She shouldn't 'a done that!* was all Stag could think, the words crimson against a crimson background emblazoned on a crimson field of blood that backed his eyes. He reached.

He caught her by the ponytail and dragged her up against him, and she got her nails into one cheek, ripping down, leaving three blood-welling furrows and one shorter, shallower one where her little finger had traveled ripping through the skin. Stag howled.

In the bedroom, Shelly heard her first scream, and the Scotch spattered against the wall as he dropped the glass and leaped to the door. He wrenched at the knob and shoved inward but it only bowed slightly, and would not give. He threw himself against it, realizing Stag had barricaded the door, and terror flicked like a running greyhound through his mind as he heard Stag bellow in pain, then the rip of something tearing, and shorter more painful shrieks as Stag did *something* to the girl.

"Open this door! *Open the door, you sonofabitch!*" he screamed, slamming his fist against the solid paneling. "Stag! Stop it, stop it you bastard, let her alone! Open this goddam effing door, you stupid rotten—*open this* DOOR!"

In the living room Stag took his hand from his reddened, watering eye, and wrapped it in the material of what was left of the peasant blouse. He put one hand in the girl's face and shoved her as hard as he could. The blouse ripped away completely, leaving two huge strips hanging down her back and a fistful of fabric in Stag's hand. She screamed again, very high, like a bird in pain, and stumbled back against the wall. Red welts appeared on her skin. There was open, unhindered terror in her face. The red hair was flying loose now, the body a hopeless, unmuscled jumble of thrashing legs and arms.

"Stag! *Open the door!*" Shelly bellowed as he threw his shoulder against the paneling. Unlike the movies where it seemed so easy, he bounced back, a shattering pain in his shoulder. He hit it again and once more rebounded. A third time, a fourth. One of the panels began to bow outward, then split. He launched himself at it again, fanatically, lost in any thought but getting out into the next room where the screams were coming closer together—like labor pains.

Stag advanced on the girl and wrapped his arms around her in a bear hug. She tried to bite him, pleading incoherently now, not giving a damn if he *was* Stag Preston, out of her mind with horror at the mauling and the blood all over her—but mostly *his* blood. They wrestled for a moment, stumbling backward, just as the paneling of the bedroom door shattered and Shelly's face appeared in it.

The publicist took one look and his face went white as the shock wave of violence smashed him. He screamed wordlessly, and ripped at the chair blocking the knob. It fell away.

Stag and the girl caromed off the wall, still locked in each other's arms, her legs covered with abrasions and blood from where he had tried to wrap his legs about her. They hit the wall a second time, bounced off it and fell back, striking the French doors leading to the balcony.

They crashed the doors open, snapping the delicate tiny lock-decoration and thrashed out onto the small balcony over Broadway. He had a grip on her shoulders, was digging his fingers into the white flesh where the blouse had torn away, and this time all the songs in the world could not win this girl for him.

Shelly reached through and turned the knob, came storming into the living room just as—

Stag tried to pull her close, to drag her back inside, but she shoved against him, as hard as she could; she was redolent of an animal fear that only signaled she had to stay out of his reach. He tripped on his own feet and his grip on her broke . . . the force of her pushing against him hurled her backward, and she hit the low balcony railing with her buttocks; the force of her fury to remain untouched pulled her up onto the railing and for a moment she flailed there, her arms now reaching for her idol, Stag Preston, to help her regain balance.

He took a confused half-step toward her, even as the scream came silently, filling her eyes with endless wide-open falling, and then the force of her backward fall threw her weight across the railing, and in a flash of legs she went over and was gone.

From where Shelly stood, transfixed, in the middle of the living room, he could hear her screams, all the way to the sidewalk.

It sounded like a ride-out ending to a rock'n'roll number.

SEVENTEEN

Time hung suffocating. It did not move though it struggled inwardly, to grasp air, to reach sanity. Then, in an instant, *everything* moved:

Stag fell backward, his eyes maddened, wide, bloody, unbelieving, hot and frantic, utter disbelief on his face, a rag of peasant blouse still in his hand. His other hand was in midair, at the point where it had rested on her shoulder when she'd pulled loose. He bumbled forward, staring down into the street, in clear view from below, and Shelly could hear other screams drifting up from the street now.

A flight of shrill birds, deathly white, rising on wide-spread wings into the sky. Screaming. Screaming.

Shelly took three steps and reached Stag. He grabbed him by the back of the neck and violently threw him back into the room. He looked down, and so many eyes stared back up at him it was frightening. She was down there, all twisted up into herself, and at the same time spread out, with the red hair against the dirty gray of the pavement. There was a tight little circle around her.

He saw the ash-colored faces of the Secaucus Stag Preston Fan Club turned toward him. Or were they turned to watch their sister go to whatever Heaven was reserved for foolish rock'n'roll fans? Even as he stared down at them staring up, a girl with a camera flashed light at him, and he knew the whole thing had been recorded.

They had waited for Marlene to step out onto the balcony with her God, to wave the tiny souvenir he would have given her. They had stood, staring up—

—as she fell, twisting, screaming, trying to fly the way they do when there is nowhere else to go but down, and too ripped up the center with their own screams of horror as she plunged down amid them, barely missing a passing tourist. It was all there, and the fat girl with pimples had it on film. Black and white or color Kodachrome, she had it, and it was that thought, only that thought, filling all space and sucking up all air, not a thought but a goddamn *black hole*, that sent Shelly scurrying back into the suite. In a panic, he closed the French doors tightly and relocked them. Then he thought better of it and unlatched them again. This was going to have to be fast, perfect. He would have to snap Stag out of it . . . cooperation was the most important thing, now.

Stag was braced against a high Chinese breakfront, the bit of peasant blouse still wrapped in his fingers. It was a scene from Hogarth, full of madness and the imperative of *hurry*!

"She—pulled away. She hit me and . . . went—she went *over* . . . I tried to stop—to stop her, but she—she—" The cruel mouth was a baby's now, the dark eyes dim with confusion and fright. "What'll they do to me?"

Shelly's face was made of lead. The lead that was quicksilver, melting and running slowly, reforming. He grabbed Stag by the lapels and forced him to his knees, talking intently into the insanity still lingering on the boy's face: "Listen to me. *Listen, you sonofabitch*, listen! That kid is dead in the street down there and you want to know if you're going to have to pay for it!

"I'd like to beat the hell out of you right now, you miserable effing bastard, but there's too much to do . . . God only knows why . . . give me that cloth . . . *give it to me*," he said ferociously, ripping it out of the boy's hand. "Now listen close, you ratty sonofabitch. I want you to go in that bathroom and wash all that blood off you, do you understand? I want you to put on a fresh shirt and a new jacket and comb your hair. Then I want you to come back in here and set up everything you knocked over. And then—so help me God in Heaven you'd better pull it off, you ratty scummy bastard—then I want you to sit down and compose yourself. I'll tell you what to tell the police when they get—"

"*Police!* Jesus Christ, Shelly, they'll come, won't they? They'll come—Jesus, you gotta help me, Shelly, you got to help me—tell me what to say to them 'cause I don't know I mean you're my friend and you've got a piece of the action and it'll all go down to hell if you don't—"

Shelly let go of one lapel and cracked him fiercely in the mouth. It brought Stag's eyes back into focus.

He dragged the singer erect and propelled him through the bedroom into the bathroom. "Move, you ignorant bastard! *Move!* And leave this door open." He indicated the shattered bedroom door. "If it's against the inner wall I might be able to keep them out of there and they won't see it. Now do what I told you, and pray, no, forget that, you dirty sonofabitch, just forget it."

Shelly ran out of the bathroom—it had only been a matter of seconds since she had fallen, though it seemed centuries, slowly dragging—and grabbed up the piece of peasant blouse. He could not chance running down the hall to the incinerator in the maid's cubby, but there was the kitchen. He pulled the half-filled bag of garbage out of the pail and thrust the cloth down into the bottom. Then he plopped the bag of garbage on top of it.

Stag had not yet emerged from the bathroom, but in a few minutes the hotel staff, the police, crowds of curious peepers, the world . . . they'd all be in the suite. He stood the pedestal table upright; the one the girl had knocked over, retreating from her idol. He picked up the ashtray and the unbroken Swedish vase and set them in place. He fluffed the pillows on the sofa. Now, no one had sat there.

Stag came out of the bedroom, his hair combed, his face pink from having been scrubbed. Only the wild light in his dark eyes and the hollows in his cheeks belied the naive adolescence of him.

He was buttoning a fresh blue piqué shirt, a Scotch plaid sports jacket under his arm. "That thing's too bright. Take it back and get something black, something dark blue. *Jump!*" Stag turned on his heel, almost an automaton, and a few moments later re-emerged wearing a dark blue blazer with brass buttons. He looked good . . . reserved . . . not like the sort who would cause a girl to fall to her death escaping a rape.

Shelly shoved him down in a chair. "Now look," he said, carefully, so it would penetrate, "when the cops get here your story is that she was invited up for an autograph, a souvenir, a talk because she was the president of one of your fan clubs, and you like to take personal interest in these kids because it's good business relations and—are you listening, you simpleton?"

"She—she just—fell . . . " His eyes were glazing again.

The slap across the cheek brought him back and Shelly tried frantically to get it across again. "They will take your ass out and string it up, do you understand, Big Man? They will kill you the way you killed her unless you get control of yourself and start doing some of that acting the critics raved over. Now, dig: she flipped at being with you, tried to make a pass and rip off your jacket, you jumped and she caught you with her nails." He touched the four furrows still livid on Stag's face. "You shoved her away and she started chasing you . . . "

Shelly snapped his fingers, disengaged himself from Stag, and moved on to a floor lamp plugged in by the breakfront. He moved it near the French doors and laid the cord out on the rug as though it had been pulled from its socket.

"Now you get it? She chased you, tripped over the cord, and went out through the French doors. The force of her fall threw her over. You're *desolate* with sorrow that one of your fans should have such an accident. You'll pay all funeral expenses and the family will never have to worry again. You got that?"

He nodded tightly. He was starting to come around.

The doorbell went off like a gunshot.

Had he been just another slob on the scene, just another faceless guy brought to official attention, it might have been an Inquisition, and downtown to the Tombs for questioning. But he wasn't.

He was Stag Preston. Had the Colonel been around (no one seemed to know just *where* he had gone) even the mild questioning they suffered might have been averted. One call by The Man to his contacts downtown, and like a stream being diverted, they would have talked to intermediaries, left Stag alone. But Shelly had been forced to handle this little performance, and he handled it well.

It didn't take much talking at all, but what there was—was fast. Shelly caught them as they came through the door, juggling them like sterling silver globes. They spun madly, faster and faster, until the publicity man hurled them over to Stag.

Easily Academy Award quality. He acted the role of the half-crazy-with-torment star so well that at times Shelly had to stop to correct his thinking: *He is acting. He isn't actually sorry, or innocent, or in anguish. This is an act.*

But what an act:

"We're sorry to bother you, Mr. Preston, but the girl *did* fall from your balcony." Heavy irony in their voices; an idol was an idol, and they knew their steps could only be so many, so far, so hard; but it didn't preclude irony, heavily, in the voices. "Now what, Mr. Preston, exactly, happened?"

Shelly had told it, but it had to be told again.

Then again.

And a third time. (And still no sign of the Colonel.) But simply told it was simply told: Mr. Preston had seen the young lady—he didn't even know her name—at the theatre. She had been making quite a spectacle of herself, apparently. Mr. Preston had invited her—under Mr. Morgenstern's chaperoning—to stop by for a souvenir and an autograph. Mr. Preston always takes special pains with his fans, because every fan is something special to him. Once in the suite, the girl had acted very badly, pawing and trying to kiss Mr. Preston—aw, hell, fellas, you can call me Stag—and had even clawed at him in an attempt to rip off a piece of his clothing as a memento. She had made embarrassing advances and Stag had tried to get away. In the scuffle she had tripped over a lamp cord and fallen through the French doors.

"The force of her fall must have just thrown her over," Stag concluded, desolation and misery in his eyes, the timbre of his voice. "I—I didn't know what, what to do . . . she was there one minute and the next . . . " He shuddered eloquently.

A sharp-eyed plainclothesman, who had been examining the nap of the rug, the placement of the lamp's trailing cord, and the way the French door had snapped open the flimsy lock, stood up, and made an, "Uh, Stag?" of attention.

The singer turned to him, and Shelly saw in that face of the law what he was hoping not to see. The man was not fooled; he knew the girl had been struggling ferociously, had not fallen as accidentally as Stag Preston told it. "Uh, Stag, where's the piece of her blouse?"

The boy came through beautifully. There was a briefest flicker of the dark eyes, and a recovery so swift there might never have been a fumble. "What piece of her blouse?"

The detective's jaw muscles bunched and he said very smoothly, "The girl's blouse had been ripped down the front. We thought it might be here in the hotel somewhere."

Shelly leaped in abruptly: "She must have, uh, she must have ripped it on her way down, or perhaps on the door handle here—" He stepped across theatrically, very much like a schoolteacher or a television announcer, pointing to the product, directing (or misdirecting) everyone's eyes. He pointed to the door handle. The plainclothesman turned back to Stag. The man was no dummy.

"You didn't see the blouse, is that it?"

Stag shrugged and spread his hands in all directions, turning. "No, you can look if you like." They didn't look.

"Perhaps one of her friends grabbed it up, those nutty teenagers, you know," Shelly said, interceding again, misdirecting. "She was with some fan club, a whole bunch of them . . . you know how they are . . . maybe one of them grabbed it up."

"Perhaps," the detective murmured, turning away; he knelt down again to study the patterns of ruffling on the carpet.

It went on for some time. Shelly managed to get away once and hit the phone in one of the bedrooms. "Hello . . . this is Shelly . . . let me talk to Joe.

"Joe? Shelly. Listen, we've got it and bad this time. The kid had a groupie up here . . . " He launched into a *Reader's Digest* condensation of the episode, concluding, " . . . they've got us sewed-up here. I told them I was calling The Palace to cancel Stag's performance. Do that, but get with the columnists. Every goddamn busboy and maid in this joint has found some excuse to breeze past the door or the dumbwaiter while the fuzz've been here. It's probably with every stringer in the city by now. Get with them and keep their mouths shut. I don't care how you do it, just *do* it!"

When he reappeared, his face was a twist of sadness. "Captain," he addressed the senior investigating officer, "this has been a helluva strain on the kid. He's pretty much attached to his fans, you know. We've canceled the performance at the theatre, but I'd like to see him in bed for the day. Do you think you've got enough for now?"

The Captain, a man with over twenty years on the force, and a staunch believer in the old saw, *You scratch my back and I'll scratch yours*, a man who knew the Colonel and what he could or could not do, thought he very well might have enough for now. There would, of course, be more questioning later, and the coroner's inquest, but he was sure everything was just as Mr. Morgenstern and Good Old Stag had it.

The girl must have had some kind of unbelievable strength to throw herself out a window like that, but hell, anyone could see Stag was really broken up about this thing, and yes, it's terrible, and sure, we'll refer the newsmen to you, Mr. Morgenstern, I guess you want to handle the way they talk about this thing . . . some of them got real nasty mouths on them, and sure, we understand, and you betcha we'll pass along the Colonel's regards to the Commissioner for his interest and his help. Thanks a lot, gang.

Then the door was opening and closing and people were leaving. If they had arrived and been juggled like silver globes, then their leaving could only be compared to fog. They left like fog.

Great gouts of them left at one time—harness bulls, the police photographers, the analysts, the reporters, the plainclothes detectives, the Captain. Then smaller wisps drifted away, unseen: the morbidly curious ones who had heard the terrible news and who wanted, for a few instants, to bathe in the glow of the famous, the notorious, the colorful. They were the gray ones, like fog itself, who drift and are never really seen. Who derive all their glamour vicariously, all their color by reflection and refraction, like the oil slick on asphalt after the rain. They disappeared, but only when they were certain nothing more was happening . . .

Then the last of the hotel staff, the toadies, leaving the royal chamber, genuflecting and bowing out backward, hoping Mr. Preston and the Colonel would not feel the management had acted in bad faith by calling in the police so quickly, after all, the girl *had* fallen from one of their suites, and their hands were tied, it was only the *natural* thing to do, because they had to maintain their repu—

"G'wan, get the hell out of here!" Shelly snapped.

(Was it his imagination, or did they all have huge, gnome-like pointed ears, to hear all the more, to tell all the more?)

And where in the name of Jesus Almighty was the Colonel? Or were they one and the goddamn same?

A splitting headache cromped down on Shelly the moment he had slammed the door on the toadies. They would open their mouths, he was sure of it. It was bound to leak out; after all, midafternoon on Times Square, a header into the street, a little chick from Secaucus of all places, and her crowd standing there watching. This was going to hit every penny-ante fan-mag in the country unless the payola was spread thick as peanut butter. The headache grew more intense the harder he thought. He leaned against the closed door, ignoring Stag Preston in the center of the room, still onstage, and he tried to think it out.

The effort was simply too much.

Forget the thinking and let the reflexes take over. It was synapses time, and he was the Old Sheldon Morgenstern, as he had been all afternoon. Was it inevitable, then, that he was doomed to return to that hideous shell of hipness, that shallow shell he had thought cast off? Every time the alarm went off, would he once more revert?

It was too horrible to consider.

The poor man's Jekyll-Hyde, he thought, wildly.

Break. The story was going to break. Click click click. It was going to get out all over the place unless he acted. He jumped, then, and found the phone again.

Once he had the number, and the dial tone had broken, he barely waited for a voice on the other end. "Joe? Me. Did you take care of it?

"Yeah . . . yeah . . . uh-huh, yeah . . . what about Atra Baer?

"Yeah, yeah . . . okay, good. Have any trouble with Kilgallen or Wilson?

"Yeah . . . yeah . . . right. What? Sullivan hadn't heard? Good, that way we tipped him ourselves. Maybe he'll figure we're playing tight with him.

"Now look: get with Herman and Buddy on the Coast and have them get to the columnists—trade and otherwise. Particularly the second-string *schlock* magazines; the ones we deal with won't screw us, but the others'd sell a story like this to our audience in a minute if they thought they could get away with it. I want them all sewed up. *All* of them. Have Herman and Buddy work on it all night if it takes that long and get back to you. I want a statement on how we stand by morning. Don't forget, they're three hours behind us out there. They've got—" he glanced at his watch, "—five good hours before six o'clock.

"Yeah . . . right . . . right . . . *now* you've got it!

"Look, Joe, I want this sewed up tight before you go home tonight, you got that? Yeah . . . yeah . . . that, too . . . yeah . . . okay, keep on top of it, and ring me if you come up against anything *boygus*.

"Yeah, it's Yiddish. It means tough. And I'll have your *tuchus* in a sling if you don't cement this thing up.

"What? How the hell do *I* know why the moron picks days like this to get in trouble . . . ? I'm only paid to wipe his ass for him. No, that *ain't* Yiddish. Now *jump*, willya!"

He hung up and walked back into the living room. Stag was standing by the French doors, now closed. He was silent, with a drink in his hand.

Shelly slumped down into a chair. Suddenly, it was very quiet in the suite and he felt utterly drained. It had not been an easy afternoon.

At that moment the door opened and Colonel Jack Freeport came in. Shelly started to speak, but never got the words past his throat.

"What has been going on here, today?" The Colonel was furious. "Everybody in the lobby was rushing up and saying how sorry they were it had happened. Did this miserable kid do something big again, or is it just another minor emergency?"

Shelly started to speak again. To tell the big, white-haired Messiah that his pride and joy had tossed a teenaged fan out the window. The words would not come.

"Well, it doesn't matter, anyhow," Freeport said, without waiting for an answer, "I've sold the kid's contract."

Did you know there *are* bombs that make no noise at all?

Eighteen

A healthy, red apple, with one bite out of it, turns brown and stinking in the air, inside a few minutes. Stag Preston turned around to face the Colonel, and his healthy, red face went brown and stinking within a matter of seconds. Someone had taken a big bite out of him.

But Shelly's question preceded the singer's. "You *what*? You *sold* his *con*tract? Are you kidding?"

They were inane responses to an extraordinary statement, but easily on a par with the inane answers to extraordinary pronouncements down through the ages. Now that it had been said, Shelly was not certain he had really heard it. Men do peculiar things in the peculiar world Shelly Morgenstern inhabited, but they did not throw millions away. Underarm *or* sidearm.

"Tell me what went on here today," Freeport demanded, laying his pearl-gray fedora on the table. He studied the boy in front of him, and his glance narrowed down as he turned his eyes to Morgenstern.

"You, Shelly. Tell me."

Shelly recapped it, hill-and-valleying it for speed and attention to such details as his calls to Costanza in re the columnists. The Colonel, however, seemed peculiarly disinterested; his attention was more clinical than personal.

When Shelly had concluded, Freeport moved across to the French doors, examined them carefully, stepped out onto the balcony and took a fast look down. He re-entered the living room and sat down in an upholstered straight chair, as though he had something brief to say and wanted no part of momentary comfort till he had said it.

"Boy," he said, aiming a blocky hand at Stag, "you have an apartment of your own, I believe. I'll expect you to be out of here as soon as possible. If you have any clothing or possessions I'll have the management send them over to you."

He steepled his longshoreman's hands and puffed at his lips. "Shelly, you still own a block of Stag's stock, don't you? Hmmm. I thought of that this afternoon. Well, of course, it's your decision, but there's always a job open with me if you want to market your share of the contract. I couldn't retain you on my staff with your interest in—" He did not finish the sentence, merely aimed two steepled fingers at his ex-talent.

Then Stag Preston, silent and bottled up during the explanation by Shelly and the comments by Freeport, exploded. He threw the drink across the room.

It shattered just under a Utrillo oil the Colonel had brought back from France, and the stain smeared down the wall in helpless, offensive trickles.

"What the fuck you think you're doin', Mr. Freeport *suh*! Just what the hell you think you're doin'? Whaddaya mean you sold my contract? You think I'm some kinda shit to sell or somethin'? I got a lot to say around here, and you ain't sellin' Stag Preston to *no*damnbody! Not till I say so, y'heah?" His eyes, dark a moment before, now actually glowed and flashed as he saw a bit of the situation out of his hands. All that drive, all that power and success and money, and he was still nothing more than an item on the slave-block for the more muscular traders.

Freeport contained himself. The mask of imperturbability stayed fastened firmly. He aimed the steepled index fingers at Stag Preston and amended the boy's speech. "You *had* something to say."

Stag assumed a pose that could only be called *snotty*, legs apart, arms akimbo, neck thrust forward. "Now what is *that* supposed to mean, Big Man?"

The Colonel seemed almost to be relishing the exchange. The

years with Stag had been ones of inner annoyance for Freeport. He had taken this raw Kentucky dirt and made a star of it, yet had seen himself maneuvered too often by circumstances manufactured out of poor public relations, recklessness, and outright immorality. Now he was exercising his pleasure at cutting Stag Preston to his own mold. Now he was seeing the cockiness and the smart-mouth drop away into fear and uncertainty. He was pleasuring himself at last.

"It means that your antics for the past four years, and in particular the past nine months, have drained your assets. You have sold me thirty-three percent of your contract in return for certain considerations—I'm sure you'll remember some of them—over a period of two years, and this, added to my original thirty percent makes me the controlling investor in the stock known as Stag Preston, Incorporated. Sixty-three percent is a good bit over majority."

Shelly had not known it had gone that far. He remembered how Stag had been hit brutally by taxes and expenses; he recalled how the boy had had to scrounge to make the payment to Trudy Quillan and Golightly. He even knew things were shaking seriously when the payoffs came due for various stringers around Hollywood and Broadway. (The half dozen who kept quiet monthly, for a fee, totaled close to eight thousand dollars.)

And then there had been Stag's parties, his romances, his exorbitant expenses for cars, apartments, gifts. All that money came from somewhere, and there were enough entourage-leeches hanging around to take another sizeable bite from the apple that was Stag Preston.

And finally, the monstrous chunk to quash the stag movie scandal. That had started the decline and fall of the Roaming Empire in earnest. But to have only seven percent of his own contract left! That was almost frightening in its implications.

A madman, spending with both hands, would find it almost impossible to waste a constant fortune of that sort. The only investments Stag had made were in a music publishing company dealing almost exclusively in nothing but his songs; and the profit from *that* venture had been blown on the celebration party Stag had thrown. It was in the red for decades.

Seven percent. A measly seven percent. Shelly was now a larger contract-owner than Stag. Thirty, still in Shelly's name, still pouring money into a bank account on a carefully lawyer- and tax-regulated basis to extrude the last possible cent of gain. Shelly might quit working that moment, and never have to lift a telephone again.

Why, then, was he still beating the drum for Stag?

It had nothing to do with money. He had explained all that to himself months before. There were days like this, when by all rights he should have quit cold, rather than bailing the kid out. But he stayed on.

Seeds of rot are planted deep.

Responsibility is a tenacious plant, too. It can grow from the most rotten of seeds, and cling to a barren, arid personality. So he stayed on, listening.

"And so—?" Stag demanded. "So?"

Freeport smiled a wafer-thin smile. Depending on who was describing it, perhaps even a smirk. "So I have just realized a profit from your contract by selling it to the highest bidder."

Stag pulsed with fury. Sold, like a side of beef. "And who the hell'd you sell it to?" He was shouting now. Completely out of control.

"To a group of small, but consolidated, businessmen from all walks of life, boy, who will manipulate the strings with a good deal more tightness than I did."

Shelly recognized the pattern. Freeport had unloaded what was fast becoming a harrying proposition, in favor of a juicy, quick profit. Stag had been purchased by a group of *schlock* operators; entrepreneurs who would milk him fast, build him up greedily, and then dump him as soon as it looked as though his mode was running out. Like a green club fighter, he would be overmatched, overexposed, overplayed, and then resold, right down the river. Or right down the drain . . .

Nothing as shadowy and sinister as a "syndicate," but a group of mutually interested parties who owned blocks of the boy, held meetings to decide policy and direction, and controlled the purse strings. Stag was now no longer his own man. He was owned. They would get in touch with Shelly soon enough.

Did he want to stay around and see what would happen?

He had to think about it. Not now, but later, when he could think without wincing, when the noise level in his skull had lowered. Not now.

Freeport was still speaking, slowly and distinctly, and still with great relish. "I think I pulled out of this cursed arrangement just in time, my boy. I feel your escapade today was enough to make you a very unsure property. In this connection, please get out of my suite."

The thin smile that might have been a smirk broadened, and a coarse laugh—too coarse for the pose Freeport affected—escaped him.

Stag leaped. The afternoon had been too much. Adding insult and rejection had done their part. He swung at the seated Colonel, his fist an awkward device that took Freeport high on the cheekbone, just under the right eye. The Colonel again demonstrated the hidden depth of his physical strength, half-rising from the chair and throwing himself to the side, even as Stag's blow caught him.

He reached out a huge hand, clawed a vicious hold on the boy's thigh and crotch—causing Stag to scream like a woman—and in one sinuous movement wrapped his other hand in the boy's collar and lifted him bodily off the floor.

He hoisted Stag once, as though about to heave a sack of coffee beans, and hurled him across the room. In a mass of uncoordinated flesh and limbs, the almost six-foot length of Stag Preston did a flat-dive over the sofa and crashed into the table halfway across the entrance chamber. The table—unlike breakaway furniture Stag had encountered in Hollywood—barely gave at the impact, and his back was bent over it, sickeningly, as he crashed onto it. Stag slipped off the table, taking with him the mosaic ashtray, the enamel statue of two gulls in flight, and a decorative bowl of pierced glass balls.

They landed in a glass-shattering heap at the base of the table, and Stag Preston's eyes rolled up in his head.

"Shelly, get him out of here. Call me when you've made up your mind." Freeport started to turn away, to gain the seclusion of his bedroom and bathroom, to wash away the perspiration and change his clothes. He paused and added, "Take your time, Shelly. I can always use you. See how the wind blows with him, and if it looks as though he can last, there will be no hard feelings. But I've been feeling it in the air; he's wearing off, and today may have been the finishing stroke. Don't get caught when the building falls in."

Then he turned and left Shelly to prop the half-conscious, bleeding Stag to his feet.

"C'mon, Meal Ticket," the flak-man murmured, mostly to himself, "let's leave Waterloo to the big artillery."

He rang the bell and Carlene opened the door. Her eyes widened momentarily at the sight of Shelly's burden, but she moved to allow them entrance. Shelly helped Stag to the sofa, but the boy staggered erect and disappeared into the bedroom. The sound of a leaden weight striking the bed came through to the living room distinctly.

Shelly looked around.

"You're living a lot higher than when you roosted with me, baby," he said to the girl.

She ignored the slap. "Is it true?" she asked.

"Is what true?"

"About that kid falling out the window."

"Correction: balcony."

"Balcony, then. Is it true?"

"Why?"

"Because I *have to know*!" she howled, infuriated by his fencing.

"So you can check out and find another nest high above the city if this pigeon's about to be gobbled by the hawks?"

"Is. It. True?"

He grinned maliciously. So there was a part of him that still gave a damn about the hipster life. "Yeah, Princess, it's true. But don't worry, we've got it hushed. It won't interfere with your dinners at The Four Seasons."

She bit her lower lip in concentration.

"Well, so long, Mommy. Your baby boy's dattaway."

He was halfway to the door when she said to his back, "He's all finished, Shelly."

Shelly turned. "How do you know?" There was fun and games, and there was seriousness, and Carlene's intuition (compounded of a sensitive feeling for the scene and its warm air currents, and tips from knowledgeable friends) was seldom wrong. It was past time for fun and games; it was time to dig her closely. "How do you know?"

"I know," she answered cryptically. "He's had it. You can't keep what happened today quiet. It'll get out."

"Not if we keep the columnists and fan mags in our pocket."

"There are other voices, and much louder," she said.

"I don't believe it; not in this country, anyhow."

"You'll see," she assured him, turning and finding her way to the bedroom. The words hung behind her mystically, almost a pronouncement of doom, and they bothered Shelly more than he cared to admit.

He was certain she was not soothing Stag in that bedroom. She might be checking the condition of her luggage, but she sure as hell was not soothing Stag Preston.

It was like a brush fire.

It began very slowly and in no time at all was completely out of control. Attendance was down at The Palace all the rest of that week. It was actually possible to get seats.

Fan mail assumed a different tone. A questioning tone, without really asking any questions. There were fewer requests for photos.

A copy of a photo, mailed from Secaucus, reached Shelly. It showed Stag and the dead girl, Marlene, thrashing on the balcony, but it could have been interpreted as Stag had related it to the police. There was no return address on the envelope. No amount of private detective pressure or investigation could uncover who the girl was, or who had taken the pictures. And there were more. One arrived each day, five in all. One of them was an out-of-focus blur that could have been a body, falling toward the camera. Another showed a man looking down from the balcony.

There was no letter attached to any of them. There was no hint of blackmail. It was simply FYI—For Your Information. Shelly began to shake.

Stag took no notice. He was above it. He had bigger things to worry about. The "syndicate" of little merchants had gotten in touch with him, and with Shelly. There was going to be a stockholders' meeting.

But the wind was rising. It told in the little things:

Stag had to wait for a table at The Harwyn Club.

They were evasive at the record company about things like the sales curve on the new album, when the next cutting session would be, whether Sid Feller would take it, what promotion was swinging with at the moment. Little things . . . things that had always been Am-Par's business, of course, but which they had gladly shared with Stag and Shelly.

Carlene disappeared. There was a rumor she had found a playboy from the Dominican Republic and was yachting south.

All the tables were reserved at the Stork.

Stag's tailor presented his long-standing, glad-to-put-a-star-like-you-onna-cuff-Mr.-Preston bill.

Stag stopped drinking heavily, tapered down and down and finally abstained altogether.

Cabdrivers no longer turned around to ask, "You're that Stag Preston, ain'tcha?"

To Stag the air was hot, close, barely moving.

But for Shelly, it was a swift current, chilling and eddying and heading out to sea. He went to the stockholders' meeting with trepidation.

He needn't have felt trepidation, for the "syndicate" of small merchants was just that. Money was a self-conscious garment to them. Tiny operators with Yiddish accents, Italian hand gestures, Polish sets to their eyes and lips, uncommunicative, questioning, altogether charming and friendly. They made their wishes plainly known.

No more boozing.

No more wenching.

No more bitching.

And lots of money into the group kitty. They addressed their property in his presence as "Stag" or "Mr. Preston" and called him "the property" in his absence. Shelly had seen these men on Mott Street, had known their inflections and their desires back home—they had been friends of his father. These were the men who ran the shops in the lower middle-class sections of the town with signs that read GOING OUT OF BUSINESS! POSITIVELY LAST DAYS! all year through. They were the ones who felt the tomatoes and the melons before they bought them. They were the men who backed quick operations, who sliced in and up and out like a switchblade.

The promoters.

The men who cut the ends off their cigars rather than throw away a chewed stub.

The entrepreneurs.

The men who sold when the market was five points higher than when they'd bought.

The *schlock* operators.

The men whose teeth, when bared, were not fangs but more rodent-like, who could never be cornered nor put out of business; for there was always a slipperiness to them, a small-time, niggling eel quality that carried them from quick operation to short change maneuver, and who hit only below the belt, because little men can reach no higher.

Though Stag Preston may only have sensed it, Shelly knew it to be a fact. When Freeport had pulled out, the operation known as Stag Preston, Incorporated, had dropped instantly to the minor leagues. And the wind was rising.

NINETEEN

The decision was not demanding enough, on a deeper level. Had
he not made a small fortune, wisely invested, and had he not been
assured that he would never again have to pound the Manhattan
pavement to make a buck, and had he not been guaranteed that he
would never again miss a meal or have to wear last year's topcoat,
it might have meant a great deal more.

But Shelly *had* made his pile from Stag; he *had* gained a large
measure of financial security; so it was still a matter of inner turmoil, or more closely: how ethical he could afford to be.

The vindictive strain in his conscience said, *Sure you can afford to
be righteous and get out! Certainly. You've got yours; I'm all right, Jack.
Let's see how honest you'd be if you were broke and the payment was due
on that hot rod of yours. Now you've made it and you're suddenly devel-
oping a streak of ethics. Hypocrite! Charlatan! Fink! As soon as there's
trouble, you grab and run. Creep!*

Was that the case? Had he milked Stag for all he could, used him
till the bank book bulged, and then on the first discordant note split
for the hills? Was he still the phony hipster with ideas of fame and
fortune predicated on the cut of a suit, the turn of an ankle, the size
of a tailfin, or the push of an engine? Was he still the animal? Was it
only a momentary relapse that had convinced him this life was a
pit? How much *was* he fooling himself? And if he *was* pulling a fast
one on himself, how empty a gesture would it be, to drop Stag's
contract? Would it be the smart thing to tag along further, pull as
much loot as he could out of the scene, then sell short like Freeport?
Who, after all, was looking out for Number One?

And the reassuring strain in his conscience answered, *You aren't
the same man you were when you found him four years ago. You've*

changed. Your values aren't the same. Don't be a greedy fool. He used you as much as you used him . . . now get out from under. You've done all you can. He's out of your area of responsibility. The money changed you, but for the better . . . for Stag it was only a spur to his rottenness; it corrupted him all the more. How guilty can you feel?

How much longer can you punish yourself, eating your heart out at every stinking stunt the kid pulls off? You're not alleviating the evil, you're only corrupting yourself again. A man exposed to Plague doesn't allow himself to be contaminated again, once he's been healed, unless he's a fool. Are you a fool, Shelly?

Don't believe it. You're a decent guy; get out of this and go cover your scars with some honest muscle. You're a good publicity man . . . You can make a living anywhere. Get out now. It's got to get worse, and no indication that it will get better.

You don't owe it to anyone back there. They're animals, Shelly. They know no allegiances. They'll eat you alive. The money isn't a factor in any way. You'd have to cut even if you were penny-poor. But do it now.

And from that teeth-grating inner conversation came a philosophy. A very simple one, yet one that brought with it a sense of reality; a rationale for existence.

Money is freedom.

If you have money you don't need to sell yourself. You can sell your services, but only to whom you want, for those ends you feel worthy. It is possible to bring from the dry-rot of a hipster existence a flowering decency by which a man can be his own man and live. The money had been made: don't think about it. It was a tool. A tool can be neither good nor evil. It is only to be used.

Money is freedom.

Shelly realized he might limp for a while, for after all, he had been lame a long while. But living in a leper colony was possible only for another leper. He was out of the scene now. For good.

One stray tie bound him, however faintly.

Jean Friedel. When he had decided there were no debts owing to the animals of Jungle York, did that also mean Jeanie? There had been nights when they had talked . . . the time after Ruth Kemp had been turned away . . . the evening Stag had tried to rape her . . . other times since then. She had been a useful companion in running Stag Preston, Incorporated. Was there a debt still owed?

He didn't know. He decided he'd have to find out.

She was on her knees before a filing cabinet, shuffling stacks of papers and file folders, hanging them into the sliding racks more in gobs than in particular. Her skirt was very tight across her rump, and once again he marveled at the mechanisms of modern women's undergarments that had introduced the unbroken, one-cheek backside. He wasn't certain he altogether approved of the innovation, though there were times—and now was one of them—that the sight was distinctly appealing.

He ran through his memorized list of clever mental openings, for one he had never used on Jean Friedel, and came up with, "You look like a girl who'd like an intensive six-week course in karate."

She turned her head and smiled, still cramming great sheaves of documents into the file drawer. "Hi."

"Hi, yourself," he replied, perching on an edge of the desk. It was a new desk; an inexpensive modular unit that poorly copied a Knoll design. It was typical of the furniture in this new office: an office whose bills were paid by the syndicate of small-time operators. It was flashy on the surface, but underneath merely borax. Freeport was oak and gold; the little men were borax and gilt.

"Oooo," she exhaled heavily, rising. "What a job! Transferring records from the Colonel's office to this joint has been almost more than I could take." She kicked the bottom file drawer closed with the tip of her Capezio.

"Didn't they have a records transporting concern do it?" he asked.

She gave him a lopsided, rueful grin and said, "Oh sure. Lotsa luck.

"I did it all by my lonesome. I've been up and down Fifth Avenue maybe ninety-two times in the past week." She held up a grimy pair of hands. "How would you like to take The Soot Queen out to lunch?"

He grinned despite the tenseness in his stomach. "Mah pleasuh, Ma'am," he imitated Stag's phony Kentucky drawl. While she washed her hands and put on fresh makeup he lit a cigarette and walked around the office.

It was going to be difficult. Was there anything between them? She had once told him she wanted everything there was to want, and if she didn't want it, it wasn't worth having. That might still be true. There had been moments when they had communicated, when they had shared something, however small. But whatever it was, did it really have any meaning to her? Shelly had run with the pack in Jungle York long enough to know their hungers were monstrous, and small pleasures were exchanged, shared, accepted only when they did not interfere with the running, or the eating. It was going to be difficult.

He took her for schnitzel and dark beer at the Steuben Tavern on West 47th, and in a back booth, surrounded by the deep reassurance of dark woods and good smells, he lit cigarettes for both of them and settled back, waiting for openers.

"How's the rogue of the rock'n'roll set doing today?" She smiled at him. When she smiled, small creases appeared at the corners of her eyes. Shelly thought he liked that very much. It wouldn't be difficult looking at this girl first thing every morning for the next fifty years . . .

"Oh, hey!" She cut him off before he could speak. "We got the transcript of the coroner's inquest this morning. Did you have to give anybody anything for that testimony? Stag looked solid gold when it was over."

Shelly did not feel it was necessary to tell her the syndicate of small-time operators had made their deals. Stag had indeed looked like solid gold. The verdict had been accidental death. Even Marlene's parents from Secaucus were convinced, and when Stag had gone to them at the inquest, put his arms around the dead girl's mother, and wept unashamedly, it had won the day. Suspicions had disappeared like morning mist.

Stag had even given the dead girl's parents a handsome check to cover the funeral arrangements. The heaviness of the check would have provided for the burial of a maharajah.

"To me, that girl was *more* important than the King of England," Stag had said, wiping his cheeks of tears. "I sung before some of the biggest people in the world, but that little girl was the best of them all." It had gone over very well.

Shelly had considered offering the script to *Theatre Arts Magazine* for an unabridged publication.

Shelly dragged his thoughts back to the girl across the booth. The inquest was over, Stag had been exonerated. Now Shelly had to make his decision to check out, stay, or take her with him in either case. He avoided answering the question about bribing the witnesses at the inquest. "Listen," he said, "I've got some things I've got to say and I'm embarrassed."

She looked at him archly. "You're kidding."

"Now c'mon," he said sophomorically, blushing, "it's hard enough being serious for a change, and twice as hard when you sit there putting me on. I'm about to unbare the tortured inner surface of my soul, so pay attention—"

"*Jeezus!*" She shook her head.

"Look, Jeanie . . . " Shelly leaned toward her. He wanted to take her hand, but they were both holding cigarettes and the awkwardness of shifting hands and smokes would have destroyed what he was trying to build. "The kid is on his way out. I know for sure, and so do you if you've been taking as good care of the office as I think. But it's there. I heard from Universal that they're going to drop his option . . . "

"Whaat?"

He nodded. "That's right. The morals clause. They've got him, if they want him. And they may just decide to dump. This thing with the chick who took the brodie is just too hot to shut up. We may have kept it out of the papers, but his fans are leaking it. That bunch in Secaucus—we've tried to hush them, but no good—they've even mimeographed some innocuous gossip sheets and they're mailing them to every Stag Preston Fan Club in the country."

"Anything libelous?" she asked, more concerned than he thought she would be.

He shook his head, pursing his lips contemplatively around the cigarette. "They must have had a lawyer dream it up for them. Safe as a Copa girl having her period. But it's doing the job; that, and word of mouth. It's circulating, Jeanie. The word is out, and even Am-Par is getting edgy. I tried to get through to Sid, but he's been 'conferencing' like mad.

"I'm getting out, Jean. All this I've said about the wind rising has nothing to do with why I'm checking out. It was only offered as reasons for your leaving Stag, too."

"Why *are* you checking out?"

He snubbed the cigarette and blew out the final blast of smoke. "Because I'm having trouble with my dry cleaners."

She looked at him questioningly.

"They can't get the stink out of my clothes," he explained.

She bit her lower lip as she nodded understanding. In silence. In deep. She was thinking.

"And you want me to come with you." She stated it more than asked it. He nodded. "And do what?"

"And get married, maybe, we'd see."

"And live in Bucks County or in Riverdale out in the Bronx, in a big rich house, and raise kids between us?"

"There's worse." He was defensive now; her tone . . .

She shook her head with stately deliberation. "Uh-uh, sweetie. You're a wonderful guy, and you've somehow found the secret of it all, but it won't play."

"Why not? Anything as simple as—you don't love me?"

She looked pained at that. Her jaw muscles clumped for a moment, then relaxed, and the cosmopolitan veneer slid sickly back across her eyes. "That too, Shelly. You're fun to ball once in a while, and you're nice to talk to, but I *don't* love you. And even if I did, it would *still* be a no."

"Why, for God's sake? Do you *like* this life?"

Her smile was patronizing. He finally understood. "Now you understand. Yes, Shelly, I *do* like it. I love it. This is my way. Everybody's entitled to go to hell in his or her own way, and this just happens to be mine. We aren't alike anymore, Shelly, you and I. We've changed in the past weeks, but you more than me. I've seen it happening. You can't con or swing with the Lindy hang-ups any more. They hurt you . . . here . . . " She tapped his chest.

Then the food came, and they ate without talking.

When it was gone, the *schnitzel à la holstein* and the applesauce, and the *strudel*, and the coffee, again they lit their cigarettes and shared smoke, perhaps the last thing they *could* share.

"I don't know what I'll do with my share of the contract," Shelly said.

"Well, sell it, of course," she advised him. "What else?"

He toyed with a fork. "I don't know," he said softly.

"Shelly . . . "

He looked up. Hoping.

"N-nothing." She shook her head, as if to clear it.

He exhaled deeply, as though washing his hands of the entire matter and expelling the last air drawn while it was under consideration. "Do me a favor, will you, Princess?"

She smiled softly, sweetly, affirmatively.

"Call a meeting of the stockholders for tomorrow night, will you? Eight o'clock at their usual stand." He folded the linen napkin from his lap, very neatly, and laid it on the table. He started to rise.

"Do me a favor, Shelly . . . no, *two* favors." She waited.

He nodded acquiescence.

"The first is please always remember what I told you that night I called you, and you came over to help me with Stag. Some of us can't help ourselves, Shelly. You don't curse a steam whistle when it blows; that's what it's built to do . . . "

"And the second favor," he said cutting in sharply.

"Let me come to the meeting."

Shelly had finally made up his mind. Or rather, it had been made up for him, by his conscience, by his philosophy, and by Jean Friedel, who had denied whatever they had shared, and who had decided to remain on the deck of the sinking ship.

Sinking. *While Shelly was escaping?*

At the meeting, when Shelly announced he was getting out, the eyes of the members of the syndicate of small-time operators gleamed ferociously. One man's bald head began to sweat. It shined like oil, slick and moist in the overhead lights. Another thirty percent open to them . . . up for grabs.

Teeth began to gnash, sharpening, silently.

They began dry-washing their hands almost in unison; it resembled some wild Rockette routine, employing old, anxious, greedy, senile men.

Old they were. And anxious. Greedy, as well. But hardly senile. Teeth flashed, hands dipped toward eyes, shading them so emotions could not shine out.

The sweet odor of the animals about to feast filled the room, filled Shelly's nostrils, spurred the old men on.

Stag leaped up and slammed his hand on the table. "I wanta talk to you, Shelly. I wanta say something to you." He waited for Shelly to give some indication, then strode around the table into the other office. He pulled the door tight behind him and turned on Sheldon Morgenstern.

There was open fear in the boy's eyes.

"Shelly, they gonna cancel me at The Palace. You heard!"

Shelly nodded. He'd heard.

"I need you, boy. I need you bad. You been with me from the first and if you take off and leave me I'm gonna be out in the open for them lousy kike bastards in the other room there." He noticed Shelly stiffen, but had no idea why.

"Sorry, Stag. I have to go away."

Stag Preston's face became a grimace. "You can't! You can't just jerk out and leave me sittin', man! I need your help. You been mak-in' a pile . . . look, I'll give you a couple of my shares of the contract . . . that way you'll have a bigger bite than any one of them."

Shelly actually felt sorry for the boy. It was down to the wire now. He could feel it in the air. Everyone was running away from him and he knew he was slipping. Now even his monumental self-assurance, the driving hunger that had made him as big as he was, could not help.

Stag abruptly altered his expressions and his nostrils flared as he threatened Shelly, "Look, you sonofabitch, I'm tellin' you this: you leave me and I'll have you blackballed in every city in this country. You'll have to go to Russia to get a job, you smart-aleck sonofabitch, you hear me?"

Shelly shook his head sadly.

"What you gonna do with all that contract, you bastard? What you gonna do with that thirty percent . . . give it to those slobs out there to use against me? That what you're gonna do? Sell it to them?"

He stood with fists clenched at his sides, panting, the blood drained out of his hollow-cheeked face, his eyes black and intense, glowing, glaring.

Shelly spoke very softly. "No, Stag, I'm going to put it where it belongs, give it back to the one who deserves it most." He reached into his jacket pocket for the contract.

"That crummy Ruth Kemp, thass who! That's who you gonna give it to . . . that mewlin' sonofabitch woman come around here suckin' and cryin' till we don't know what all . . . ".

Shelly cut him off as he handed the contract shares across to the boy. "Here, Stag, you take them. It's a gift. A little piece of your soul back again. I held it too long."

Then he turned for the door, and said very quietly, without capitals, "excuse me now, i have to go take a bath."

TWENTY

Shelly was undecided about the scene. He was not surprised when he read the item in *Variety* a week later that said:

> *Personal management of Stag Preston has been undertaken by Miss Jean Friedel, recently of Colonel Jack Freeport's staff. Miss Friedel announced the shift in positions at a press conference called to refute a rumor that ABC-Paramount Records had severed its contractual obligations with the young twenty-two-year-old rock'n'roll star whose meteoric rise to fame was . . .*

He was not surprised at all. Jean had told him she was one of the animals. She was still prowling, and though the cat and the canary can smile at one another occasionally, coexistence is no existence at all. She had broken the last tie to the hipster life for him.

He had to get out of New York, that much he knew. For a while he considered going back to Freeport, but that would have been another dead end; or rather, a cloverleaf running up and over and back down onto the same road he had traveled with Stag Preston.

It had been four years, and more. He was thirty-eight years old. No longer a hotshot, hardrock flak-man who could sell sandboxes to Arabs. He was a tired guy of thirty-eight with a lot of good years ahead if he could find the way.

So Shelly went looking for jobs. With money in the bank, he went looking for jobs. Good jobs. Honest jobs. He rejected a nightclub account, because it catered to too many people he knew. He accepted personal management of a quartet of commercial folk singers, recently graduated from Yale, because they still smelled clean, and it was possible he could do something for them before they got too cocky and too slippery and he would be forced to move on.

But he kept track of Stag and Jean.

In the trades, by word of mouth, through friends at the clubs where Stag was now playing, and at the small label for which Stag was now recording. It had been phenomenal; within a year after Shelly had left, Stag could not be booked into any of the big money venues. Vegas was stillborn for him. Forget television. Atlantic City: no-price. Hate California, for him it's cold and it's damp, that's why Staggy is a tramp! He was losing a mint; and none of it belonged to him. The syndicate of small-time operators was hardly as lenient as Freeport had been, but they had been conned into accepting much of Stag's wastrel manner as "front."

Then a further blow was struck in the face of Stag's waning popularity. A print of the movie he had made that night for Porter Hackett got loose. No one was able to pin the blame, and really, no one tried too hard. They were having a bit too much fun showing the flick at parties. It was copied and recopied, and though none of the big exposé rags picked it up (for some strange reason; possibly because Stag was on the way out in any case, and there was bigger game afoot), it became a Hollywood joke. A running gag that had nasty undertones. The sentiment toward Stag took a sharp downward dip after that. Even sharper than before, if that was possible.

One weekend when Shelly was in the city, he lunched with Jean, and noted that she was weary, very weary. "I'll be pulling out soon," she said. "I've made my contacts, and I'm on my way." Shelly had thought, *Yeah, on your way, honey.*

Going my way?

No, the other way. Straight down.

"How's the kid?" Shelly had asked.

"He's been getting into hock more and more with the little men. They keep biting into his thirty-seven percent. I don't think they'll put up with these losses much longer. They've got a peculiar trapped look about them, Shelly."

He had known what she meant. They were losing money, and that was losing life to the syndicate of small-time operators.

And still Stag lived high. Clinging to all he had left—his delusions of grandeur—he lived high, and the little men spent.

Then one night, in Kansas City, Shelly picked up a newspaper and it was on the front page. It was laid out there like an epitaph, only it wasn't as clean and neat and final as an epitaph. It had a stink to it; it smelled of the four years Shelly had spent selling his soul under the delusion he was "making it." It smelled of the year he had been away from Stag . . . a year so short it had seemed like only the turning of a page, but some years are like that . . . free and open and clear and perhaps even clean. But the story on the front page of the *Kansas City Star* wasn't clean and open. It was murky and the photos accompanying were all full of darks that might have been blood.

The article told how Stag Preston had been found face down on a lonely Connecticut road, his throat and face slashed—apparently by determined amateurs—and his career just as effectively slashed. The *Star* compared it with the gangland knifing of Joe E. Lewis, many years before, but said this was no such shady operation. It said Stag Preston, the singing idol (who in the past year had withdrawn more and more from public life), had been robbed and mugged. It was shameful. It was terrible. But nobody cried. It also said he had been taken to SuchandSuch Memorial Hospital.

It was all there, all they had to do was read it. Why had Stag been taken to a public hospital, rather than to a private admittance? Because he no longer had backers to foot his bills, and in fact, if you read it right, his backers were the ones who had put him there.

The article concluded with the information that the singer was fighting a life and death battle in the emergency rooms of the hospital.

Shelly faked an excuse to his folk singers, bracketed them with instructions about finishing out the gig in K.C., and hopped a plane to New York after a telegram to Jean Friedel.

She met him at Idlewild and they Hertz'd it out to Connecticut.

The expiation of guilt is a sometime thing, and a spotty process at best, taking longer than a year.

He sat in the waiting room of the hospital for three hours before they would allow him to go in. He sat for three hours, the entire time spent trying to understand just why he was here. It wasn't enough, apparently, to say, *I'm finished, goodbye, and end.* It wasn't enough when the human being lying in there was a part of your creation, part of yourself. Stag Preston lay stretched out between sheets and inside bandages, but it was also Shelly Morgenstern. Left outside, but cut up just as badly, bleeding just as profusely, suffering even more, for he was denied the peace of coma.

Three hours and three hundred thousand thoughts; faces from memory gliding past like blind crayfish in a subterranean cavern, unseeing but living their brief lives behind his eyes. Faces of Carlene, of Trudy Quillan and Golightly, of Asa Kemp and Ruth, of the Colonel, Joe Costanza, Jeanie, and last of all, falling away, diminishing, growing smaller smaller smaller as it faded past and was gone, the girl Marlene.

So many faces. All touched with a stain of rot, and all from the touch of the boy who lay inside, gasping deeply, trying to breathe air, not blood, a tube down his throat, the strained stitching along the throat, across the cheeks, down over the larynx. That boy in there. How much of his touch had left the brown rot? How much of it was him and how much was Sheldon Morgenstern, who bore his guilt heavily, painfully?

Three hours wandering in a wasteland of question marks shaped like crosses, of dark images that pointed accusing fingers, of helplessness and turmoil. It was very bad; and even when the doctors came out and told him he might look in for a few moments, that the boy would live—but never sing again—it wasn't finished. He did not walk into the room alone. Insubstantial shapes, ghosts with grins drawn up like the death rictus called *sardonicus* of lockjaw, heavy bodies that pressed at him—these followed, silently, watching.

He looked down at Stag Preston. The boy was covered to the chin with the white sheet, almost unruffled by crease or wrinkle, solemn in silence. His head was completely swathed in linen, a male nun in a Bedouin's headwrap, bound tightly closed, sealed in, a cocoon, deepest quiet, the breathing out of a painfully white face as regular as soft breaths lightly drawn could be.

And the eyes were open.

Those dark, piercing eyes that said, *I am me; I am always me; if I close my eyes, me ceases for a moment, so I keep them open; I am watching you.*

The sight of the dark eyes staring up shocked the older man. For a moment he thought Stag Preston might have died, the eyes reflexing open, remaining that way, studying for an eternity the cracks in the ceiling. But then the eyes blinked moistly.

Shelly moved closer, made a pistol with thumb and forefinger, and fired it in salutation. Stag moved his head imperceptibly in recognition.

Then he spoke.

If the croak of a frog can be called speech, then he spoke. If the moan of a strangling baby can be called speech, then he spoke. If a crippled and struggling thing on its back, trying to turn over, can be called speech, then by all means Stag Preston spoke.

He rasped. He ratcheted. He croaked. And he spoke:

"I want to tell you," he said. It took him the better part of a minute to utter those five words; they were almost totally incomprehensible, and Shelly understood him instantly. It was painful to watch the boy. He had to talk; whatever else happened in this room, this night, right now he had to tell someone he trusted, had always trusted, as much as he could trust anyone. But the sound was a bubbling, broken-gear thing.

Shelly kneeled beside the bed and listened. It took Stag Preston nearly fifteen minutes to say it:

"They owned me, all of me. I had to borrow real heavy from them. I—I had to keep up a front, couldn't go back to that friggin' poor. *Had* to, don'tcha know? Then when they—"

He rattled it out like lengths of chain.

He had borrowed till he was into the syndicate of small-time operators up to his eyebrows. Then when his records were gathering dust in the distributor's bins, when Am-Par and Universal and The Palace and all the big clubs refused to book him, when his drawing power was so low they couldn't sell him even as a minor act on a twenty-bill tour, they knew they had to sell short, had to get out, but not till they'd collected their money. They demanded it. They demanded it from a person incapable of being ordered about, a human being who had twisted himself so much in five years that he could no more be demanded at than he could hold his breath till expiration. Stag—arrogantly clinging to the emotional vestiges of his popularity in a world that suddenly wanted no part of him— refused to pay. He had called them the names they called themselves, *among* themselves; names they could use to one another but names no one else could use with impunity. He had called them *schmucks*, he had called them *kikes*, he had called them *sheenies* and *mockies* and *wops* and *dagos* and *spaghetti-headers*; he had called them *finks* and *crooks* and *bastards*. And *motherfuckers*. Oh, yes, that too. They were not gangsters, these little men with small goals and tiny ambitions. They were not "The Combine" and they were not "The Mafia" and they were not "The Syndicate" as the tabloids think of The Syndicate. They were only what they had always been, a consortium of small-time operators (in lower case) and they were not familiar with beatings and killings and vengeance; but this money-losing property with his vile language, his snotty manner, his big mouth, had called them the names they could not be called openly (not to mention motherfucker); and had taken their money— *their money! their blood!*—and had refused to pay them back. Unacceptable behavior, the little *putz*!

So they did something they had never done before. They hired two men, for a price, and those two men took revenge for no financial expedient, but only by transmitting to knife, boot, and cleaving fist the fury and helpless revenge of small men with small desires . . . and large insecurities.

They had left Stag Preston bleeding and unconscious on a lon-ely Connecticut road, with the debt still unpaid, but satisfaction extracted. Pound of flesh, an incision for every smart-aleck word he had called them.

They had managed to save Stag Preston's life, but he would never sing again.

"I can barely . . . barely talk . . . Shelly . . . " The boy ended his relating of the facts. "Get them for me, Shelly. Tell the p-police, huh?"

Shelly stood up, then, and looked, as deeply as he could force himself to look, into the face of Stag Preston. Time rolled back, thoughts rolled back, the light and the sense and the immediacy of it rolled back. He was standing on a deep, empty plain, charcoal-gray and only a lance in his hands, with all the windmills gone. He was there by himself, and as the wind came up, swirling the sand and the bits of rotting leaves too tired to make fertilizer, he heard the voices of emptiness. Voices reciting the *kaddish* in Hebrew the way only his father could speak Hebrew, with the S's sibilant and tiny bits of spittle flying; the goodbye that was mouselike and passing away as the bus left home going out to the big city; he heard the first voice of the first hipster he had ever known with the "Hey, now! Like I cert'ny don't wanna put you on, fella, but if you wanna make it in this city you got to put somethin' down . . . you got to *say* somethin', man. That way everyone knows you are with it and on the scene. Do I make myself clear, I mean, do you understand?" and his own voices so many voices answering fading into one another, "Yeah, uh, yessir, uh, yeah, I under—I understand I *dig*, right? I *dig*!" And his voice changing, changing so subtly, he could never tell just when the change had come, except perhaps it was the first day he said a word he had previously only read on the walls of toilets, and said it without being self-conscious. That word with the first letter an F, the one he had always shied from, he now said without feeling chilly inside about it. Was that the moment?

Whenever it had been, now he said the word again, softly under his breath, hungry to know, just that one word that began with an F, and he felt chilly again . . . and he knew he was free.

It can happen that simply.

It can happen, just with a word that begins with an F and nothing more profound. It only takes something small.

"Goodbye, Stag," he said. He smiled, a very thin smile, the grin of the razor; and then so resigned, half-sorry, because he could not help it; a smile that was just a pressing together of the lips. He did that, saying, "And goodbye, say goodbye to Luther for me. I heard him sing once, a long time ago in a hotel in Louisville, and I liked it very much. Goodbye."

He left the hospital room, and found the doctor in charge of Stag's case and asked him how much the bill would be. The doctor did not know, and tried to refer Shelly to the cashier's office, but Shelly asked the doctor to estimate, so he did, and Shelly wrote a check for one hundred dollars over that amount and gave it to the doctor to pay the bill.

Not because it was Stag Preston in there.

Not because he had known his ordeal by fire with Stag in there.

Not because he had come out of this terrible thing a person whose life was worth living.

For none of those reasons, but simply because in there was someone he had once known, and a right guy doesn't turn down a buddy when he's in need.

Then he went out into the night, and went looking for his muscles. He had found his soul, now all he needed was to burn off the fat of guilt, and get some muscles.

TWENTY AND ONE

Life is not art. In art, they go into the sunset arm in arm and live happily ever after. Fade to black, and credits. In life they go into the sunset, argue about whether the furniture will be Swedish Modern or French Provincial, whether the baby's name will be Frederick Alan after *her* father or Timothy Tyler after *his* father, and inside two years begin the path to Reno. In art it is all clean, neat, final, tied up in a socko exit line and a clear moral point. In life it is messy; the ex-lovers see each other a few more times, drag it out, do it sloppy. The guy who rebelled slips back and takes a few more jabs to his ethics, his manhood, and his pride. The nice black-and-white punch lines get muddy and gray and insubstantial. The Fastest Gun in the West grows old and wets his bed. The Wicked Witch of the East gets psychoanalyzed and turns out to be a latent dyke. The beautiful princess gets a little too heavy and the prince cheats on her with a scullery maid. It happens. That's life.

And because it's life, can't be anything *but* simple true life, it had been no more than life for Shelly Morgenstern. It might have been nice had the time in the hospital room been the last time he saw Stag Preston. But it wasn't. Stag's rise had been fast, his descent even faster, but the ends were not cut off that neatly. There was one more time, two and a half years later.

Stag had disappeared upon release from the hospital. For his own good, and to dodge the hundreds of thousands of dollars in debts he had accrued. Shelly had at first tried to get a line on him, follow him by a close reading of the trades, but it was as though the boy had unzipped the Earth, popped in, and zipped it back over his head.

The moral responsibility Shelly had felt drained almost completely. Time heals. Etc.

Then, two and a half years later, on a publicity junket in New Orleans, Sheldon Morgenstern encountered one of the loose ends of his life. On Bourbon Street with a group of press agents, merely walking, going for a pot of jambalaya, a nice crawfish etouffée stew, a big bowl of andouille gumbo, Shelly passed a strip joint. Kandee Barr was peeling in the joint. The name aroused Shelly, for in half a dozen other buff shows down the strip he had seen billboards boasting Candy Barr, Candi Bahr, Kandy Bar, and Candy C. Barr. In smiling at this particular Miss Barr's photo, life-size and voluptuous, his eyes met someone else's. A dark, intense, lingering look, even in the photo, that held his glance.

It was Stag Preston.

He was singing in the strip joint. He was alive, and working, and *singing* in this strip joint. Shelly excused himself, suggested the fellows go on up to the restaurant, not waste those reservations, have their gumbo, and he'd meet them back at the hotel.

Then he entered the club.

It had no name.

He didn't want to know the name.

What sights beyond vision in such places; the trysting places of meaning, where men test their souls, and the vista must be conversant, sympathetic with the mood. What places are these, where great tries are tried, great ties are tied, and great treaties formed. What importance they have, and how seldom they fit. Seldom.

It was dingy, soggy, frayed, splayed, smoky, smoked-out, just damned weary in the nameless strip joint. Artificial as a plastic leg. The walls were of an unidentifiable wood, paneled as though to signify something—perhaps at one time intimacy or relaxation—but saying nothing. The smoke eddied and misted and drifted, a heavy low-hanging cumulus that made Shelly's eyes water. He had been a smoker all his life, and for the first time of which he was aware, cigarette smoke was making him uncomfortable. The veil was partially drawn, and he wanted to see, to *see*! All of it.

Just beyond the bare semicircle in which he stood, separated by a worn velvet rope and two tarnished brass posts supporting its flaccid droop, the tables began. Four chairs to a table, all filled with dark shapes hunched in toward the center, or sprawled away from the nucleus, touching female thighs and knees and arms. The men were mostly alone, but some had been hooked, some had been pinged by the unerring sonar of a B-girl slathered with pancake makeup into the hairline. Some of these men had been picked-up, some had been lucked-out, some had been cleaned-out . . . and some had even brought the wife to this naughty place. But mostly the men were alone. They would, probably, *always* be alone. Lost in the cumulus.

Just beyond the tables was the raised stage, and on the stage a girl of—why bother to mention them—attributes was peeling. Her flesh was yellow, very yellow, blue, very blue, then red, very very red and back to yellow as the gels spread their diseased light across her empty face, her swollen thighs, her meaningless breasts. She was doing things. They had no interest for Shelly.

"Table, Mister?" The maitre d' was pear-shaped, out of a comic strip dealing with pugs and hipsters and fat little men in checked suits who spoke from the recesses of their noses. Shelly reached into his side pocket, brought out a bill, and waved it through the maitre d's immediate venue.

"This, when you tell Stag Preston that Shelly Morgenstern is out here and wants to see him." The pear-shaped man nodded at the bill, puffed a cheek in empty meditation, and turned away. He threaded his way among the tables, into a curtained archway, and out of sight. Shelly lit up and waited, seeing the girl because there was nothing else to see. She had split nipples and stretch marks on her belly from a tough pregnancy.

A little bit of time passed and the pear-shaped man returned, hand first. Shelly gave him the bill and the maitre d' unhooked the velvet cord. He fastened it behind Shelly and led him to a table off to one side, with only two chairs, neither occupied.

Shelly sat and the pear-shaped man inquired about a drink. Shelly shook his head, turning the scene off as easily as a shower.

He waited, and continued waiting until he felt the hand on his shoulder. "Hi, kid," he said, staring straight ahead.

The body moved around him, a hand reached into his line of vision, pulling out the chair, and then the body in its tuxedo lowered into his sight, first the waist, then the stomach, then the chest, the shoulders, the neck, the chin, the scars, the face, the eyes, and he was there, once more, completely in Shelly Morgenstern's life.

He was no longer the golden boy of the rock'n'roll world. He was no longer even a boy. If he was a man, he was some kind of man that did not exist in the world of reality, of sight and sound and emotion. He was something else completely. The ravages of his own sins and sour living had caught up with him, beat the hell out of him, and left him for gone, but he had fooled them. He had saved the hulk, pieced it together with Scotch Tape and gin and grapnels thrown into the cliff because it was a long drop.

He was on the verge of alcoholism. The abyss lay in his eyes.

The end result of what he was now, living in the Bowery, on the Embarcadero, on every Skid Row from Bangor to Bangkok, was called a "wetbrain." He wasn't that yet, and he probably never would be, because the scream was still there, like the abyss, in the eyes, in the cruel mouth . . . but it was bad, very nasty, very bad indeed.

There was even the faint stink of the junkie about him. There? Yes, there, that faint odor, is that it? High-tech crematoria, autopsy rooms, dumpsters outside slaughterhouses.

It was obvious Stag Preston had gone in search of artificial stimuli to bring back tumescence to the limp dick of his dead dreams. In the high flights of liquor and junk he was still Stag Preston. On Top. Up There. *Pow!*

The scars were covered with a heavy layer of No. 2 theatrical makeup, and the hair worn longer over the ears to cover one free-sliding furrow that rode onto the cheek. But the mass of them just under the right ear, covering the underside of the chin, the back of the neck where hair would not grow, these stood out in bold, pink rat-tail relief. Good enough for men with limited budgets. His hair was thinner now, combed over a little, for camouflage.

Stag Preston had healed badly on the surface; how had he done inside?

"What's shaking, kid?"

The boy was looking at him intently, almost ferociously, with open hunger. "Shelly Morgenstern." It was a prayer. "Jeezus, it's you. I thought for, for a minute it was maybe a gag, a thing, y'know, but Jeezus, it's, it's you."

"Yeah." Shelly laughed nervously. "So how goes it?"

Stag spread his hands like the wings of a small bird. "Not to complain."

Shelly nodded and waved broadly at the joint around them. "This isn't much."

"Not much," Stag agreed. Then added, "Jeezus, it's *really* you."

It was getting awkward. Shelly had wanted something . . . he wasn't quite sure what . . . a feeling of import? A feeling of some change, something happening that would form a great epiphany to his world-view: see the boy, get a bit more of "the message," the way it really was. But nothing was happening. Stag was sitting there with a peculiar, almost worshipful look on his face, and it was starting to smell embarrassing. It was like a reunion with an old buddy whose interests are now totally divorced from yours, and the empathy is gone. It was absurd. But he was trapped, hooked, there.

"Well, listen," Shelly said, half-rising, "I've got some people down on a promotion, I've got to get back to them, so you take it —"

"Hey, now, wait a bit, hey wait."

Stag was suddenly galvanized, intent on holding this together till it was done; but not yet, wait a bit, come on; just a few more minutes till I get up the nerve. "Listen, I, uh, I want you to hear something. I been training myself, and uh, hey I know—" He rose, looked around, spied the pear-shaped man, and yelled over the brassing, booming music of the trio backing the stripper, "—Hey! Mario! Hey, Mario baby, c'mere."

He sat down, smiling to reassure, a surprise just ahead of us if you'll sit a minute, huh, just hold on. The pear-shaped maitre d' put down an empty glass on a passing busboy's tray and maneuvered to their table and waited for Stag's word. It was obvious he wanted to serve the singer, didn't feel put upon.

"Uh, hey, Mario, what's good . . . give uh, give him the Tornado Special, huh. You like that, you think, Shelly?" He looked appealingly at the publicity man.

Shelly did not want a drink, especially not one of the cloying Southern bourbon drinks with too much mint, too much spice, too much greenery; not even in a hurricane lamp mega-glass with umbrellas. But he nodded a yes.

Mario scuttled off like ambulatory pastry from a cartoon, and Stag grinned with familiarity at Shelly. The alumni in the fraternity house. Unsure, trying to relate, trying to capture a piece of someone else's past.

"Listen, Shelly, I want to tell you something, y'know."

He was leaning across the table.

The French cuffs peeping from his sleeves were moist with humid sweat-stain, sootiness, frayed. The links cheap.

Shelly nodded imperceptibly. "What?" he asked.

"Y'know, I'm not finished, Shelly. I mean it. I mean, really. You know when they cut me up they thought I was done, they thought that. But they didn't know, Shelly. They didn't *know* I could come back.

"I can sing, Shelly! I can sing.

"I'm better than ever. You know? I mean, like I sing different, because they cut my cords pretty bad, but I worked out, I sang, and I learned to do it all over again. I lived all over for a long time, and I got myself back in shape. I can sing, Shelly, all I need is one damned break, just one little push, one little thing, you know, and I can make it bigger than before."

What was there to say? What do you tell a blind man? That he can see? Do you tell a leper his toes can be stitched on again, just give me a real big Singer Double-Bobbin? Shelly only nodded and smiled patronizingly, mouthing words like, "Gee, that's swell, Stag. I'm really happy for you."

The boy's expression changed with the instant mercurial instability of the true, practicing paranoid. "So you think I'm bullshittin' you, huh? You think I'm conning you, trying to make a touch. Well, listen, Big Man, I want you to just stay there. You just *sit* there. I want you to hear me . . . just *sit* . . . now *damn it, sit* there, and I'm gonna let you hear if I'm boning you."

He got up and moved quickly through the tables to the curtained archway, disappeared into it, and Shelly rose to leave fast, and Shelly sat back down heavily, and Shelly waited, because Shelly had to wait, because he *had* to wait—

Mario brought the drink. He pushed it away, ground out a cigarette butt in the already reeking, filled ashtray; and he lit another, and he waited.

The broad finished suffering.

The lights dimmed and a hollow P.A. voice announced:

"The Rampart Club Is Proud To Introduce That Star Of Stage, Screen, Television And Records, The King Of The Rock'n'Roll Beat, The One, The Only, Special Attraction To The Rampart Club, The One And Only . . . Stag Preston!"

The spotty applause was suffocated by the imperious comping of the trio, then the spot went on, and it was five and a half years before, the stage of The Palace, in New York, and there he was again.

It was terrifying.

It was the same recurring nightmare.

Stag Preston, with guitar and with face and with the same stance, except now it was more matured, more deliberate. And he began singing.

He had regained his bravado. It was all there, again. The song was something low, something vaguely dirty, with heart and movement, though. Something he was doing specially for Shelly that said, I was at the bottom, and I made the top, and then found out the bottom had been the middle, because then I really hit bottom, and this is what it looks like, from the floor, from the underside. I've seen it all, I've even eaten the corrupt flesh of it; cupped here in my hands, want a look? Just a peek? All right, here, look!

It was all that, and a great deal more.

It was the voice of Stag Preston, grown larger.

Deeper.

More meaningful, because now it was more than the trickery of someone who has eidetic feelings, who emulates others' suffering or triumph or courage or cowardice, others' *true* emotions. It was something he had been and suffered through, and come out better for having learned.

If anything, Stag Preston was more commanding when he sang.

He can still do it, he can still charm them, Shelly thought, with a flash of sudden fear.

All he needs is a break, one little shove, that's what he said. Now as a professional talent scout, as a man who knows what will play, can he?

When he was seven years old and his tonsils had been removed, Shelly had been under ether on the operating table and had heard someone say his name, "Shelly," and in his unconsciousness it had seemed to be reverberating down and down and down a long hall, a corridor, endlessly. It was that way now, as the answer came back to him, up and up that long corridor, lost till now, lost since he was seven, the word of unassailable truth.

And the word was yes. Yes yes yes yes yes . . .

Over and over again, beginning, in fact, to reverberate within his mind, the answer was unarguably Yes, Stag Preston can do it again. All he needs is that one-handed push.

He is something larger than life when he sings.

Even standing in front of a brain-dead, rowdy, inattentive, hung-over derelict crowd in a shitty strip joint, in front of the roughest audience imaginable—make-out artists, hookers, tourists, winos, psychos, perverts, Shriners, screamers, loud old ladies, deadbeats without honor and drenched in boredom and cynicism—a Roman Coliseum crowd that wanted bare tits, bear-baiting, and disembowelments—he had a potent holding power with his voice. How he had done it, slashed that way, Shelly could not imagine. But he had done it. He had trained himself to sing around the broken areas. He commanded, he ruled, he *subjugated* that rabble.

Shelly felt his mouth beginning to water. There it was, the power, the inarticulate monarchial *power* that Stag had always possessed. The rabble *listened.* No matter how stupid or blasé or tone-deaf, they heard him. Not just between their ears, but in the marrow, in the DNA of dead fingernails, to the roots of their pubic hair. Like a prime number, Stag Preston's necromancy stood alone, undimmed by space or time or previous condition of servitude. There it was, that damned talent, ability, artistry, conjuration . . . whatever the hell it was, there it *was.* And Shelly felt his mouth actually begin to water.

Somehow, by dint of work and sweat and naked rage at having his kingship wrested from him, the naked hunger for revenge, for the sweetness that came only with getting back everything taken from him . . . and more . . . a bit more than the best, the top, the ultimate, a bit of lagniappe . . . Stag Preston had done what legions of Olympic athletes could not do, what armies of showbiz-hungry starlets could not do, what pantheons of rejected gods could not do: he had managed to transcend disaster, had bared his fangs and chewed his way out of defeat, had clubbed and eviscerated and smashed in the skull of the Just Desserts life had visited on him. He had pissed on the floor of Heaven. He had beaten God. He had throttled Justice and all those concepts of evil-gets-its-comeuppance. Stag Preston had managed to train his damaged vocal cords. He had screwed the odds and transcended disaster, had shaped his own destiny once again.

He wasn't as wildly infectious as before, but he wasn't a kid any more. Shelly watched as that rabble in the strip joint became one with Stag, watched as they paid the price and he *owned* them.

There wasn't a sliver of doubt in Shelly's mind that Stag could be huge again, bigger than before, because not only did he have that genuine magic not even pukey music critics could attack, but now he had the potential for being the Very Essence of The Comeback Kid. His story was sensational. Down, all the way down. Cut and sliced and flushed. But back! Back again and better than before, more mature than before, stronger than before because of his travail, his tragedy, his pitiful fall and determined, anguished rise. Not a sliver of doubt: Stag Preston could be on top again, more powerful and important than before ... and all he needed was that one tiny break. That gimme-a-shot that he wanted more than his soul, or his posterity, or a light to guide him through the darkness.

Not a sliver, shard, scintilla of doubt, because Shelly was there seeing how the rabble listened, absorbed, just purely *dug* it. Fingernails, palates, to the roots of their hair.

Stag could be back ... and Shelly could go all the way.

He was one with the rabble, he was part of that single giant ear that was tuned only to Stag Preston, part of that gestalt the singer created when he worked a crowd. Shelly was one with him again, once more in the bear-pit, down there with the rabble that loved Stag, wanted only to be ear-fucked by him till the end of eternity ...

And then the Angel of Truth touched Shelly Morgenstern with her magic wand. In a heartbeat, the Good Blue Fairy sprinkled him with mind-awakening dream dust, and he knew in that instant the true nature of the epiphany he had been seeking.

The rabble.

He had thought of them as the *rabble*. The herd. The pig crowd that could be bought with a song. He had become one with Stag Preston, indeed. He had thought through Stag's mind, had seen through Stag's eyes, had reviled the rest of humanity as the rabble, just as Stag did.

In that Angel of Truth, Blue Fairy, Delphic Oracle clarity Shelly understood exactly how dangerous Stag really was. Because Stag owned *him*, had always owned a piece of him, the *best* piece of him. He despised what he had done, what he had become in Stag's service, because he was no better than the monster he had served.

His mouth stopped watering at the potentiality of success greater than before. His mouth went dry.

He gulped at the Tornado that had sat unnoticed on the table, but the dryness in his mouth remained. He sat there ashamed to his soul, frightened of his thoughts and desires, petrified with horror at how close he had come, how easy it would have been, how much he wanted it.

Stag was that part of him that had succeeded, that had transcended life and capacity and insecurity and even tragedy and the hot blood of his own destiny. Stag was that part of the failure named Morgenstern that could not be intimidated. And he wanted that Mr. Hyde to rule, to subjugate the rabble.

If he could have cried, if he'd known where to search inside himself for the purity that would permit tears, he would have dropped his face onto his forearms and cried like a coward.

But he was trapped inside Shelly Morgenstern and didn't know where to find the key to let himself out of solitary, to find that purity that permits absolution.

And Stag was riding out the end of his song. He chorded a finish and left the small stage with the audience of drunks and slatterns and boastful bullies and insipid tourists banging glasses, tapping swizzle sticks, clapping hands, whistling with little fingers in the corners of mouths, cheering and hooting and begging to be allowed to rejoin the great meat gestalt again!

Stag had intended a demonstration. He had provided the parting of the Red Sea during the Second Coming as a prelude to The

Rapture and Armageddon.

Stag plowed through the hands trying to touch and congratulate him and made it to Shelly's table. He leaned the Gibson against the wall and sat down. Looking smug. Stag ruled. He hunched toward Shelly and the smile of power, of satisfaction was there, just the way it had been so long ago. He wasn't a shadow, nervous, unsure, unable to gain the right feeling for the situation. Stag ruled. He had done the one thing in this life he was able to do better than anyone else, and now he wanted to throw it at Shelly.

Just as he had, almost ten years before, in a hotel room in Louisville, Kentucky. He was older; he was wearier; but he was still Stag Preston.

"Well . . . ?" He grinned imperiously. "Didn't I tell you?"

Shelly smiled and felt his gut constricting; the kid was going to say it. Don't say it. Please, don't say it, I may not be strong enough, it's been a hard fight, I don't want to re-enter that arena. I'm not strong enough to fight them off any more. The animals still prowl, they just don't like my brand of flesh. Please . . .

"You gonna help me, Shelly?"

He had asked, was asking again:

"You gonna help me get outta here, get back on the track? We can make a mint, Shel baby. I know I got it again. I've been workin' the toilets for about eight months now, just seeing if I could put myself in shape, and I'm ready. I'm really ready. Whaddaya think?"

Answering was difficult, he was so frightened. It would be so easy. So terrifyingly easy. Was this the way the bombardier had felt as he sighted on Hiroshima in his Norden, got ready to send that first hell bomb on its way? Was this the feeling:

Chilled clean through.

Empty of everything but fear.

Unable to answer but trapped by eyes dark as pencil points. Was this the way it felt to know you could destroy the world with the flick of a finger?

He heard himself talking . . .

"Listen, kid, I think you've got it better than before. Sure, I'll give you that break, Stag. I've got to make it now, but I won't leave town till I talk to you again. You just wait, kid, you just wait . . ."

You just hold your breath.

You just sit and stare.

You just keep cool, I'll be back.

And somehow, he was getting out of there. Somehow he was getting out of the line of those two radiating beams of black light from Stag Preston's eyes. Somehow he was stumbling over chairs in his rush, and ducking under the velvet cord before Mario could unhook it. Somehow he was out into the cool and humid and sweaty neoned street, striding quickly away and around a corner and down a block and around two more fast corners in case he was being followed for more words, more glances, more pressure.

Finally, on a side street in New Orleans, down in an eddy in the swamp of life, Shelly Morgenstern stopped, and leaned against a building, and drew in breath raggedly. He pulled out a cigarette and his lighter, and joined them the way they had been intended.

He moved away from the building, under a street light, alone in the darkness surrounding that baleful spot of brilliance, and he pulled at the cigarette. It had not been as clean and neat and finished as he had thought. Life wasn't like that. You ran into people again. You saw them straight up, singing, healed, the eyes dark and the hollows in the cheeks, and you knew they weren't finished; that with the right touch, with the shove you could give them, with the power you could put in their hands, you could turn them on again, like a robot, ready to tear into the scene and start gnawing at people's throats.

It could be done.

The power, the way, the method was there. If you wanted to do it.

Shelly Morgenstern stared up at the night sky of New Orleans, this last whirling eddy in the swamp that Stag Preston had made of his life, and the lives of too many others. Too many. And Shelly Morgenstern came to a very bitter, very brutal, very simple conclusion:

There are those people in this world who were born for evil. They never bring any real happiness to anyone; they can only cause misery, heartache, and trouble. The Hitlers, the Capones, the little people with a touch of rot about them. Everyone knows someone like that. But few of them have any range and power; they're limited. What if they get loose, gain status?

He drew deeply on his cigarette, and the glowing tip of it was like Stag Preston, back in the sleazy strip joint, glowing, waiting to be thrown into dry brush, to start the fire all over again, to burn out good ground and good crop and good timber. It was that easy.

He realized, quite clearly, that just as once before, when he had turned Stag Preston loose on the world, he was perhaps the only person who had the power to do it again. Few people would listen to a scarred guy singing in a low dive, and the chance of anyone with influence crossing the singer's path again . . . well, it could happen, but that was art, fiction, not life. No. Stag was here to stay, unless . . . unless Shelly set him loose again.

All it would take would be that one little favor, that one little push, that one little nudge and break.

That's all it would take.

"Sure, Stag," he said to no one at all, "sure, I'll give you a break. I'll give us *all* a break. You can count on it, baby." He took one last puff on the cigarette—the cigarette seemingly so harmless, like Stag Preston, but capable of cancer—and flipped it into the gutter. It landed with a shower of sparks, and Shelly walked away into the night, looking for a hot bowl of gumbo, leaving the cigarette butt and Stag Preston behind, to sink forever out of sight, each in its own gutter . . . harmlessly.

A Belated Note
of Acknowledgment

MIRIAM LINNA, dowager princess of all things rockabilly, and the various rotating staff of the ROCK AND ROLL MUSEUM, the former in New York, the latter in Cleveland, have been long-time admirers of this novel, and have clarioned its worth unceasingly for decades.

That I have not, till now, tipped my hat in affection and appreciation is no less than "my bad," and if you happen to cut their trail, would you mention to them that I really really am grateful as hell.

HARLAN ELLISON
12 February 2006

Oh, and by the way, long before Alan Freed, I was introduced to "race records," r&b, and soul by a Cleveland DJ probably none of you ever heard of, so let me toss a wink into the Hereafter for him,

OLE DOC LEMON

BIOGRAPHY: HARLAN ELLISON

This was not Harlan Ellison's first novel, but it was the first after his discharge from the U.S. Army (1957-1959). It is now included in the collection of the Rock and Roll Hall of Fame at the museum in Cleveland; and the great R 'n' R critic Greil Marcus calls it "the best novel ever written about rock 'n' roll."

Harlan Ellison was recently characterized by *The New York Times Book Review* as having "the spellbinding quality of a great nonstop talker, with a cultural warehouse for a mind." *The Los Angeles Times* suggested, "It's long past time for Harlan Ellison to be awarded the title: twentieth century Lewis Carroll." And the *Washington Post Book World* said simply, "One of the great living American short story writers."

He has written or edited seventy-six books; more than seventeen hundred stories, essays, articles, and newspaper columns; two dozen teleplays, for which he received the Writers Guild of America most outstanding teleplay award for solo work an unprecedented *four* times; and a dozen movies. Currently a member of the Writers Guild of America, he has twice served on the board of the Writers Guild of America West. He won the Mystery Writers of America Edgar Allan Poe award twice, the Horror Writers' Association Bram Stoker award six times (including The Lifetime Achievement award in 1996), the Nebula award of the Science Fiction Writers of America three times, the Hugo (World Convention Achievement award) eight and a half times, and received the Silver Pen for Journalism from P.E.N. Not to mention The World Fantasy Award; the British Fantasy award; the American Mystery Award; plus two Audie Awards; and a Grammy nomination—for Spoken Word recordings.

He created great fantasies for the 1985 CBS revival of *The Twilight Zone* (including Danny Kaye's final performance) and *The Outer Limits*; traveled with The Rolling Stones; marched for civil rights with Martin Luther King from Selma to Montgomery; created roles for Buster Keaton, Wally Cox, Gloria Swanson, and nearly one hundred other stars on *Burke's Law*; ran with a kid gang in Brooklyn's Red Hook to get background for his first novel; covered race riots in Chicago's "back of the yards" with the late James Baldwin; sang with, and dined with, Maurice Chevalier; once stood off the son of the Detroit Mafia kingpin with a Remington XP-100 pistol rifle, while wearing nothing but a bath towel; sued Paramount and ABC-TV for plagiarism and won $337,000. His most recent legal victory, in protection of copyright against global Internet piracy of writers' work, in May of 2004—a four-year-long litigation against AOL et al.—has resulted in revolutionizing protection of creative properties on the web. (As promised, he has repaid hundreds of contributions [totalling $50,000] from the KICK Internet Piracy support fund.) But the bottom line, as voiced by Booklist last year, is this: "One thing for sure: the man can write."

And as Tom Snyder said on the CBS *Late, Late Show*: "An amazing talent; meeting him is an incredible experience." He was a regular on ABC-TV's *Politically Incorrect* with Bill Maher.

In 1990, Ellison was honored by P.E.N. for his continuing commitment to artistic freedom and the battle against censorship, "In defense of the First Amendment."

Harlan Ellison's 1992 novelette "The Man Who Rowed Christopher Columbus Ashore" was selected from more than 6,000 short stories published in the U.S. for inclusion in the 1993 edition of *The Best American Short Stories*.

Mr. Ellison worked as creative consultant and host for the radio series 2000^X, a series of twenty-six one-hour dramatized radio adaptations of famous SF stories for The Hollywood Theater of the Ear; and for his work was presented with the prestigious Ray Bradbury Award for Drama Series. The series was broadcast on

National Public Radio in 2000 & 2001. Ellison's classic story "'Repent, Harlequin!' Said the Ticktockman" was included as part of this significant series, starring Robin Williams and the author in the title roles.

On 22 June 2002, at the fourth World Skeptics Convention, Harlan Ellison was presented with the *Distinguished Skeptic Award* by The Committee for the Scientific Investigation of Claims of the Paranormal (CSICOP) "in recognition of his outstanding contributions to the defense of science and critical thinking."

To celebrate the golden anniversary of Harlan Ellison's half a century of storytelling, Morpheus International, publishers of *The Essential Ellison: A 35-Year Retrospective*, commissioned the book's primary editor, award-winning Australian writer and critic Terry Dowling, to expand Ellison's three-and-a-half decade collection into a fifty-year retrospective. Mr. Dowling went through fifteen years of new stories and essays to pick what he thought were the most representative to be included in this one-thousand-plus page collection. Along with *The Essential Ellison: A 50-Year Retrospective* (Morpheus International), Mr. Ellison's first Young Adult collection, *Trouble-makers*, is currently available in bookstores.

Among his most recognized works, translated into more than forty languages and selling in the millions of copies, are *Deathbird Stories*, *Strange Wine*, *Approaching Oblivion*, *I Have No Mouth & I Must Scream*, *Web of the City*, *Angry Candy*, *Love Ain't Nothing But Sex Misspelled*, *Ellison Wonderland*, *Memos from Purgatory*, *All the Lies That Are My Life*, *Shatterday*, *Mind Fields*, *An Edge in My Voice*, *Slippage*, and *Stalking the Nightmare*. As creative intelligence and editor of the all-time best-selling *Dangerous Visions* anthologies and *Medea: Harlan's World*, he has been awarded two Special Hugos and the prestigious academic Milford Award for Lifetime Achievement in Editing.

In October (2002), Edgeworks Abbey and iBooks published the Thirty-fifth Anniversary Edition of *Dangerous Visions*.

In the November 2002 issue of *PC Gamer*, Ellison's hands-on creation of the CD-Rom game *I Have No Mouth, & I Must Scream*, based on the award-winning story of the same name, was voted "One of the ten scariest PC games ever." ("I Have No Mouth, And I Must Scream" is one of the ten most reprinted stories in the English language.)

June 2003: A new edition of *Vic & Blood*, published by iBooks in association with Edgeworks Abbey, collected for the first time both the complete graphic novel cycle *and* Ellison's stories including the 1969 novella favorite from which the legendary cult film *A Boy and His Dog* was made.

December 2003: Ellison edited a collection of Edwardian mystery-puzzle stories titled *Jacques Futrelle's "The Thinking Machine,"* published by The Modern Library.

October 2004: A new edition of *Strange Wine*, published by iBooks in association with Edgeworks Abbey.

The Science Fiction and Fantasy Writers of America (SFWA) has named Harlan Ellison its Grand Master, 2006. The award is given to a living author for lifetime achievement. (The SFWA was founded in 1965. The Grand Master designation is awarded no more than seven times in a given decade. It is conferred rarely, as an author's peers recognize a career at the highest level. Since the Grand Master Award was first presented in 1976, there have been only twenty-two recipients. Those recognized include Robert A. Heinlein, Arthur C. Clarke, Isaac Asimov, Ray Bradbury, Ursula K. Le Guin, Alfred Bester, Andre Norton, and A. E. van Vogt.)

He lives with his wife, Susan, inside the Lost Aztec Temple of Mars, in Los Angeles.